THE LONG CAPER

THE LONG CAPER

A TIME TRAVEL NOVEL

Charles Paul Reed Jr.

Storybook Adventures LLC

Copyright

Dedication & Acknowledgements

This novel is dedicated to the Reverend Charles Paul Reed Sr. and Mary Holifield Reed,
who blessed me with an appreciation for reading, spiritual awareness, and a sense of adventure.

Cover Art by Stan Dresser and Cover Design by Pepper Reed, with all rights to Charles Paul Reed Jr.
Storybook Adventures LLC

Also, by Charles Paul Reed Jr.
Tracks to Harlon County-21 Tales of Life and Adventure
Trouble in Harlon County -1stt Novel in the Pursuers Series
Mission in Harlon County – 2nd Novel in the Pursuers Series.
Justice in Harlon County – 3rd Novel in the Pursuers Series

I very much appreciate the following individuals who read and provided valuable input in every aspect of this novel
(In alphabetical order)
Gary Buscombe
Mark Church
Martha Weatherl

1

I first met Bryan Nappy at a roadside park between Tulsa, and Claremore, Oklahoma, on August 29, 1963. I noticed him right away for two reasons. First, he had bright red hair like mine. Second, he was picking weeds. Of course, there are quite a few redheads out and about. The spectrum of reddish hair color ranges from auburn to coppery red, to carrot red, to blazing red. But, take my word for it; hair like mine is rare. It's so red; well, given the gray that started creeping in about fifty years ago, I should say that it was so rare that even redheads commented on it.

Of course, a good deal of it is missing now that I'm older. I'm one hundred and five years old today. That doesn't make me the oldest man who ever lived, but it's still a pretty small club. Since I'm writing this in 2021, that means that, as far as I know, I'm the only fella you're likely to run into who will admit to having lived in four centuries. Yep, four centuries. I know. It takes a little while for folks to absorb that.

On November 23, 1918, I was born in a hamlet in northwest Arkansas called Pea Ridge. We may get back to some of this later, but you'll have to stick around for a spell. This year, the Pea Ridge Historical Society decided to put together a time capsule to celebrate the two hundredth anniversary of the Battle of Elkhorn Tavern.

Since I'm the oldest person they could find with local connections, they asked me to write something.

"Anything you want to write about," they said. The time capsule is supposed to be opened in the year 2062. Obviously, only you fortunate few get to read about my adventures in 2110 and 1865 a few years in advance. I'm looking forward to when they open it. In any event, on the day I met Bryan, I was headed back from Tulsa toward Claremore, Oklahoma, where I practiced veterinary medicine back then. I had just finished giving a veterinary workshop and was already tired when I started. I was a large animal veterinarian and planned to take some time off to run over to Arkansas to visit friends in my hometown. It was a hot day and humid. Despite the little car's air conditioning, my shirt stuck to the back of the vinyl seat. I pulled into a roadside rest stop and got out to stretch my legs. A 1962 two-tone blue Ford Country Sedan station wagon was parked nearby, but the owner was not in sight. I suspected he was off in the bushes taking a leak. It seemed like a good idea, so I stepped out of view of the road and took care of my business. When I finished, I walked over and sat with my back against a concrete picnic table for a few minutes.

The heat wasn't so bad in the shade. I let my mind meander over odds and ends in my life. I wasn't married, nor did I have a steady girlfriend. I wasn't rich. I did love my work, so one out of three didn't seem so bad. The most dangerous thing I had done up to then was to visit Italy as a guest of Uncle Sam in 1944. That's a different story. Maybe we'll tell that one some other day. Noon was approaching, and the hottest part of the day was still ahead of me. It was a pleasant spot, and the light and shade dappled the area under some large burr oak and smaller chinkapin oak trees. As I stretched my arms overhead, I stared up into the cloudless sky for a couple of minutes and was about to get back in my car when I spotted an older guy approaching from around the curve of the road. As I mentioned before, he had flaming red hair. He was a relatively small fella, a least six inches shorter than me, and looked to be a decade my senior. He had heavy eyebrows and a thick shoe-brush mustache. His blue and white checkered shirt was open at the neck, darker in the armpits from sweating in the heat. He wore faded blue jeans, whereas I wore wheat jeans, which were popular at the time. He was carrying a bushel basket and filling it with a weed I had noticed growing by the side of the road while I was tooling along the highway. I grew curious as I watched him approach. He stopped a couple of times along the way and nipped off a weed stem or two with hand clippers to add to the basket. Eventually, he reached me.

"Mind if I join you?" he asked but didn't wait for me to reply. He dropped the basket on the other end of the picnic table and pulled out a wrinkled handkerchief to wipe his brow. "I'm Bryan Nappy." He stuck out his hand. We shook.

"Paul Canute," I said. "You collecting weeds?"

"Well, I am," he said. He picked up one of the delicate white-flowered plants from the pile in the basket, held it aloft, and looked through it. "Pretty, don't you think?"

" It is," I said. "Can't say I have ever paid much attention before, but it is pretty when you look at it close-up."

"It's Daucus carota, popularly called Queen Anne's lace, or wild carrot." He lay it back in his basket. "It's late in the season. It's an interesting plant. It has a two-year life cycle. It flowers the first year and then goes to seed after the second year."

"I guess my name for it has always been noxious-weedious," I joked.

Bryan grinned wide beneath the mustache. "That's probably what most people call it."

I saw him glance up at my hair while he scratched the back of his head. I waited for some comment, but he looked away, picked up a couple more of the weeds, and lay them on the table. They were lacy enough to earn their fancy name. Being a curious sort, I had to ask.

"So, what do you do with those?" I fingered one.

"Well, I dry them and sell them to flower shops to use in flower arrangements," he said. "It's a pretty good business."

I nodded. I could recollect seeing filler plants in arrangements. I was about to ask Bryan if he lived nearby when there was a squeal of brakes out on the road. A big black Cadillac series sixty-two hardtop did a squalling deceleration from sixty to zero, leaving a long black streak of rubber on the asphalt and twice as long a trail once it hit the bar-ditch. The ground was still soft from rain the day before. The car turned a little sideways as it came to a stop.

"Oh, oh!" Bryan's first reaction was to duck down, but then his eyes turned toward the Ford station wagon, which suddenly seemed a long way off. "I gotta go." He grabbed the basket and took a step. A gunshot rang out. A pine cone landed on the table, and a small limb dropped nearby. One of the men had taken a shot at us! Bryan moved as if to head for his car but stopped when another gun fired. "You've gotta go too!" His face radiated anxiousness.

"What's going on?" I looked from him back to the black Caddy. Two mean-looking thugs were throwing the doors open. They were both holding pistols. They were big guys, big as me, and I was six-four back then before old age shrank me. The scowls on their faces told me a lot. The car's momentum had carried them south of our location, so they were maybe a hundred and fifty yards away.

Bryan's head looked back and forth from them to his blue station wagon. He seemed to be calculating the men's distance from us and his distance from his car. He looked at my AMC Rambler, sitting only a few feet away. "I'm not kidding! Quick get in your car!"

I could feel my eyes widen. I looked at the two men. They seemed to anticipate that we'd run and started toward us in long loping strides. Another bullet thudded into a nearby tree. I looked over at Bryan. He pushed the basket toward the center of the table as if to straighten things up before leaving. "Let's go!"

I hopped off the table and opened the driver's door. Bryan grabbed the Rambler's little tail fin and swung himself around the far back corner. He jumped in just a half-second behind me. "Gun it!" Even with bullets flying, I kind of chuckled at that expression when applied to the Rambler. I turned the key, and the motor turned over twice before she started. If the men were going to chase us, I was plenty doubtful about the practicality of a road race between my little six-cylinder and the Caddy. I could imagine the size of the engine under that humongous hood. I twisted the steering wheel and gave her the gas, and we hit the asphalt going about twenty miles an hour. The two men were at an equal distance between my car and theirs by then. They seemed to do a quick calculation of their own and decided to retrace their steps. As I floored the pedal and sped up, I could see them tuck the guns inside their jackets. They had to turn their car around to pursue us, so we'd gain a few seconds with that.

"What the hell?" I glanced over at Bryan. He held the door handle with his right hand and the front seat cushion with his left. Both hands had a death grip, and he braced his feet against the floorboard. The set of his jaw and the scowl below the big mustache told me a lot.

"You from around here?" He glanced over at me.

"Passing through," I answered

"This is going to be close," he said. "With this curvy road, we might have a chance."

I swerved around a chuckhole in the road. "You wanted by the law?" I had to ask, although the black Cady smacked of something more sinister than law enforcement. Bryan looked, and his demeanor seemed law-abiding enough, but who knew?

"Yes, I'm wanted, but strictly speaking, not by the police." He turned his head toward the rear window. We were entering another curve, and I looked back again. The Caddy was lurching forward to make a U-turn as the doors swung shut. The ominous vehicle disappeared as we continued around the curve. He looked back again, and I checked the rearview mirror.

"This is going to be a short chase," I said. I had a bad feeling in the pit of my stomach.

"Could be," Bryan said. We cleared the extended curve, and the Caddy was still out of sight. Then he pointed. "Quick, pull around to the side of that barn!"

By that time, we were doing maybe fifty. Immediately, I spotted a lane leading across the ditch. I tapped the brake, and we went across the culvert, still slowing down. I was afraid I'd lose control when we hit the weedy graveled yard, but we were down to maybe twenty-five by the time we reached the front side of the barn.

<h1 style="text-align:center">2</h1>

"Pull further in and turn over there!" Bryan motioned while he threw himself around in the seat to look out the rear window. I twisted the wheel again, and we came to a bouncing stop in wagon ruts near a rotting fence behind the barn. I sat there, grasping the steering wheel with white knuckles for a minute before I looked toward Bryan.

"Did we lose them?" His hand was on the door handle.

"Shoot, I don't know," I said.

Bryan opened his door, and I did the same. I looked around the area of the barn. It was an old two-story structure painted red about half a century earlier. Even standing a distance away, I could smell the stale odor of spoiled hay and rats. In my profession, you spend a lot of time in such places. I admit that the suddenness of our flight shook me up. A lot of "what ifs" and "how comes" were churning around in my brain. Why were they chasing us? What if there had been a gate when we whipped around that last corner? What if I had missed the culvert and ended up buried to the hubcaps in the bar ditch? What if the black Caddy came roaring around the corner of the barn just now? The question of why we were being chased circled in the rotation again.

Bryan jumped out of the car and ran to the corner to peer around toward the road. It was dead quiet save for the wind whistling through the cracks of the old building. As my brain caught up with my racing heart, I looked at the little man for some sign. He straightened up and rubbed his jaw. He seemed to be pondering something. I figured he had some explaining to do

"Let's get back to my car?" he said.

"Okay." I was fine with that. I was interested in getting on my way, as well. I climbed back in my vehicle while he stood watch at the corner again and gave me a high sign. I backed around, so I was pointing toward the road, and then pulled up to where he waited. He came around the front and hopped in.

"You don't think they'll be back?" I asked.

"Well, they are not the smartest goons I've ever seen, but eventually, even they will suspect we gave them the slip." We looked both ways as we reached the road. No black Caddy was in sight. He turned toward me. "I'm heading toward Tulsa. How about you."

"Claremore," I said. I had headed that way when we exited the rest stop since it was my intermediate destination, and I would have risked a bullet trying to go south right past them. It seemed likely the goons were well on their way north to Claremore by now. I drove over the ditch again and headed back south to Bryan's car.

"I hate that I put you in a dangerous situation," Bryan said. "But if they stake out the road outside of Claremore, they could pick you up if you continue."

I wasn't that worried about the goons. I thought it more likely they'd head back toward us than park and wait. I was pretty sure I knew the area better than they did. There were several secondary roads I could take to slip into Claremore and reach my apartment unobserved. My original plan was to drop by my place for some clothes and head on over to Arkansas. Their guns guaranteed that I wanted to avoid the two men. How long would it take for the fact that we had slipped them to sink in? I thought that there might not be a lot of time to play with. I pushed the peddle to the metal, and the little Rambler perked up a bit.

"I hate to ask, but if you aren't on the run from the law?" I let the question trail off. I moved my eyes from the rearview mirror toward Bryan.

His blue eyes were intent. The scowl on his face was a fair imitation of an English bulldog wearing a fake mustache.

"I can't answer that without lying to you," he said. "Let's just say it's a national security issue with the understanding that I'm lying." He looked back at me with a half-smile.

"You're saying you can't tell me." I slowed as we approached the park. I scanned the parking area out of an abundance of caution and saw no sign of the men or their car. I looked into the rearview mirror a last time before turning in. I pulled up to the picnic table. The basket was where he had left it. The scene seemed pretty benign. I didn't expect that situation to last long.

"They are probably between Claremore and us by now," Bryan warned. I nodded. I had a plan. I'd take a side road to highway twenty and go into town from the west. But I needed to get started. I looked over my shoulder again. Bryan reached over to shake my hand and take his leave.

"Thanks for the help." He opened the door, took a step toward the basket, stopped, and raised his hands. That's when I spotted one of the big guys as he stepped out from behind the same tree I had peed on earlier. I got a slight sense of pleasure, knowing he had probably been standing in it. Then a revolver was shoved against my left temple by big guy number two. That cut my gloating short. He pulled the driver's side door open and motioned for me to get out. I guessed that he must have been hiding behind the blue Ford.

I followed directions and moved to the hood of the car. I felt the gun prod me between my shoulder blades a few times. It was getting pretty irritating. The first goon marched Bryan over closer to me.

He wore a black T-shirt that spread impressively across his broad chest; the shirttail lapped over black pants. He could have been either a mortuary employee or a bouncer in a bar based on looks alone. He had a scar over his left eye that I suspected was a battle wound from said bar. I turned my head a bit to the left to get a better look at his partner. They could have been twins based on apparel. He wore the same outfit but minus any scars on his mug.

"What's this about?" As I turned a bit, I felt the gun barrel rake across my back. My big guy took a step away.

"Charlie, we got a bonus," he said to the other man. "Do we get extra points for two?" he grinned. The other man smiled as well. They didn't look any less intimidating with smiles on their faces.

"Probably not." He took handcuffs out of his pocket. "You two are coming with us."

Bryan had a desperate expression on his face. He hugged his fists to his chest rather than putting them behind his back to accept the cuffs. I heard the minor scrape of the second pair of cuffs slide open beside me.

"Hold it!" I pulled my hands away. "What's this about?"

The man grabbed my left arm and tried to twist it behind me, one-handed. Reflexively, I jerked my arm away and brought my left fist down on his gun hand as hard as I could. Though never arrested before, I knew the routine from watching *Dragnet* on television. 'Friday,' the lead investigator was supposed to identify himself and tell me what the charges were. Their departure from the accepted script got my dander up. The other man was so distracted by my actions that he swung his gun toward me. From the corner of my eye, I saw Bryan slip his hand into his jacket pocket. He pulled out what appeared to be a tube the size of an old-fashioned fountain pen. That was weird timing! With more time to analyze, I still wouldn't have a clue what he was about to do.

Instead of opening the pen, Bryan twisted the six-inch-long tube in half. He pitched one end to me. Four pairs of eyes watched it travel end over end in what seemed like slow motion. It seemed to hypnotize the two goons. I was mesmerized, but I still caught it. Bryan palmed his part of the tube. Suddenly, I heard a loud sucking sound, like a vacuum cleaner struggling to pick up something too large for the nozzle. Bryan yelled one instruction.

"Over there!" He knocked the gun from his entranced goon's hand and ran toward the blue Ford. I lunged to follow, and we ended up flat on the ground about fifteen feet away. I couldn't see how we had helped ourselves. Then I felt encircled by some invisible force. Everything around me went as black as night except for what looked like cryptic pin-sized zig-zag symbols like lightning flashing just out of reach. Reflexively, I closed my eyes for about half a minute. The sucking sound stopped, and I opened them a little and squinted.

3

It was still black, really black because the lightning and flashing symbols had stopped too. I flitted my eyes around and pawed a little at the area surrounding me, trying to pierce the darkness. Then I heard a rustle nearby. I tentatively reached out my hand further in that direction and almost poked Bryan in the eye.

"Yowl! Be careful!" He reached up and grabbed my hand, and pushed it away. It was then that I realized that the "fountain pen" had grown warm in my hand.

"What is this thing?" I opened my hand palm up. My half of the six-inch-long bar-thing was glowing from the separated end. Bryan plucked it out of my hand. I could see his fingers seat the two sections together in the last rays and give a twist. The blue light went off. I heard rather than saw him stick it in his pocket.

"Homing device," he said. Without that light source, we were in pitch black darkness again. He spoke again. It almost seemed like an afterthought. "Light!" The indirect lights went on. He pushed himself to his feet and grabbed my arm at the elbow to help me up.

"Well, this is a fine how-do-you-do," he muttered. The expression reminded me of Oliver Hardy of the old *Laurel and Hardy* comedy team playing every afternoon on television.

"Well, here's another fine mess you've gotten me into," I retorted.

"Huh?"

"Never mind. Where are we?" I said. The room looked like a cube, approximately ten by ten, with dark gray walls that absorbed the light rather than reflected it. There was no furniture, no décor of any kind. It reminded me of the close confines of an elevator without any sense of motion.

"Decontamination will start in about ten seconds," he announced.

"What? Decontamination?" I barely had time to respond, and then it started.

Decontamination smelled a lot like the hot steel of horseshoes on a blacksmith's forge, intermingled with a slight whiff of lavender. Alternating gusts of wind buffeted us from four sides, from head to shoelaces. It sucked our clothes away from our bodies. It stood the hair up on the top of our heads, and I felt like the air was being sucked out of my lungs. I clamped my mouth shut and grabbed my nose. Decontamination only lasted maybe ten seconds, but I didn't know that, and I could feel my panic rise after the third second. Bryan flapped his arms out into a cross-like position and nodded to me. I followed his lead but still fought the feeling of having the air sucked out of my lungs. When it was over, I could hear my ears ringing, a series of high-volume noises along with the sucking, and I didn't like it a bit.

"Okay," Bryan said. "I'm going out that door," he motioned to a faint door outline flush with one of the walls, "and I'm going to be gone for a few minutes. I'll be back soon. Just have a seat, and don't worry about anything."

His look seemed benign. I nodded dumbly, only half understanding. And, given my experience so far, half expected a chair to appear. When it didn't, I let myself drop into a cross-legged position on the floor. The floor was dark gray with a kind of a pebble surface.

While he disappeared through the sliding door, I unfolded myself and lay out entirely prone to rest my back.

I waited. I thought about what had just happened, although my mind refused to accept it fully. It felt like a puzzle that I only half understood. I had been bodily removed from a roadside park halfway between Tulsa and Claremore, Oklahoma, and deposited in this room. I looked closely at the floor. It was solid but still pliable. I could press on it and make small indentations, but it was resilient and came right back. I got to my feet and examined the walls—the same material. The surface of the door was the same. I sat down again and waited. What had one of the big men in black said? "Do we get paid extra for two?"

What the heck did that mean? Two what? Two crooks, two bodies, two red-headed guys? Did they think we were aliens from outer space? Given what had just happened, it occurred to me that maybe one of us was. The kind that I'd read about in comic books and sci-fi novels for about thirty years. That gave the big man's words a different tint. Abduction? Bryan? He sure looked and sounded like a human. I thought back on his speech pattern. It sounded like America-speak to me. I took exception to their suspicions if that was what they suspected. I was born in the good old USA! I was born less than three hours from where they attacked us. I decided I needed to tone down my imagination. But that didn't eliminate the question, what the heck was going on?

I'm a pretty organized person, so I started assembling my questions while lying there on the floor. The first was, where was I? How did I get here? When was I going back? Why did the men think they needed to handcuff us? Were they with the government? I was still coming up with more questions when the door reopened, and Bryan returned.

A tall, middle-aged man and a woman followed Bryan in. I got back to my feet. I guessed that she was in her thirties. She was a beauty, wearing an outfit I might expect to see at a 1963 costume party. It looked like tights with a short skirt that stopped well before it reached her knees. Pretty face, sky-blue eyes, and hair that could be from my head? I reached up and touched my hair to be sure I still had it. Yep. It all seemed to be there. All three of them smiled when I did that. Then I realized why the lady's outfit nudged my memory. Except for the lack of a prominent symbol across her chest, it was a perfect match to the clothes women wore on Krypton in the Superman comic collection I had when I was a kid. Admiring her in that outfit reminded me of the old high school saying, 'it left nothing to the imagination.' The hair was shoulder-length, parted in the middle, lovely rounded bosom, slender waist, legs that went on forever, and her pale complexion glowed in the room's white light. The man was wearing clothes a little closer in style to my own. He had baggy-legged pants that seemed more so because they had three pleats from his shiny red belt halfway down each leg! Bryan was still wearing the blue checkered shirt and blue jeans, and I was glad. After all that had happened, I needed something to look normal.

"Mr. Canute? The man with the young lady was a couple of decades older than she and maybe a little older than Bryan. I put his age at fifty. He had a florid face, flaming red hair half down to his fancy collar, and perfect teeth. He could have just done a Colgate commercial on television. He had eyebrows thicker than my own. He was blue-eyed, just like Bryan and the girl. Yes, and like mine, for that matter.

I just stood there and waited awkwardly for the answers to my questions to come before I asked them. They were all shorter by varying degrees than I was. The girl was about the same height as Bryan. She smiled and stuck out her hand.

"Hello, my name is Louise."

"Paul Canute," I said. Her hand felt small in mine. The wrist, forearm, and biceps were slender and firm. She could have been a tall gymnast. The older man stepped forward and extended his hand. He was the tallest of the three and bore the self-assuredness of a man-in-charge. He had no facial hair. His long-sleeved knit shirt was pale blue.

"Preston Andrews," he said. His grip was firm. His hand was not quite as big as my thick-fingered paw but close. His eyes seemed to search my face. "I suspect you have questions?"

"And how," I said.

"I thought so. Let's go somewhere more comfortable, and we'll tell you all we can." Before I could respond, he turned abruptly and walked to the door. Bryan and Louise followed him, and I followed them. The automatic door opened when he reached it, and he and Louse went through. Bryan stood to one side so I could pass through before him. I wondered if the intention was courtesy or to keep me contained. I hoped that I would see something on the other side of the door that would enlighten me. I was disappointed. The door opened onto a hallway that carried the same ambiance as the room. We continued to the end of the hall, where another door opened. The sound of many voices washed over us like surf at Big Sur that I had seen on television. I could see forty or more men and women through glass partitioned rooms of various sizes reclining in chairs. Many were wearing devices that seemed to be permanently attached to their foreheads. Preston led us to a corner grouping of chairs. He pushed a button on a table, and partition walls seemed to flow out of the floor to rise to the ceiling. He motioned for everyone to sit. We did. A silence enveloped us.

"Mister Canute, we apologize for the inconvenience." Preston's blue eyes swept the others and settled on mine. I was sitting with my elbows on the arms of the chair. I made a shrugging motion with my hands and waited. I wasn't feeling as much inconvenienced as unsettled. Mainly, as I said, I had questions. I took the silence as an invitation to speak up.

"Where am I?" My mind leaped ahead. My earlier reflections had settled on an answer to that question. I waited to see if my guess was correct. An abduction suggested something else. I could see no windows. "Is this a spaceship?"

Preston smiled. "No, this is good old earth." He patted the arm of his chair.

"Good to know," Those six words were reassuring. So far, so good. It helped that the three looked like earthlings. I stood. "In that case, see you later, alligator," I said. I headed toward the door we had just come through. They were so surprised that I reached it before anyone responded. All I needed was to see an "Exit" sign, and I intended to be gone. "Whoa!" Preston said. He leaped from his chair, hurried to me, and put his hand on my shoulder. I twisted away and felt around for a release on the door. It did not automatically open for me as it had for Preston earlier. I glared at him.

"Look, I want to go back where I was. I want to leave now!" I remembered *Dragnet,* "Keeping me here against my will is kidnapping!"

I thought I saw a bead of sweat on Preston's previously placid forehead.

"Please, just sit, and we will answer all of your questions." He looked almost pleadingly into my eyes. He motioned toward the chairs. "Please?"

I made a face. I looked from Preston to Bryan and Louise. They both looked shocked at my actions. That was a very satisfying reaction and gave me a feeling that maybe I had some leverage. I walked back and sat down.

"How did we get here?" I looked toward Bryan.

He glanced at Preston, who nodded. I noticed that Louise sucked in her lower lip in a very provocative way. I enjoyed looking at her. Beautiful lady. Another good reason to be patient?

"Well, we capered," Bryan said.

"We capered?" I knew my face looked as baffled as my brain felt.

"Yes." He paused.

"Correct me if I'm wrong, but I have a vague memory from my botched school days that caper means to dance, skip, or hop." I paused.

"And leap," Preston interjected. "You and Bryan have done just that. Given the surroundings, I guess it may help for you to know the when as well as the where. You and Bryan leaped from 1963 to 2110, as you reckon dates. The two of you capered one hundred forty-seven years into your future." He leaned forward and seemed to eye my hair. "You shouldn't be alarmed. It was quite safe."

"Baloney!" The ire rose in me. I hated when people lied to me. I leaped up again. I thought I smelled a trick. "There is no way we changed time zones in that half a minute, let alone went a hundred and forty years into the future. I don't know if you knocked me out to get me here or what, but I'm tired of it. Take me back where you got me!"

Louise roused then and leaned forward. There seemed to be real concern in her eyes. "We'd like to do that, Paul. We would love to send you back right now, but we can't. The minimum rest time after a caper is five days."

"Sure, it is." I sat down again. "So, I'm a prisoner," I said this with some finality, and I was already wondering what the chances were of finding an escape route from wherever I was. I was bigger than any of them, and sometimes size matters.

"Sir, you are only a prisoner of circumstances," Preston interjected. "Bryan brought you here for your protection. The men you encountered could have been dangerous. Bryan says they fired weapons on the two of you. He was concerned for your safety if he left you behind. Bringing you here was against protocol, and we will be happy to get you back as soon as we can."

Their continued insistence on my travel through time gave me pause. My natural curiously caught up with my anger, and I realized that these people were in charge, at least for the moment. I forced myself to relax a little. I wasn't missing any work, and no one was waiting for me at home. I didn't have a dog or a cat to feed. My planned vacation stretched ahead for a couple of weeks. I had some time available to be "inconvenienced" if it was interesting enough.

"What we'll do," Bryan said, "is let you rest up for the five days, and then we'll caper you back to your car within a couple of hours after you, and I left. That's so the thugs we left behind will have time to vacate the area. So, although you will spend at most a week or so with us here, you will only be 'missing' from 1963 for about two hours." He looked at the others.

"How do you expect me to believe any of this?" I waved my hand around toward the four walls.

"It would probably help put things in perspective if we show him what 2110 looks like," Louise said. She looked from one man to the other.

Preston and Bryan nodded, and the older man pushed a button on the arm of his chair. Suddenly we were sitting on benches in the middle of a pine forest. I could smell the pine needles. I could move the brown pine straw at my feet with the toe of my shoe. Looking up, I could see the blue of the earth's sky through the canopy. I looked at the three kidnappers. They were watching me with faint smiles. Preston pushed another button after a moment or two, and I observed my chair leaving the floor and moving slowly and smoothly in a vertical path that put us just above the treetops. I felt the pine branches brush against my shoulders; the air rearranged my hair. I glanced down toward the ground, and down was a very long way. My legs were swinging over an abyss. I had a death-grip on the arms of my chair.

"This is the earth? We're still on earth?" I searched the horizon for a sign of a building and the sky for some type of aircraft. All I could see was a flock of sparrows. As if reading my mind Preston pushed another button, and we commenced to skim over the tree-tops. There were lakes and rivers, grasslands and marsh. On we moved. I extended my foot, expecting to encounter an invisible floor. There was the disorienting feeling of touching nothing but air, although I assured myself that it all had to be an unbelievable optical illusion. But this seemed more than visual. I was sailing through the air in an open chair, and feeling the wind against my face when doing so was impossible!

Our journey continued over the peaks and through the valleys of tall mountains. I could see the deep snowpack approach and watch the shadow of my chair carry me across the landscape and then disappear with each new drop-off into the valley. It was exhilarating but scary as hell. But nothing could compare with our descent from the foothills to wing our way along a beach. Birds dotted the sand as waves crashed against the shore. Craggy rock formations jutted out into the water. My sensory system was experiencing overload. No one attempted conversation. No one even pointed at anything.

"Enough!" I couldn't take it any longer.

Preston pushed another button. We were instantly back in our original places. I pressed the palms of my hands against my temples and closed my eyes to let my mind settle. I flexed my fingers and straightened and flexed my legs. I even opened my mouth experimentally so my tongue could lick my lips. I opened my eyes and looked around. A question was nagging at me. What was real, what was imagination, what was a dream? Then another question flashed to mind; if what I had seen was real and this was earth, where were the people. We had just covered hundreds of miles.

4

I'm sure that the look in my eyes when I opened them was pure panic. Louise pressed ahead quickly.

"What you just saw was real. A multifac drone acted as our eyes. A finely tuned environmental control system surrounded us with all the smells, air movement, and virtual vantage points." Louise said. "We never left this room. The scenes you saw are a part of the rehabilitated earth."

"Rehabilitated? People! What about people?" I said, almost plaintively. Sure, there were people in the adjacent rooms, but we encountered no one during our supposed simulated travel. "How many people are on the earth now? Has something drastic happened?"

"The human population of earth proper, colonies, star-gliders, and such is about twelve billion." Preston steepled his fingers.

"Twelve billion?" Next to the spaciousness, we had just experienced, the room was beginning to feel claustrophobic. "Why didn't we see any people on our "trip"?"

"Two-thirds of the population lives in one of the revolving cities. Only about a third live permanently on the surface or the interior of the planet," Preston said.

"Interior? Revolving cities?"

"Yes, almost everyone except those here in the Caper Center and some other institutional complexes, a few million vacationers, and about two hundred thousand park rangers live and work either beneath the earth's surface or in a revolving city. But, of course, there are lots of science projects on the surface as well. Perhaps you will understand if I show you." Preston looked at me questioningly, probably remembering my white knuckles earlier. I nodded. Preston moved his hand on the chair arm. "Brace yourself." We were again virtually transported to a view of the exterior. But this time, we were much further away from the earth's surface. Now I could see hundreds of huge round transparent bubbles. Each seemed to contain a city. They were strung together like beads on a string. From our position, I could see the orb of the earth rotating beneath us. From our perspective, one orbiting string appeared to circle the globe from the North to the South Pole, while the second seemed to follow the equator west to east. Preston pointed at the world beneath us. But only when Preston spoke was the illusion broken, and I realized I was holding my breath.

"You see, earth almost died fifty years ago. The oceans were waste-lands of debris, and the cities were unlivable. We manufactured potable water from scratch from hydrogen and oxygen. Our planet was at death's door. Eighty percent of the ecosystem was on the verge of extinction. We lost half of our population to pandemics. To put it colloquially, we as a race were a blight on the earth, and she rebelled."

Louise nodded in agreement. "Due to our failure as custodians, half of the amphibian species and twenty-five percent of mammals disappeared and would have been lost forever. Then caper was born. Our overall project is to rectify hundreds of years of neglect as much as possible."

I felt my eyebrows go up. I could tell that Bryan was looking for an interjection point. I had a question long unasked.

"Why were those goons after you?"

"They belonged to a religious cult that seemed to see the devil in everything." He pointed at his head. "Red equals demons to their minds," he smiled. "I just wanted to mention that this is a huge project that will take another hundred years to complete."

Preston nodded, "Caper has taken on three missions; first, restore the planet to a healthy interdependent ecosystem. That means traveling to the past and obtaining specimens of botanical and zoological life that were lost. Second, we retrieve history lost during the turmoil throughout the twenty-first century. We send expeditions to observe and gather on-the-spot details of historical events. Third, we recover missing historical documents."

I looked at Bryan. "What were you doing?"

He grinned, "just what I told you. I was gathering selected plants. However, the 'selling to florists' part was a ruse. The destruction of the ecosystem affected plant life even more than animals. From the giant Sequoia in California to the roadside weeds, it was all part of the environment before the death spiral."

"Don't tell me the Sequoia was lost!" I leaned forward, remembering my awe of the enormous trees, their texture, their smell.

"No, the Sequoia has survived, man, even at his worst," Preston assured.

He brought us back to the sitting room. "Once we retrieve the necessary components, we hand them off to experts to reinstate the botanical and biological life. We insert retrieved documents and debriefed experiences into the historical record. These are time-consuming projects on their own. All of the plants and animals that we 'resurrect' must be carefully reinstated. An exaggerated example of a mishandled reinstatement would be to plant cactus in a rainforest. It is often a delicate process and a time-consuming one."

"Based on what I saw during our trip through the forest, it appears that most of the work there is done," I said.

"What you just saw was somewhat deceiving. All life starts with the oceans," Preston said. "Those are now fairly stabilized. Even so, we are still removing heavy metals from the ocean sediment along the coastlines—the remaining cleanup involves billions of tons of plastics and other non-biodegradable artificial formulations and toxins. The forest we saw earlier was the first to be re-established forty-five years ago. There are millions of square miles of less mature plantings. Planting the right plants in the right places, at the right time, is a very complex and time-consuming process."

"At present, our efforts in this division of the institute are focused on mammals. We are working with plains animals. Bison, deer, sheep – obviously, a long list." Louise said.

My ears perked up at the list of larger animals. "Horses?"

"We had a massive setback with our horses. First, the species was almost extinct. Then, all existent horses were rounded up many years ago and kept in a single herd in Wyoming. As a result, the distinct breeds are lost. Then there was the mutation."

"Mutation?" I felt my heart leap. I've always had a love affair with horses. The beautiful symmetry, the noble head, and gentle eyes first touched my heart when I was fifteen years old. The smell of them, their contentment expressed in a snort or a nuzzle against my chest, has always made my heart glad. Just the day before meeting Bryan, I inspected a beautiful Arabian. He was magnificent at fifteen hands. I remembered running my fingers down his neck and the length of his short back. He had a deep chest and powerful legs. I felt wary of broaching my question.

"What was the mutation?"

Preston nodded. "Their lifespans have been reduced to about five years. They discovered the change two years ago when the staff detected the first affected animals. With all of the animals in a single herd, several generations passed before the old age characteristics became apparent and long before their chronological age should have warranted it. Of course, their biological ages affect their ability to reproduce. The resulting herd contains only a few mares thought capable of carrying a foal. There are about thirty stallions to service them, and of course, any newborns will only carry the mutation forward. It is a frustrating failure of our stewardship."

"Failure?" I felt my heart leap. "So, all of the horses as I know them are lost?" I could scarcely believe such a tragedy could occur.

"Our scientists were pulling their hair out. It took them a while to come up with an understanding of the problem and a plan. So, our teams will be capering back in history in a few weeks to obtain the starter seed of new herds. Our goal is to obtain the sperm of twenty different breeds. We are readying expeditions as we speak."

I was hanging on to every word. The thought of the near extinction of what was, in my opinion, a noble animal was more than I could stand. I noticed that Bryan was watching my face intently as we listened to Preston's explanation. "You said sperm. What about ovum?"

He glanced at the others. They nodded, for they too had noticed how caught-up I was in the story.

"We will use IVG technology to create both sperm and ovum at least until the program is on its way. You seem more than a little interested in this project."

"I should. I'm a large animal veterinarian," I said. "Tell me about IVG."

Their three mouths dropped open in unison. They looked at each other again and back at me. Preston cleared his throat. "That is very interesting. IVG stands for in vitro gametogenesis, manipulating cells to produce either ovum or sperm from other kinds of cells. In this case, having recovered sperm, we will utilize it to create the ovum.

"Huh? That's possible?"

Preston nodded. He looked at me with a speculative expression. "You know, we have about twenty-five veterinarian candidates lined up for the equine capers," Preston said.

"I can't imagine that with twelve billion inhabitants that there could be so few veterinarians," I said. I didn't pick up on his inference at first. I was too bound up in my questions and didn't know where to start.

Preston smiled. "Ah, I guess it does seem odd, doesn't it? But you see, the criteria eliminate a lot of prospects. First, you may have noticed that everyone in this room has red hair? Capering further into the past, more than twenty years is limited entirely to red-headed people. A very narrow spectrum of red-headed people."

I started to question why that was so, but he ran his hand through his locks and continued. "Second, even at the height of the veterinary profession, in the twenty-first century, there were only three hundred fifty thousand vets in the world without regard for hair color. Third, since the biological renewal project has been going on for some years, almost all of our large animal vets are already occupied by important work dealing with our existing animal population problems. Finally, capering is viewed by many as dangerous work, and for a good reason. As we said before, it is not dangerous for someone like yourself with the requisite hair color, but because in many cases, we are visiting societies highly suspicious of strangers. And believe me, the hue of our hair makes us strange!" Preston paused, allowing me to ask my other question.

"Why is capering limited to redheads?"

"A mutation causes redheadedness. A century ago, it was thought that our red hair was associated with interbreeding between humans and Neanderthals. It's a lot more complicated than that. Redheadedness affects less than two percent of the population. Within those two percent, there are varying degrees of redheadedness. Only five percent of that two percent are within the spectrum of redheadedness that the four of us possess. Only people like us are capable of surviving a long caper." He watched to see if I understood the implications of his statement

"Being capable of a long caper doesn't guarantee participation. Many of those who have physiological potential are interested in other things. There is a recruitment effort going on, but the pool is still quite small." Preston paused again.

"The red-headed mutation I mentioned has many effects on us. We have light skin making us susceptible to a variety of skin cancers. Red hair seems to affect our tolerance to certain types of pain, and we are inclined to bruise. We have known these things for a long time. Of course, with the advent of capering, our mutation's effects became apparent in that regard."

Bryan looked toward Preston. "I just thought of something. Couldn't Paul be a candidate if he was interested? He handled himself well during our little adventure today. He has the requisite medical training, he has the requisite red hair, and he has already survived a long caper."

5

I leaned back in my chair. My adrenalin level shot through the roof. The idea of personally participating in time travel was so foreign that I barely grasped it. Then Preston's dubious expression amid a litany of negatives annoyed me a lot.

"Not so fast," Preston said. "This requires some serious consideration. Successfully interacting with the natives during a caper requires a bit of training. A minor factor to consider is that although we can return to our own time with very small lapses, our biological clocks are still running the whole time we are away. Wherever we are in time, we refer to our "here" time. Everything that may occur elsewhere is "there" time. So we are substituting caper time for time spent at home." He looked at me closely as if trying to determine if I fathomed his meaning.

As I considered Preston's words, the whole subject was mind-boggling. My first reaction, aside from my annoyance at him for trying to say "can't" without coming right out with it, was pure fear. I imagined being in a strange world without even the illusion that my life was totally under my control.

Preston's argument didn't fly. Yes, I did have responsibilities back home, but Bryan's explanation that I could return to 1963 with very little time lost filtered out that concern. Two hours seemed pretty insignificant. No, I assured myself, that wasn't a factor of importance. Considering that we spend a third of our lives sleeping, I couldn't regard a few days lost because of a caper as a problem.

I had indeed survived capering once. But did I get through it unscathed? I took a moment to check myself out. I ran through the obvious concerns. I examined my body from head to foot. I couldn't detect any changes. I tried my memory. There were no prominent blank spots. I thought about my academic abilities. I still seemed to understand the contents of the last article I had prepared for publication in *Equus* the month before. I came out of my review unable to detect any damage. But the fear lingered. It was the primal fear of the unknown. I stood up and walked around the room. I looked toward the door that I was so anxious to exit through just an hour before. The three citizens of a different century made no effort to interrupt my thoughts or intercept me. I wondered if they were as self-assured as they appeared.

"You are serious about this?" I looked around. Their faces were suddenly expressionless as if attempting to remain neutral. I had to ask myself the same question. Was I serious about this? I remembered the Arabian I inspected at home just that same day. I felt the love well up. But that was raw emotion. Didn't I need a rational reason to put myself in danger? Didn't I need some assurance that these people were on top of things? What guarantee did I have that I could depend on them to make the right decisions on their end? Most importantly, didn't I need some confidence that I could rely on myself? I thought again of the world without horses. I pictured a grassland herd of horses sweeping across the plain with tails high, manes flowing! I tossed reason aside. I wanted to be part of saving them. My mouth was dry when I croaked, "I think I'd like to do it!"

Preston's face lit up, and I realized that he was on my side after all. "Excellent! We'll run some tests to verify that you don't have any physical abnormalities that might make multiple capers unusually dangerous. He looked at Bryan. "It seems like we have stumbled onto a good addition to our mission."

Bryan grinned below the thick mustache. "Resourceful, aren't I?"

Louise stood, and the rest of us followed.

"It does seem miraculous. I'll get in touch with Professor Ortley." She turned to me. "He is the science head of the mission. You two should be spending a lot of time together over the next three weeks."

"Why isn't he going himself?" I had to ask.

"Because his hair is as black as your boots. He'd never survive such a long caper."

My supposed decision did not settle everything. My head was still whirling. I had just semi-obligated myself to a "mission" without knowing any of the details. Where were we going? What year was I about to experience firsthand? Who would be going with me? What famous historical figures was I to meet or at least see along the way? My heart leaped at the thought of just seeing Aristotle, or Julius Caesar, or George Washington.

Preston interrupted my racing brain. "First, we need to get you settled in. "Bryan, would you go through the mechanics of finding Paul a place to live, and we'll meet back here for lunch. Second, Louise, would you coordinate Paul's initiation and training. He'll need a full array of vaccinations as soon as possible. He'll also want to join the meeting with Professor Ortley for initiation training today. Finally, Paul needs to become fully knowledgeable concerning the rules of capering."

"Rules?" My head was spinning again. Of course, on top of everything else, there were going to be lots of rules. I looked around the room where I had already experienced things I'd never even dreamed of. I would soon learn that there were not only rules but strange new gadgets, tools, doodads.

"Wait!" I needed something concrete to settle my agitated brain. I turned to Bryan. "That thing you tossed at me in the park. Let's start with you explaining that."

Bryan seemed bemused. He glanced at Preston and Louise and pulled out the two halves of "fountain pen."

"Okay, this is a homing device. We call it a Homey. You can see that it is about six inches long and oval down its length." He didn't compare it to a fountain pen, but it looked to be the same size. He pushed it to start it rolling, and it continued to turn a couple of revolutions until one of the broader sides lay flat on the table.

"If you look closely, you will see that it is segmented." In addition to the center twist apart division, I could see another division about an inch from each end. They were barely discernable even in good light.

"The homey has two distinct parts with two separate yet identical functions," He pointed. "You can see that this male-end is lightly etched. The female-end is not. Rotating the male end into the female end activates the homey at the start of a mission. When the two ends are screwed together, the Seeker knows your precise location for scheduled pickup. Separating the female and the male is an emergency maneuver." Bryan twisted the Homey, so it became two segments. "Separating the two ends activates the male end, automatically requesting immediate pickup. When I tossed one end to you, I made you a target for pickup as well as myself." Bryan twisted the two segments apart. The familiar blue light I noticed earlier glowed from the female-end. Yellow light glowed from the male-end.

"Notice that the two lights are recessed about a quarter of an inch. When screwed together, there is a little chamber between the two ends. The two lights meet there and combine, creating the trigger.

"What is the etching for?" I peered closer.

"The etching is so you can know which end contains the penlight in the dark." He gave the mal-end a half twist, and a small wide beam of blue light glowed for a moment until he turned it off. I had hunched over to observe. I leaned back, but Bryan wasn't finished.

"Wait, there is more." He pointed to the end of the female segment. "Okay. Notice that if I rotate the little one-inch section here," he demonstrated, "It contains a translator that automatically converts any spoken language recognized in the database to English. Once activated, it mutes the spoken language, so all you hear is the translation. That makes for almost seamless communication." He twisted it back to its original location. "I'd demonstrate, but we're all speaking English already, and my French is very limited. *Est-ce que tu comprends?*" He smiled.

"My French is rusty too, but *Oui*," I grinned, quickly remembering my painful French class so many years before.

6

Comprehensive, Anonymous,
Pre-pandemic Era Research

The sign covered the wall behind the speaker. I was sitting in a conference room with fifty other red-headed people. Professor Alfred Ortley, the only dark-haired person present, pointed to the sign. "This is the story of this Institute. Five words that say everything about our mission." He turned from the wall. His deeply tanned face brightened as he surveyed the group before him. He was two decades older than the median age of his audience. He wore clothes I found somewhat akin to my own time. His pants sported cuffs four inches wide and were of bright kilt-like material. His shirt of solid blue had a sort of double collar. Odd, but close enough for me. His square jaw dominated his face except for the eyes. They were a piercing blue, alive with amusement. I had seen that look before on people who enjoyed their work. He touched a place on the oval pad worn on his wrist very much like a watch, and the image of a pretty dark-haired girl of about thirteen flashed on the wall beneath the sign.

"This is Camilla Windsong. She is the biology student who toured our facility with her class about twenty years ago. She looked at this title, and realized that within the title lies an acronym. C.A.P.E.R., which means to leap. Ladies and gentlemen, that is what you will do. This one word explains the entire mission of the Institute. We take leaps through time and move among our ancestors to perform research in pre-pandemic times. In many ways, we are historians. At times we are archeologists. Sometimes we are detectives. At all times, we remain anonymous." He looked out at the group suppressing a smile. A hand went up. Professor Ortley nodded toward a pretty lady on the first row.

"Shouldn't we be concerned that we might change history prowling around in the past? Couldn't we mess things up for our present? I've read stories."

Professor Ortley looked closely at a young lady with her name tag emblazed above her heart, a safe distance above her ample breasts.

"Thank you for the question, Miss Manfred. You are very quick. It usually takes another ten minutes into my lecture for someone to ask that question. The answer is no. Everything any of you will do in the past, big or small, is already built into our present. Jump from a tall building and make a small crater in the New York City sidewalk, killing yourself and a pedestrian, and nothing will change for us here. Marry a handsome gladiator and have six kids. Nothing will change here. The past is the past. There may be past events that we do not know about. There may be past events that changed the world. It does not matter to us here and now. Everything you do in the past is, in our time, already done. It is already a building block to bring us to our present. Want to caper into the past and save a historical figure from assassination? Try as you will; you will fail." He held up his index finger.

"However, there are many unknowns in history. Perhaps you succeed in saving him, but it is so covert that no one knows. It may be unknown to other people of that day and to history for centuries. One hundred years later, some inquisitive soul may come across a box of letters, a tape recording, a video record that exposes what happened. But nothing changes for us except a correction in the record. Our little civilization goes on, and so do our little lives. That is not to say we are not careful. We are careful because we do not want to create hazards or conflicts among the people we encounter. That brings up another question, doesn't it? In addition to being careful, why are we circumspect and anonymous?" His eyes searched the room. They fell on me.

"Doctor Paul Canute, can you surmise why we are anonymous and circumspect in our journeys?"

"Because we don't want to put ourselves in danger?" I asked. That sounded a little weenieish when I said it out loud, but there it was.

"Very good! Yes, that is an excellent reason! Everyone who wants to be a victim of a stabbing or punched or put in a chokehold or shot with an ancient revolver because you are a monster from the future, hold up your hand. Everyone who wants to scare people into running into and over each other escaping from a crowded room to get away from the monster from the future, hold up your hand!" He smiled. "Let's try an experiment. Ladies and gentlemen, I am happy to introduce Doctor Paul Canute. Doctor Canute is from our past. He is one of our ancestors that a set of unusual circumstances have conspired to bring here to us. He has done something that neither I nor any of you will ever do. He has moved through time into his future."

There was a stirring, and fifty sets of eyes craned around to look at me. There was a low hum of exclamations. "Now, how many of you noticed Doctor Canute before I called on him? Show of hands!" I looked around. The lady directly behind me raised her hand. The man to my right raised his hand. All of the other hands in the class remained resting on the tables. "Enlighten us, Miss," said Professor Ortley, "why did you notice Doctor Canute?"

"He's so big," the young lady burst out. "I was afraid I wouldn't be able to see the lecture trying to look around him!" The class laughed. I looked around at her and grinned.

"I hear that a lot," I said. The class laughed again.

"And you, Mister Swift?" Professor Ortley read the name tag and pointed at the fellow beside me.

Mister Swift pointed at my feet and grimaced. "I've never seen boots like that before in my life. I've seen pictures but never the actual boot. They look like they're made mostly of animal hide?"

I looked down at the black boots and realized how important that detail could be. I looked around the room. Everyone was looking at their own feet before they craned around again to look toward me. Some of them were making a face of disgust. I realized that for many of them, I was an antique for wearing apparel made from the body parts of another being. I exhibited habits and beliefs that they felt that civilization had long abandoned. What else might be "odd or disquieting" about me? Of course, I didn't point out my equally antique leather belt.

"They are not totally animal hide!" I said defensively.

Professor Ortley smiled. "Are you beginning to see why anonymous circumspection can be so important? Doctor Canute, like the rest of you, is preparing for an important caper. His visit to the past is to restore the horse in our time. To you, he is an anomaly, a curiosity from our past. Imagine your reaction if you had no idea that a caper was possible and learned that you had run into someone from the future. Ponder that for a moment. Think how exposing the truth to an uneducated populace could jeopardize you and your mission." He pointed at the board. "Your safety and our mission are all important considerations."

Across the room, another hand shot up. "You said that Doctor Canute is from the past but that none of us can go into our future. Why is that?"

Professor Ortley pursed his lips. "There are complicated mathematical equations to explain that. I'll take a stab at it without the math." He went to the board and drew a dot, and from it, an arrow left to right. "Imagine that you are on a glideship that is moving very fast toward some distant location. At every point in time and space, you know where you are and where you have been. You think you know where you are going. But which is more certain? Where you have been is certain. There is a permanent disturbance in the space/time continuum like the trail behind an ocean-going ship. Where you are going on that ship is much less certain. There are unknowns ahead of you."

There was a general nodding of heads. I wondered if such knowledge was freely expressed in the schools, among the tracts kept in libraries, and as subjects of special lectures.

"Today, this minute, this second, this nanosecond is now. From the fixed place of now, our force fields can create a bulge in the space-time continuum and follow a trail of now's to the past through all the previous now's to any place, any time we choose on that trail. There is no trail to follow going forward."

Someone spoke up. "Then how did Doctor Canute go forward to get here?" There was a murmur of agreement. "How!" Many voices challenged him all at once.

Professor Ortley grinned. "Excellent question. But the answer is simple. Doctor Canute hitchhiked here with one of us. Think of it as an anchor on the ocean-going ship I mentioned earlier. You cast it out, and you pull it back. One of us followed the trail of all the now's in space-time back to Doctor Canute's time and place and then returned following their trail through space/time. That is the second phase of all capering events." Professor Ortley brushed his fingers through his dark hair. "Well, because he shares your unique physiology. Note that I do not. Doctor Canute was attached to our caperer's anchor and pulled safely forward to our time. He grabbed the anchor, or to be more precise, the anchor grabbed him via a shared homing device. If he had not had his unique physiology, he would have arrived here as a sizzling bundle of carbon." He looked around to see if there were more questions. Seeing none, he nodded.

"Okay, lunch and then back here! Thanks for your attention."

7

I approached Professor Ortley as the rest of the class headed for the exits. He shook my hand. "Welcome! Your presence in my class has been a big help in eliciting questions from our future caperers.

"So, I saw," I said. "I didn't know enough to ask questions, so the questions helped me as much as the answers."

"That is often the case with new constructs. Do you have any questions now?" He tilted his head to the side and waited.

"I do. The part of the discussion regarding someone traveling into their future didn't touch on one aspect. If someone from your future capered to this time and place, couldn't you hitchhike into your future as I did?"

Professor Ortley's eyes narrowed. "Yes, except we have a strict rule against such capers. Capers are not allowed into any past time since the pandemic dark age ended. Such journeys might open the door to all sorts of mischief. Moreover, our capers' successful trips into history depend heavily on the ignorance of those we encounter regarding our origin. As I said earlier, nothing we do in the past will change our present, but our activities certainly can affect the day-to-day lives of the people we meet. Unfortunately, our lunch period is getting away from us. Let's go eat and talk further?"

I nodded. Professor Ortley led the way out into the hall, where we boarded an elevator to a luncheon area. We spotted Preston and

Louise in the cafeteria. I supposed that Bryan spent his morning resting from his adventure in 1963.

Preston saw me look around and answered my unvoiced inquiry. "Yes, Bryan is getting some rest. The further into the past a caper takes us, the more stress it exerts on the human body and mind. That is why we have set limits regarding the rest time on both ends of a caper. Each caper is assigned a reasonable time in which to accomplish the mission."

"Where does someone get rest and recuperation in a perfectly organized society?" I asked.

"In good total-submersion entertainment, usually." Dr. Ortley smiled.

"Of course, Bryan has been trotting around in nineteen sixty-three for five days. There was little in the way of perfect organization then," Preston said.

"That's true. The two thugs we encountered seemed perfectly unorganized. We had to roll with the punches," I said. Professor Ortley and I eased into chairs to join the others.

"So, what was the big news the day you ran into Bryan?" Preston asked?

I thought about that for a second. "Can't think of anything special happening August 29, 1963, but the day or two before might turn out..." I stopped. remembering my current year. "Might have turned out to be significant, history-wise, I think."

Louise and Preston leaned forward. Professor Ortley smiled knowingly. "Yes, August 28, 1963, was the historic March on Washington. Dr. Martin Luther King Jr. gave a speech that certainly was memorable."

I looked around the table. "Was it?" I remembered the news broadcast from the previous morning. "So many things start with a bang, end in a whimper. They said on the news that there were two hundred fifty thousand people for the event."

"It has been a long road from there to here," Preston began.

"Well, only one hundred forty-seven years." Professor Ortley laughed.

"I was thinking figuratively as well as literally." Preston looked around the table. Seeing his amusement, I wondered where he had capered and when.

"I guess it isn't that long when you can skip as many as you want," I said. "Has anyone actually seen a dinosaur?"

Preston raised his head and peered about the room for a moment, then pointed. "That fellow over there has." Preston pointed at a large man across the room. "He claims he was almost lunch!"

I leaned down on my elbows and held my head in my hands. The thought of traveling to the Mesozoic era made my head swim. Preston patted my shoulder. "Getting used to the reality of capering takes some time. My first caper was to Scotland in 1304 AD. Seeing a man's head on a pike takes a while to shake off as well. I saw more than one."

I looked up. There seemed to be genuine empathy for me on my new friends' faces. I rubbed my forehead and ran my fingers through my tangled mop.

Professor Ortley put a hand on my arm. "Getting back to Doctor King, his message has been a rallying cry ever since, as various minorities found themselves the object of one kind of discrimination or another. Seventy years ago, almost everyone in this room would have been subject to such treatment."

I looked at him, astonished. "How? why?"

Preston ran his hand meaningfully through his hair. "Can't you guess?"

"You're kidding!"

"No. After a series of pandemics, redheads were accused of carrying the virus without symptoms. That made them a threat to others. Of course, so did many darker-haired people. It is part of human nature to look for easy answers no matter how complex the problem."

I shook my head. There was just too much to fathom.

"Oh, by the way," Professor Ortley said. "Twenty years ago, aside from those in the program, there weren't more than a few thousand people planet-wide in the general scientific community who knew our program existed. Once threatened with discrimination, you didn't take any chances. Remember the fear and condemnation of witches? History teaches us that your red hair is just another excuse to be singled out."

"Do you suppose there will ever be an end to it?" I looked around the table.

"We've talked about that," Preston stage whispered. "The answer," he looked at Professor Ortley and smiled.

"Probably not!" All of my new friends nodded their agreement. "There is something within us as a species that demands clear delineation between them and us. There is something in us that seeks the majority's dominance over the minority wherever a discrepancy can be detected. Unless we manage to make every person on the planet unisexual, with standard height, weight, eye color, hair color, skin color, with the same opinions and beliefs about everything, some person or group will find a way to claim superiority with or without evidence."

"I'm not sure that all of that would solve it," I agreed.

After lunch, Professor Ortley and I returned to the class. By that time, some of my classmates had come up with more questions. The Professor handled them, and when the inevitable lull arrived, he flashed a photo on the screen.

"Anyone care to guess the identity of this person."

We all studied the face. The man was handsome, darker of skin than any of us. His dark hair fell in heavy short locks about his forehead and short of his ears. I noted the Roman nose and garment and made a wild guess. "Julius Caesar?"

Professor Ortley led the laughter. "That was too easy, wasn't it? Anyone who has studied Roman history has seen busts of the man chiseled in marble. Before the camera's invention, only notables were captured in three dimensions in bronze, marble, or terracotta. Drawings and paintings also give us an idea of the features of historical figures or beautiful men and women whose names were of secondary interest." He flashed up another photo. "Here is a harder one." A beautiful girl stood holding a baby. She, too, wore a robe. Again, the dark hair fell to her shoulders. The baby had its thumb in its mouth. The forest behind the figures gave no clue to their identity.

"Which one?" someone quipped.

"Could that be Mary and Jesus?" another voice queried?

"Good guess but wrong," Professor Ortley smiled. "That is Julius Caesar as a baby and his mother, Gaius."

"I should have known. There is no halo!" the young man quipped.

When the laughter subsided, Professor Ortley nodded and continued with the presentation. Most of the photos were from history that precluded the existence of photo equipment during the period. I watched with a growing elation. The prospect of being in the presence of men and women that I admired or even disdained all my life seemed like a dream come true. To me, to meet one or more such luminaries seemed beyond comprehension. But I reminded myself, remaining anonymous limited personal interaction to just the amount necessary to accomplish the mission.

"All right. That is all for today. Tomorrow you will break up into groups of three to review the details of your particular missions. Rest up. It will be the most important session you will have."

I caught up with Professor Ortley as we headed out the door. "My mother always called me an eager beaver. Do you suppose you could give me some work ahead of time? I feel like I'm beginning a long way behind the starting line."

He agreed and sat me down with Louise in his office to learn how to use an Autosatiscis Device. It was pretty intuitive, and in a few minutes, I knew how to tune it to my memory synaptic system.

"Here is a list of suggested inquiries. You must merely look at the list projected above the machine and determine the one you want to access. Keep in mind that you are not limited to this list. Very little of such matters are kept secret in our society now. You have access to practically any information you care to access. Those of us who caper regularly have the benefit of an information implant." She tapped her forehead. "When we run into something requiring obscure information, it is available in about a heartbeat. Have fun!" Louise smiled and left me to go back to my room and entertain myself.

8

When I reached my room, I found an Autosatiscis Device on the corner of the desk. I tuned it and then addressed it silently, and my list of suggested programs was suddenly visible behind my optic nerve. I knew that my scheduled caper was to Georgia in early 1865. First up on my list was "A History of Titustown, Georgia." I walked over to my bed and kicked off my disreputable leather boots. I started the program and learned that Titustown, Georgia, was established in 1840 as early settlers, including Amos Titus, occupied the area after the Creek Indians' simi-forced departure. He opened a store and eventually elected himself mayor of his town. I learned that the town was a backwater during the civil war as most skirmishes occurred North, East, and West of Harlon County. The Confederate government recruited heavily in the area, with most men committed to South Carolina units. The local Home Guard, consisting of those too old or young to join the regular army, operated out of Major Thomas Jones's farm until the war ended. In the following few months, the Yankees ran off the Rebels and made the farm their headquarters. Also mentioned was a marauder named John Coates, who made a nuisance of himself, leading first a group of cut-throats and then forming a group of hooded southerners that were pre-cursers of the Ku Klux Klan.

I drifted off while receiving a description of the local geography. When I awoke, I simply knew things that I hadn't known before. I rubbed my forehead and looked at my program. "*Horse care and maintenance?*" I shrugged and found out about a lot of old-timey beliefs and cures. Some of them were still considered legitimate practices in the twentieth century. Learning seemed so comfortable that I couldn't help but move on to number three, "*Operating Civil War handheld weapons.*" I was familiar with that topic already but saw no reason to slight myself. I lay back on my folded arms. Then I went back to sleep.

I awoke the following morning to buzzing from my entry. Louise was at my door. I hurried across the room in my socks and opened it. She breezed in, gave the room a cursory glance, and gave me a bit of caper gossip.

"Well, you have stirred up the slumbering bears!" She glanced around, her eyes taking in my boots.

"Oh?"

"Yes, things are starting to get political. Someone complained about your participation in the upcoming capers. Some of the second-tier veterinarian prospects are disgruntled. Preston thinks he has it handled based on your previous safe caper."

"Anything I can do?" I felt my pulse rise as I contemplated getting kicked off the team.

"Probably not. You've been working with horses for better than fifteen years, as I recall. You have developed instincts in handling them. You made a caper without a hitch."

"Good," I said." I was simultaneously shaken at the possibility of missing an opportunity to experience the nineteen-century while still secretly anxious about my decision to participate.

"Anyway, you can probably do with a change of clothes. Fortunately, this is the day we visit the outfitters."

I looked down at my clothes. I had only worn them for twenty-four hours or so. But the word outfitters suggested more than just fresh clothes. "Are we talking 1865 duds?"

She nodded. "Even those boots will have to be replaced. Though made of leather, I imagine there are parts made of materials not available in 1865. If the wrong person got hold of them, it could raise unwelcome questions."

I sat on the edge of the bed and slipped them on. "I'm ready."

We headed for the cafeteria. We didn't spot any of our group, so we sat alone. It was my first opportunity to interview Louise.

"How long have you been in the program?"

"Five years. They recruited me when I was completing my bachelor's. The Institute paid for my masters. I've been on seven capers."

"Are you allowed to tell me where and when?"

"I suppose. Most were rather mundane, like Bryan's to 1963 without the complications. I did get a look at Cleopatra from a distance. Pretty woman. Her hair was not suitable for me to bring her back with me." she smiled. "You have no idea how unique you are in that regard, do you?"

I shrugged. "I figured I was common enough that the perfect society had a set of protocols ready to go when I got here," I said. I smiled and eyed her questioningly.

"From my knowledge, you are the fifth. Of the other four, three were shipped back at the first available moment; one was the pre-verbal pile of smoking carbon. He jumped our guy just at the return caper was beginning. But unfortunately, he was a Norseman with blond, not red hair," she grimaced.

"Crispy-critter," I said.

Louise was silent for an extra nanosecond. "Ah, kind-of." Her concentration ended. "A joke derived using a new product, Crispy-Critter, a breakfast cereal first manufactured in 1963."

"Yes, the power of advertising," I said. I stared at Louise for a moment before I asked the obvious question. "How did you know that?"

Louise tapped her forehead. " Remember I told you that, like Bryan, I have an information chip embedded in my head. We refer to it as an appliance."

"Pretty head," I said without thinking. "I don't see any scars."

"That's the idea." She leaned back at my compliment. "And thanks. You finished eating?"

I looked down at my neglected breakfast. "Two more bites." She nodded, and I dug in. Five minutes later, we left the cafeteria and jumped on a conveyer, which told me that we were going a good way down the hall, and after a quarter mile or so, we entered a building that reminded me of an airplane hangar.

Louise led me to a device and looked thoughtful for a moment. I felt a brief tingle in my frontal lobe. Instantly, I knew what I needed in wearing apparel. I was directed into a small room. My directions were to go through my measurements, starting with hat size, after swiftly ticking through my arm length, waist size, inseam, shoe size, and color preferences. I sat and waited. Fifteen minutes later, I heard a whoosh of air that reminded me of my entry into the year 2110. It was subdued in comparison, as it was coming from inside the wall. A door opened, and a basket slid out containing a complete 1860 wardrobe, including two changes of clothes.

I dressed, and with my apparel attended to, I left the room and found Louise waiting outside. I looked at her questioningly.

"There will be twenty capering groups leaving over the next few weeks for this mission," she explained. "The Equus Commission wants us to do some serious catching up on our losses. Each team will be searching for a specific breed."

"Teams? How many does it take to comprise a team?

"In your case, two. It will be you and Bryan."

"Does his shoe-brush mustache fit into our period?" I grinned. I tried to recall photos of the Civil War period. The facial hair options I could visualize consisted of full beards and droopy mustaches.

"I'm not sure. Bryan may have to re-train it beforehand," Louse said. She grinned.

"That makes for an entertaining visual, doesn't it?" I stood. We headed back to our classroom. I allowed Louise to walk a half-step ahead of me. She was a beautiful lady, and I've always been sensitive to the scarcity of those. She also radiated intelligence. I wondered how reliant I might be on the innate intelligence of Bryan in the coming days. I had already seen an example of his agility back at the roadside park. I felt a chill run through me. A ragged point in history was ahead. True, it was the post-war period, but my former reading, and my learning period the previous night, made me aware that this war did not end cleanly and reconstruction in the South, especially Georgia, was messy.

We opened the door, and our heads came erect at the rush of sound. A massive holographic steam engine blasted the room with its chug-chug and steam whistle. Then the image changed to a bawling calf, followed by a whinnying horse. The two raised the hair on the back of my neck. I'd been gone for only twenty-four hours my time, but the sound of the animals touched the core of me. I was thankful to be going back to when those sounds and sights were even more common than in my own time. How sweet to know firsthand the days when horses were still the primary form of transportation! Compared to these sights and sounds, the year 2110 seemed relatively quiet and even sterile. Of course, I corrected myself, animals existed in the current time, but the big draft animal we were viewing did not. Even in the 1960s, they were not a daily pleasure as they had been in the 1800s. And, I admitted, they weren't part of the daily lives of most people, even in my own time. I had to shake my head to clear my thoughts. There was so much to see and learn at the moment. We joined Bryan and Preston. The two men were gazing at the holograph as overwhelmed as I was.

After a bit, Preston drifted away to attend to other business. Bryan and Louise remained as my guides. Everything would depend on Bryan and me to accomplish our mission as quietly and anonymously as possible. I read the sign high on the opposite wall. C.A.P.E.R., *Comprehensive, Anonymous, Pre-pandemic Era Research.* Such a short name relative to the enormity of the past. So specific relative to the unknowns explored and the knowledge gained there. Was it possible for even those who experienced it to comprehend? For just a moment, a tinge of fear gripped me. What had I gotten myself into? " I thought about the Crispy-Critter conversation with Louise. If Bryan had encountered almost anyone else in the roadside park; someone who could not return with him safely; the goons could have either carried that witness off to no telling where or killed him on the spot. And I had to face the fact that no single source of danger threatened us. My red hair made a caper possible but did not absolve me of all the possible dangers "out there."

9

The days of preparation stretched into a couple of weeks. I understood that no human advance party would visit Titustown, Georgia, ahead of us. A Kladruber horse was a scarce breed even in the 1800s. We surmised that the choice of a small town post-civil war, depended on two factors; our target breed could be found there, and we could or should fit in with the native populace. I meditated on what a coincidence it would have been if my hometown of Pea Ridge was our target. A historic Civil War battle had occurred there as well. My sympathy for the beautiful animals forced into warfare tugged at me. Horses by the hundreds of thousands had perished during the war between the North and South. They were a favorite target for men on both sides of the conflict. They were larger and easier to put down than a man. They were essential as they made transportation of both men and equipment easier to accomplish. Shooting a Cavalry soldier or mounted infantryman's horse from under him reduced his effectiveness enormously, even if the fall didn't injure him. Take the horses away from a supply train or an artillery battery, and you made the accomplishment of their mission nearly impossible. My particular sympathy for horses grew from the fact that they did not have the choice to go to war. At bottom, I couldn't understand how a life-limiting mutation went unnoticed for several generations.

We couldn't swoop in somewhere and collect sperm from twenty breeds of horses all at once. First, twenty breeds of horses were not to be found in any one location. Second, our red hair attracted enough attention without arousing even more by trying to attend to multiple horses. Each breed was the mission of a separate team. Our job was to locate our likely donor and very circumspectly obtain a small flask of sperm and skedaddle as quickly as our schedule permitted. Once we returned to the current year with our prize, the sperm would be processed into sperm and ovum batches, as was explained to me earlier. For the first round, the conception of the first generation would be accomplished via a test tube. Our instructions were to wear a hat whenever we could so that our hair was as inconspicuous as possible, lay low, and finish our mission at the tail-end of the five-day time frame required for our bodies to recover from our caper. The other factor was the limit placed on our caper. We had to be ready to return in eleven days. No one asked about the consequences of missing our exit deadline. I found out why later. While every caper received what was thought to be a reasonable timeframe for completion, a lot depended on events on the ground.

We spent quite a few hours listening to recordings of what we loosely referred to as "southern speak," which gave us a feel for the cadence and everyday speech patterns of the people we would find. Northwest Georgia was not plantation country. Small to medium-sized farms dotted the valleys and foothills. Oak, walnut, and pine forests covered the higher elevations of the moderate mountain terrain. Because the area's primary industry had been logging, slave ownership had been infrequent before the war. But that had not diminished the area's enthusiasm for the conflict. As in the rest of the South, there had been many casualties. Pervasive hatred for scallywags and carpetbaggers was well known forever afterward. I was amused when told that my 'Arkansas accent' would make it easier to fit in. I could detect in my speech little that matched the recordings to which I listened. Our robotic speech linguist had one piece of advice for all of us as she monitored our practice. She repeated it hundreds of times, "slow it down, slow it down, slow it down."

Along the way, we received hands-on training with the firearms of the day. I came to know the feel of a colt-44 in my hand intimately and became accustomed to a five-inch blade on my belt. I was no stranger to firearms. Both Bryan and I had previous experience with more modern weapons. I gained my experience during the Second World War when I served in the infantry under Clark in Italy in 1943 in Operation Avalanche. Whenever I visited a beach and later washed the sand from between my toes, I remembered that beach in Italy. I knew what it was like hanging on by a thread. It was a piece of my past that I was happy to leave behind.

Bryan capered into Germany toward the end of the war on a history-related mission. Our instructor continuously reminded us to restrict the use of any weapon to life and death situations. The life in danger must be our own. We were not supposed to attempt to rescue damsels in distress unless we were the cause of the distress.

We were so busy that my five-day recovery period from my caper passed almost unnoticed. The training was constant, thorough, and sometimes tedious. Though I knew horses intimately, I had never hitched up a team to a wagon. Nor had I ever sat in the box and tried to get a team to go where I wanted. After a couple of outings, I knew that even driving the AMC Rambler did not prepare me for a long, rugged ride down rural Georgia roads in a farmer's wagon. On paper, I might have seemed a step ahead of my compatriots because of my experience and closer proximity to the time period we were to enter. But, unlike Bryan, I had never before been dropped like a newborn into a previous century

Working through our training and hanging out together in our spare time allowed us to talk about our lives. I learned that Bryan had degrees in sociology and biology with ten capers under his belt.

One of them lasted six months. He wrote poetry, had read every classic novel I could think to name, and many that had yet to be written in my time. Bryan merely raised his eyebrows and shrugged in response to my inquiry as to his social life. He said that since the death of his wife, he had forsaken a social life. I listened with sympathy. He eyed me, and I guessed he expected me to fill him in on mine. I didn't know where to start or even if I wanted to share.

While stationed overseas, I lost the woman I considered the love of my life to a captain stateside. She was a blond, beautiful pharmacy tech at the Pentagon. When I got the dear John (Paul) letter, I vowed to keep a better reign on my heart from then on. I had been successful in that endeavor for all the years since. So, Bryan and I had terrible losses in common. And we had laughter to share from lighter moments. My confidence in my ability to succeed in our joint caper grew with my confidence in my partner. The man I grew to know better fit well with my initial impression of him on the road to Claremore. That entire event had diminished in importance as we faced our next adventure. The incident illustrated how easily a caperer could find themselves in the crosshairs of a government agency or a religious or nutty political organization.

Early on, there was one loose end that tugged at my inner need for things to add up. It lurked at the door of my subconsciousness. During one of our meetings the week before we departed, I brought it up to Professor Ortley as he talked about our target horse, a Kladruber stallion.

"Professor, how do we know there is a Kladruber stallion in Titustown? I know that they were a rare breed, so this seems like looking for a needle in a haystack."

"That is a good question, Paul but believe me; we would not undergo the expense to ship you off without knowing for certain the location of your target. I happen to have this to show you." He touched the pad on his arm, and a hologram of a magnificent

Kladruber stallion stood before us. His black coat glistened. His tail swished with impatience. He stood close to sixteen hands and wore a Union Army saddle and bridle. Watching him snort and prance was thrilling. I had never seen this breed in the flesh, and the distinctive Roman nose and warm liquid eyes transfixed all of us.

"As to your question. We used several criteria in searching for appropriate horses. First, we wanted to start with twenty distinct breeds. We intend to continue each bloodline in multiple separate herds indefinitely. There will also be a combined herd. Second, we wanted to locate one in a place where our teams were most likely to fit in with the populace. The Kladruber originated in the Czech Republic. Emperor Maximilian II of Austria established the breed in 1597. Very few found their way to the Americas. A computer search of breeding records established that a stallion owned by a Union Army Officer was briefly stationed in Georgia. Further searching told us the time frame of his assignment near Titustown in 1865."

"So, we are sure that the horse we are looking for is near Titustown." I pondered that for a moment.

Dr. Ortley smiled, "Oh, yes. This animal is the horse you are seeking." He waved toward the hologram.

"How is that possible?" I asked.

Professor Ortley nodded. "Ahh. I have left out one thing, haven't I?" He grinned and reached into his pocket. He pulled out a small item that looked much like a matchbox utilized in my time and opened the lid. I strained forward to view the tiny object. I was startled when it rose from confinement. Professor Ortley pointed toward me. The little artificial creature approached me in the same manner as a mosquito. It buzzed around my head, then hovered for a moment about three feet from my face. On impulse, I held my hand out palm up. It landed, tucked its wings, and seemed to stare at me.

"Be careful not to try and contain it. Doing so will cause it to disintegrate," Dr. Ortley said.

"What is it?" I studied the tiny object and looked toward Professor Ortley.

"It's a Fleedle," Dr. Ortley said. You are looking at the one that located and recorded the Kladruber you see before you. "They are programmed to self-annihilate under various circumstances."

"Fleedle?" I made a face. "Where did that name come from?"

"Yes, flying beetle," Professor Ortley grinned. "Well, it is larger than a mosquito, and we have to call it something."

"I imagine that all of the Fleedles loosed in the Titustown area contain the same programming?" Bryan looked toward Professor Ortley.

The Professor nodded in agreement. "With the use of about a hundred Fleedles, we conducted a visual search of the twenty-square-mile area surrounding Titustown," he said. The Professor held out the box, and the Fleedle rose from my hand and flew back. Professor Ortley closed the box, slipped it back into his pocket, and waved toward the hologram. "The result is a delight to see, isn't he?"

And as our caper date came closer, I grew eager for our adventure to begin. Bryan's numerous capers were primarily to exotic places searching for lost flora or a historical mission, such as I mentioned earlier. He'd hold up a flower or piece of fungus and rattle off the Latin name and laugh when the rest of us tried to repeat it. Only the last year of his married life seemed to be off-bounds. He had lost his wife to a rare mutated strain of the virus leftover from a mini pandemic ten years before.

Two weeks before our scheduled departure, blood was drawn and analyzed to re-check for antibodies. In addition, we all received vaccinations to protect us from the many and various contagions that we would confront running rampant in the South at our arrival.

For my part, I was surprised and deflated to learn that humankind was still at risk from infections, even in the twenty-second century. Despite my medical training, I nourished the hope that the day would arrive when nature would no longer be able to throw new bacteria, viruses, and such at us so regularly. My friends assured me that much progress had occurred in the short time since Bryan's loss.

Louise was in charge of our training. I enjoyed her enthusiasm. She was beautiful, and naturally, I kept my antenna up for any sense of romantic attraction. I was disappointed. She directed her beautiful smile toward me often. Her laugh was contagious. There was warmth but no heat. The upside of our relationship was that as the weeks went by, I came to feel that at least I had ceased to be a subject of curiosity. Everyone seemed to view my small-town roots as a plus.

10

There were two mini expeditions to break up the monotony of familiarizing ourselves with "southern speak" and other preparations. The first was a brief visit to one of the cities that were strung like pearls far overhead. Though they were but dots in the distance, I commented that they seemed to have very slow orbiting velocity.

"That's because they aren't dependent on the earth's gravity to maintain their altitude," Preston said.

"How's that?" My little physics knowledge contradicted his words.

"The ability of a true satellite to maintain an orbit comes down to a balance between two factors; its velocity and the gravitational pull between the satellite and the planet it orbits."

"That's my point," I said. "The shells of the cities seem to move slower than their proximity to the earth should require."

"Your observation is valid. The same principles creating the forcefields that thrust us through time are used to stabilize the ring of cities. Would you like to visit one?" He raised his eyebrows.

"Very much," I said. From afar, the whole mechanism seemed fragile to my eyes. But I reminded myself that millions of people lived in those pearls on a string. There was no reason that I couldn't at least visit one briefly.

"I'll make arrangements. You might ask Bryan and Louise if they'd like to come along. Why don't we meet at the transport dock in an hour?" I agreed and headed for the cafeteria. I found them starting lunch. I joined them and told them of my new adventure.

"I am amazed at the technology that keeps them up there," I said.

"It's just another utilization of a new technology," Bryan said. "Give a man a new bit of knowledge, and he'll suck all the uses out of it that he can." He hesitated. "But don't ask me to explain it!" He grinned. I noticed that Louise nodded her head in agreement.

It turned out that Bryan was otherwise obligated, so only Preston, Louise, and I got in the queue for transport. We entered a glider and were soon approaching one of the cities. As we came closer, I could see a lot of vehicle movement occurring between the city globes.

"I assumed that each city would be self-sufficient," I said. I remembered the science fiction stories I had read during my misspent youth.

"I think that was the plan initially," Louise said.

Preston nodded. "Yes, but that idea turned out to be impractical in some respects. Just as different countries find themselves specializing in specific skills, so it is with the city-states. One genius or entrepreneur comes up with an idea and builds the necessary infostructure, and before you know it, he's the only source. Later, there might be copycats who can do it better, so the relative capabilities shift among the cities all of the time."

"I envisioned that they would be rotating, creating gravity," I said. My closer viewpoint made me aware that massive infrastructures connected the city we were approaching to other cities on each side. "Is that a tunnel?"

"Yes," Preston said. "It is possible to travel the entire circumference of the ring. But of course, that is an incredibly long way. That is why glide ships like the one we are on and transport vehicles exist. They can make shortcuts by cutting across and skipping huge sections of the ring."

Our gliders docked in an area that reminded me of an airport, and we disembarked with the other two hundred or so passengers.

"How long has the ring existed?" Everything was so organized that I knew it couldn't have all come together in just a few years.

"The first four cities were completed in 2090."

"I barely remember it," Louise said. She smiled, and I grinned in response. I surmised that youth was considered a valuable commodity even in the world of the future.

The tour Preston conducted took us through areas that the typical tourist would miss. There were colossal oxygen generating plants, thousands of acres of fruit, and nut orchards, vegetable farms, and dairy facilities. The living accommodations were situated in areas of vast lawns and walkways. I could readily see that bicycles were still a favorite means of transportation. For lack of a better term, the pod-cars and truck-like vehicles were electric.

I was not so much enthralled by the concept of the orbiting cities as I was by the scale. It reminded me of driving up to the Grand Canyon and looking out at the gaping hole for the first time. The difference was that you could turn away from the Grand Canyon. Here the immensity surrounded you in every direction. The term "Brave New World" occurred to me, but Aldous Huxley and other science fiction writers of my youth had merely scratched the surface.

If my enthusiasm for our mission was in danger of evaporating, our next excursion drilled home how important it was to me personally. I asked for an in-person visit to the only remaining herd of horses on planet earth. Wyoming consists of sweeping valleys and beautiful vistas, and tucked into one end of a valley was a ranch house probably built before my own time. Two sheltie dogs met us when our heli-glider landed. They seemed to sense that I was a dog lover as they joyously greeted me. I shook hands with Clyde Burrows, the herd's chief manager, and then rough-housed with them for a couple of minutes.

"Doc, you should brace yourself before we go out back," he warned me. "I know that you've seen an old horse before, but a whole herd of them is another thing altogether."

I nodded. I was not a stranger to the aging process of horses. Like us, they live their lives and ultimately pass on. But he was right, for as we cleared the corner of the house and approached the corral, I caught my breath. A mare was standing with her head protruding over the top rail of the fence. Based on my experience. I would have placed her age at around thirty if I hadn't known of the actual situation. Her lips were droopy; the eyes were sunken; her coat was rough. She turned sidewise to move down the fence to meet us, and I noticed the swayed back and muscle mass loss. This animal was an old horse. I reached out to touch her. She grunted and laid her head against my chest.

"How old is this old girl?" Even being forewarned did not prepare me.

"She's four," Clyde said.

"Four!" I ran my hand along her neck and looked past her at other horses that were just like her. They perked their ears, and a few of them limped a bit as they moved slowly to join our party. I dabbed at the tears in my eyes.

"Aren't there any young ones?"

"Not many. The hastened aging process starts soon after birth. To make matters worse, many of the mares just skip the normal years of gestation entirely. That makes for a rapidly declining herd numbers."

I gulped, "So, it's not much of an exaggeration to say that if they were humans, they'd go from baby diapers to nursing homes almost overnight." He seemed to draw a blank on my reference to diapers and nursing homes but understood enough to get my drift.

"They get old quick, that's for sure."

As the other old horses moved around and started to line the fence, I walked from one to another, stroking and petting them. It was as painful a time with animals as I've ever experienced. I've lost animals before, but the immensity of this loss just overwhelmed me.

After reaching the end of the row, Clyde ushered us into the house and threw out some stats. "Due to the lack of replacements, the herd will reach extinction within ten years." He didn't have to beat the drum very hard for me to understand that without the success of our missions to restore the various breeds, the horse would go extinct during the lifetimes of everyone in the room. Yes, there was a sense in which we could assume that our mission's failure would not be fatal. Officially, there could be more missions. But one of the things I learned in unofficial discussions with my new friends was the news that a serious political battle was working behind the scenes. From botany to biology, every discipline from history to archeology competed for the funds to keep their missions alive. Even if the missions could be kept alive, there was a constant battle to keep them on schedule. If our mission failed and others succeeded, there was always the possibility that someone in the hierarchy could eventually say, "let's go with what we have. Maybe we can add the Kladruber later." Later or never?

Back at the training center, Bryan and I lived in our nineteenth-century duds in preparation for our departure. It would not do to arrive at our destination and quickly walk our way into blistered feet. As we mingled with caperers headed for other destinations and other cultures, the variety of clothing styles reminded me of movie clips I had seen of people walking the back lots at a movie studio. We experimented with various combinations of outerwear until we felt comfortable. My new boots looked much like my old pair, except they were constructed with all-natural materials. The rest of my wardrobe was much like my clothes at home, except the pants were baggier and the underwear heaver. As far as clothes were concerned, I was ready.

Then suddenly, our date with Titustown, Georgia, loomed before us. There would be no more history lessons, no more pronunciation practice, and no more time to wonder what would befall us. Louise issued our miniature blue "flashlight" homing devices, and we waited for the door to open into the C.A.P.E.R. transport room.

At that moment, Louise gave me the biggest surprise of my short capering career. She looked up into my eyes, reached up to place her arms around my neck, and murmured, "Please be very careful." Her lips brushed my cheek. "For luck!" She was smiling as she turned away. I was simply stunned.

The door opened. Bryan smirked as he pushed me through. We placed our carpetbags of clothes and saddlebags of mission equipment in the corners and then sat down, facing away from each other. We had been shown our arrival site the night before and told horses would be waiting for us.

Bryan took the news of the awaiting horses without a blink. I was startled. "I thought we were the first to arrive there!"

"We are," laughed Bryan.

"But the horses!" Any surprise was enough to panic me at that point.

"Remember the Fleedle?" Bryan nudged me. "They've been busy scouring the countryside in an area around Titustown looking for strays. It's amazing how easy it is to herd a horse with a buzz to its ear. They will be waiting when we get there."

I started to query further because horses were supposed to be in short supply but finally managed a shrug. There would probably always be surprises coming my way. The room darkened, and the miniature lightning flashes and cryptic symbols around us began. I closed my mouth as the atmospheric pressure dropped. I closed my eyes and hugged myself. My brief second trip through space and time felt just as harrowing to my nervous system as did my first.

It was April 28, 1865; when we arrived at our destination, the atmospheric pressure rose as quickly as it had dropped. But the air was noticeably moister and heavier. I opened my eyes and turned to face my friend. Our boxy conveyance was suddenly quiet. The translucent walls seemed to evaporate. We appeared to be in a clearing. It was the misty hour just before sunrise. Birds were flitting above us. Light from the east was casting dim shadows. South of us were rolling hills. Through the old-growth tree canopy to the north, I could spot a waning first-quarter moon. It stroked my ego to observe that Bryan was as dazed as I was. I rose to my feet and moved to collect my things. As I gathered my saddlebag and carpetbag, I heard a snort. Two horses were grazing in a nearby clearing as promised. My hat flew off as our transport seemed to dissolve with a mighty swoosh of air. I approached the nearest horse. He was a big boy. His coat was a dull dark brown; the mane and tail were jet black. His color reminded me of the sorghum molasses I grew up eating in the foothills of the Ozarks. I breathed in his scent. Nothing else in this world compares to the sweet smell of a horse, even a nasty one! He was saddled and laden with dried sweat. As I got closer, I could see that his hide bore scratches and patches of loose hair. His mane was a tangle of twigs and dead leaves. No one had brushed him in a long while.

"How do the horses look?" Bryan was the first to speak. I noted that he was practicing his drawling accent, and I grinned. I moved to the second, a good-sized Pinto mare. They were both in about the same condition. I wanted to look at their hooves but decided to put that off until the light was better.

"Rough," I said. "No telling how long these animals have been loose." I stuck my hand into Sorghum's saddlebag and found a volume of Robert Burns poetry, writing materials, ammunition, and a uniform shirt for a Union cavalryman. I held it across my chest. I judged that the man's shirt size was a medium by 1963 measure. The stripes told me that the shirt had belonged to a corporal. I wondered if the soldier was dead or injured. There was no way to judge how long or how far the horses had wandered or the Fleedles had driven them. I pitched the saddlebag into the brush, intending to replace it with my own. I tied the reins to a tree and unsaddled Sorghum. There were signs of healed saddle sores under the blanket. I cradled his head under my arm and softly spoke to him as I stroked his nose and neck. "I don't know where you've been, big fella, but I guarantee things are going to be better starting right now."

We spent an hour working with the horses. After removing the saddles and blankets, we gave them a good brushing down. The nearby stream provided fresh water. It felt good to be with normal horses again. These two were rough and tough. I could only guess what extremes they had endured. But they were both under ten years of age, and aside from needing a good brushing, they were going to be okay. I was glad to be in a time that replicated my own this much. When I finished with Sorghum, I moved to help with the Pinto. "You should name her," I said.

Bryan looked at the big girl for a moment. "She's big for her breed," he said. "The oldest horse known in recorded history was named Old Billy. He lived to the ripe old age of sixty-two back in the nineteenth century." He chuckled a bit. "This century! Given what she has probably been through, I think I'll go with Billy-Anne in hopes that she can match him," he grinned.

"I thought your field was botany!"

"Well, it is, but sometimes other stuff gets stuck in there too. Also, don't forget my information-augmenting appliance." Bryan said. He tapped his forehead and grinned again.

Before we knew it, the sun was well over the horizon. I checked the horses' feet and noted missing nails on two of their shoes. We could turn them in at the blacksmith shop when we got to town. We knew our location from our pre-mission conference, so we re-saddled the horses and led them out toward the nearby road to visually orientate ourselves. Using the map Bryan drew from his saddlebag, we approached the road and noted Black Bear Mountain north of us. I was about to proceed when we heard the thundering hoofbeats of a half dozen horses heading left to right down the road in front of us. From our position in the foliage, we watched the horses gallop past. Seeing that the men were holding guns, I pulled Sorghum's bridle back and covered his head with my upper body. His head bobbed against me with nervous energy. No sooner had the horses passed than a series of shots rang out. The second group of riders was right on the tail of the first. They were wearing Union uniforms. I looked at Bryan. He was standing with his mouth open and eyes wide.

"I've heard of the old west, but I guess there was an old east too," Bryan said.

"I'm guessing that they haven't run off all of the renegades yet," I said. "Ready to head for town?"

Bryan grinned and swung into the saddle. "Let's ride!" John Wayne could have done it bigger, but he couldn't have done it better.

"Do you think we should wait a while?" I pulled Sorghum out into the dusty road.

"Well, they were moving fast and going our way. How about we go slow and follow them?"

I nodded. We rode the horses across the ditch and mounted the road. Keeping our eyes open for more riders shooting off their guns, we set out. As I fondly remembered all the westerns I had watched on television, it was hard to fathom living in the year 1865 at the end of the Civil War. I was wearing clothes very much like those of Wild Bill Hickok, who was but a few years younger than myself in 1965 if I remembered his birth date correctly. I had written a paper in a composition class about him only twenty-five years before. It was a wake-up call when I remembered that. Wild Bill had about eleven years left before his murder in Deadwood, South Dakota. As I clucked at Sorghum to pick it up a bit, I ruminated on the fact that so many people I read about as a youngster were at that moment headed for their last roundup. Abraham Lincoln was already assassinated. General Grant, the acclaimed Union general whose armies suffered 154,000 casualties while inflicting 191,000 casualties on his southern opponents, had only twenty years of his life remaining before he died of throat cancer. I suddenly realized the tragic power of knowing the future. Only four years out of West Point, George Armstrong Custer was likely riding a backcountry road somewhere in the South, having been present at Appomattox for Lee's surrender.

I glanced to my right to check on Bryan. He was holding on with both hands. Every so often, he'd brush his brow with his sleeve and tug on the brim of his hat to pull it down tighter on his head. Riding was perhaps the only skill in which I could exhibit superiority. I rode erect, shoulders back, remembering the TV cowboys. The air was clean and crisp that morning, once the dust settled, but heavier than the filtered air at the Institute. The sky was blue with a few cotton-ball clouds. We had ten days to locate and make arrangements to get our vial of Kladruber sperm. I was sure that soon after that, I'd be back on the road to Claremore. As we rode toward Titustown, Georgia, the normality of the air and sky, the sweet breeze, and dappled shade from oaks and pines made it easy to slip into the fiction that everything that happened was as natural as it would have been in 1963. How extraordinary it was for us to be in this place at this time.

11

We were both pleased to round the bend and come upon a peeling, *Welcome to Titustown* sign. My butt was tender after five miles in the saddle even though I did some occasional riding at home. Bryan was falling out of his saddle. We turned onto Main Street and rode with mounting confidence past the sheriff's office. There were few people about so early as we rode another half block to the livery stable.

A ginger-haired fellow of about fifty approached as we dismounted. He gave our hair a sweeping glance. "Howdy, boys!" He noted the army saddles and our civilian clothes and smiled a little. I wondered if he thought that we had stolen them from the hated Yankees. "You boys going to be in town long?"

I handed him my reins. "Well, I reckon we'll be here a week or more," I said. "Would you take a look at a couple of shoes?" I pointed at Sorghum's left hindquarters and Bryan's Pinto. "I noticed some nails are missing this morning."

"You bet." He gathered up the reins. "If you're looking for breakfast or a place to stay, the Lucky Star has good eats." He pointed catty-cornered to our right to a two-story building. In my time, it would have been called a hotel and coffee shop. I nodded. So far, Bryan had not said a peep. I smiled, realizing he was relying on my "Arkansas accent" to carry us through.

I pulled off my saddlebag and carpetbag, lashed behind the saddle, and set them down. I turned to Bryan, but he had already managed his. We carried our things into the small hotel lobby. A middle-aged man was chatting with a younger fellow. They turned toward us when we stopped just inside. I nodded at the clerk, and the young man turned, revealing his badge.

"Howdy, gents. I'm Deputy Shires. You fellas passing through?"

"We are," I glanced toward the clerk. "We sure hope you have a room available."

"I do. If you both will sign the guest book, the room is two bits a night. It's up the stairs and to the left." He opened a ledger and pushed it forward a bit. "You're getting into town awful early. You camp out last night?"

There were six cubby-holes behind him with keys visible. Titustown seemed to be a sleepy little village so far. I took the pen, dipped it in ink, and wrote our cover names. I was Paul Smith, and Bryan was Bryan Smith.

"We did. We just couldn't quite make it in last night."

"Well, welcome to Titustown. We have a pretty nice little town, we think." The clerk turned the book around and glanced at our information.

Deputy Shires was leaning on the counter, watching us sign. He was middle height, spare, gray-eyed. His hair was light brown. He smiled easily and seemed young for a deputy. I remembered that the Confederate Army was full of youngsters too.

The clerk lay two keys on the counter. Once our check-in was completed, he seemed to dismiss us and said something to the deputy as they continued their conversation. We grabbed our bags and hiked to the top of the stairs. Then we turned down the short hallway. Bryan opened the door to our room, and we both collapsed on the two small beds without even bothering to close the door. We lay there for a good while before I sat up.

"Well, should we get acquainted with the Lucky Star?"

Bryan gave a little moan. "You go ahead. I want to work the cramp out of my back first."

I sat up and threw my feet on the floor. As I descended the stairs, I took in the hotel's furnishings and general ambiance. After the slick synthetic feel of the institute, the place seemed homey. The walls of the stairs and lobby were adorned with attractive wallpaper. The hardwood floors were polished and dust-free. Someone was keeping the place up to a higher standard than I expected. Past the clerk's desk through the side-wall was a double-wide entry into the eating establishment known as the Lucky Star. I stopped in the pass-through and took in the place. There were about five tables with seating for four and three long tables with benches for seating for six or more. There were two tables in front of the window with two chairs each. I went to a two-place table that permitted a view of the street as I expected Bryan to join me.

An elderly lady approached me and offered coffee. I accepted and told her I was expecting a second person to join me. She asked if he wanted coffee, and I nodded. I studied the menu while the lady moved away to top off some cups of a group of locals against the back wall. I was ordering when Bryan turned up, still stretching his back. He ordered, and we looked over the room.

The walls of the Star were horsehair plaster with a chair-rail four feet high around the perimeter. Several faded framed Currier & Ives prints principally of horses, farm scenes, and historical figures. After only a few minutes. A very pretty young lady delivered our food.

When she spoke, I smiled. That was how a southern lady should sound. I murmured my thanks and asked her if the ham was cured or salted.

The girl looked a little puzzled. "Where are you gentlemen from?"

"Arkansas," I said quickly. "We expect to be here for a week or so. So why do you ask?"

"Oh, a lot of people from all over have been passing through since the war ended." She smiled at me. You being from Arkansas is not surprising, I guess." Her voice trailed off. "I've lived here my whole life. I help out my Aunt Emmy." She nodded toward the elderly lady who had taken our order. "She owns the Star. Can I get you, gentlemen, some more coffee?"

We nodded, and while she was pouring it, we saw three horses and riders through the window. A Union sergeant and two corporals tied up and appeared in the doorway. The girl looked up, and her face hardened. "They're back," she breathed.

"Oh?" Bryan said.

"Damned Yankees." She turned back toward us. "Beg your pardon. Those Yankee soldiers come in here and act like they own the place. No manners at all."

The three men shuffled over to a table just outside the kitchen door and took seats. They leered at the young lady and looked dismissively at the older one.

We watched Aunt Emmy take their orders. The young lady smiled when an older man entered the room. He carried himself with an air of authority. He was cleanly shaven except for the graying mustache. He removed his hat, noted the three soldiers, and took a table nearby. He was wearing a sheriff's star. A few minutes later, the young deputy we had met in the hotel lobby joined him. He spotted us and waved. We waved back. He pointed us out to the sheriff, who gave us a quick once over and nodded in our direction.

One of the Union soldiers made a crack, and the three men laughed. Our young waitress stopped at the sheriffs' table on her way back to the kitchen. The Union men seemed aware that the sheriff had his eye on them, and they averted their eyes while she passed. Then the biggest of corporals said something, and that bought another cackle.

"Seem kind of tense in here to you?" I eyed the three men.

"Yes," Bryan said. "We knew southerners hated the Union soldiers. But it was not just political. Seeing how personal it gets when the two sides interact is eye-opening, isn't it?"

The young lady came out with the soldiers' plates. She sat down two, and the third man reached up for his. His hand seemed to touch her arm inadvertently. She let the plate fall the last couple of inches with a thud and marched away toward our table. Laugher ran out behind her.

"Can I get you anything else?" she asked us. She ran her apron over the place where the soldier's hand had touched her arm.

"Kind of boisterous, aren't they?" I said.

"Yes, and they come in here a couple of times a week. We've complained about them before. Sheriff Beckett drops by when he notices their horses." Her eyes were blazing. "No southern man would treat a married lady like they do!"

"I noticed your ring," Bryan said.

"Yes, my husband, Jimmy, hasn't come home from the war yet." The young woman hesitated as if she was about to say more than she thought she should. "Well, we don't rightly know if he's even alive or not. None of our family has had any word for four months now. With the war over and him not coming home with the other boys, we don't know what to think." There was dread in her eyes and a firm set to her mouth that told us that she was dealing with personal feelings of loss. She straightened up and motioned toward the back of the room.

"That man back over there is my Jimmy's great uncle, Pappy Jordon. He lives in town and eats all his meals here." We glanced over. Hunched over a plate of pancakes was an elderly man. He was about Bryan's height but leaner built, with a thin mustache and bushy eyebrows. I noted that he had his eyes squarely on the Union soldiers as well. Between the sheriff, the deputy, and the old man, I could see that the girl was not without protectors. "My name is Sarah Jordon," she said.

"I'm Paul Smith. This gentleman is my brother, Bryan. Thank you, Mrs. Jordon, for the good breakfast. We appreciate you taking care of us." When we finished eating, Bryan rose, and I followed. We headed for the double doorway into the hotel lobby. We heard another raucous round of laughter behind us. I suspected that Bryan wondered how often such brash displays by the invaders would end in violence. We were on our way toward the outer door when I spied a pretty young black girl. She appeared to be no more than thirteen. Still, she was an inch or so taller than Mrs. Jordon. She was ebony black and small-boned. Her nose was straight, and her neck long and slender. The perfect teeth flashed while she talked to an older white lady I took to be the cook. I was struck by the high cheekbones and, most of all, by the large expressive eyes that seemed to radiate light rather than merely reflect it. It was but a moment's glance, and my inspection was completely one-sided, as she was attending to her kitchen duties, oblivious to my notice. I grew up in a town that did not have a back population. None of my friends were black. Playing sports against teams with black players was my first exposure to that segment of our society. I wondered if spending time with a group as hair color-conscious as the capering crowd would alter my awareness.

12

"Well, we have the day ahead of us," Bryan said as we stood outside the Star and looked down the street. We knew that the Kladruber stallion we were looking for was the property of a soldier stationed at the Union headquarters outside of town. "We need to make contact with the local military authorities. If possible, we want to gain enough goodwill for them to allow us to hang around long enough to spot him."

"I noticed a *Wagons for Rent* sign at the livery stable. Maybe we should rent a wagon and team rather than ride out there on Army horses," I said. "I'd hate to get off on the wrong foot."

"That's a good idea. Of course, everything depends on the authorities' goodwill. At best, they might take them away from us. At worst, they'd try to pin horse stealing on us."

I nodded, and we walked back to the livery stable and rented the required transportation from the owner, Bub McGee. Before long, we were moving through the Georgia countryside past the dilapidated farms. The pastures were mainly empty, and the tillable land was barren of crops.

"Isn't this planting time?" I looked over at Bryan, who was holding the reins. We could see beaten-down corn and cotton stalks in the fields, but they looked more than a year old.

"Yes, but with so many men off to war, it's been years since the last planting at many of these farms." He pointed at a shabby house close to the road. We could see a few chickens and an area where someone had started a garden. "When there is no cash crop, this is what subsistence farming looks like," Bryan said.

"I've been thinking of that young girl we talked with at the Star," I said. "I've read that there are a lot of women in that fix right now. The war is over, but a lot of their men aren't coming back. Or they are coming back with lifelong handicaps." I hesitated as I remembered a man sitting alone on a bench near the street as we rode out of town. His crutches were leaning against the back. He was missing a foot.

We were several miles out of town when we met a wagon and two cavalry troopers headed in the opposite direction. The wagon carried a driver, and a man with his left wrist manacled to the seat. He was tall and may have been a healthy young man at one time. He was wearing a Union Army cap. And he was missing his right arm below the elbow. His gaze passed over us from woebegone eyes. But they weren't vacant. They held an undercurrent of contained anger. That anger was unmistakable.

"Horsethief?" I looked at Bryan and grinned.

"I hope not!" He twisted around and looked back at the retreating wagon and riders. "I wonder where they are taking him."

A couple more jolting miles brought us to a makeshift sign announcing the U.S. Army Headquarters. There was a multitude of negros camped beside the road as we neared the lane. I suspected that such places were considered safe havens and were common in the south. This was a time of great upheaval in the south. Thousands of blacks traveled north toward cities or west toward hoped-for homesteads outside the south. We headed up the long curve of the drive until a large house came into view.

"What, no columns?" The structure reminded me of the old farmhouses back in Arkansas. It was built of lumber; the house and the plank fence that surrounded it were whitewashed.

"This isn't plantation country," Bryan reminded me. "In this part of Georgia, the farms are smaller than those east and south and situated in the valleys and foothills. There was a booming lumber business before the war, and I think it resumed afterward. Having cheap lumber available probably contributed to this farmer's ability to afford such a large house."

As we pulled up to the hitching rail, we could see the dilapidated barn and outbuildings. Past the barn was a corral, and behind that, a pasture. A flagpole held a large flag, the stars, and stripes. I knew that, in all likelihood, that same pole had flown the Confederate flag only weeks before. There were two guards stationed on the porch, one on each side of the door. There was a buzz of activity that seemed outsize given the rural setting. It was quite a contrast given the deathly quiet we observed passing farms on our way out. Bryan pulled up the team of horses, and we climbed down.

I opened the gate, and as we approached the guards, I felt a quiver of apprehension for our first contact with the military authority in the area. This meeting was very important for us to establish a basis of cooperation with the local commander. I reminded myself that this was a perfect time not to screw up.

"My brother, Doctor Smith, and I are here to see the Company Commander," Bryan announced.

The two guards looked spiffy in their blue uniforms. Their appearance was a far cry from the rag-tag state of some of the returning southern warriors we passed in the road. They looked us over. The corporal nodded, and the private opened the door. The large parlor was furnished with some seedy-looking sofas and chairs. There was an unframed printed portrait of Lincoln on the wall over the fireplace. It was draped in black. I guessed that there had not been time to replace it with a similar likeness of Andrew Johnson, Lincoln's Vice President, and successor. I gazed at the portrait, realizing that at this time, I was less than a month away from a living, breathing Abraham Lincoln, the sixteenth President of the United States.

A huge man wearing Corporal's stripes was sitting at a desk across the room in front of another doorway. Soldiers moved briskly down a hall and into and out of another door a little way off to our left. In all, the scene reminded me of a beehive. There was even a buzzing sensation to go with the constant movement.

We approached the desk. The corporal did not look up. There was a plaque on the desk that read *Corporal Yates, Company Clerk.*

"Good morning," I offered.

His large head rose from his task. He looked us up and down, "Morning."

"We'd like to see the Company Commander," Bryan said.

"Well, he's mighty busy right now. What is it about?" The man had dark eyes, looking out over fleshy cheeks. His hair was black and hung down over his ears. His one nod to fashion was a shapely handlebar mustache.

"I'm a veterinarian," I said. "I'd like to offer my services to look over your horses."

"What's a veterinarian?" The big corporal looked a little bewildered.

"I am an animal doctor. I treat large animals like horses and cows," I explained. I was afraid that I was pushing his comprehension uphill, but he seemed to understand. It wasn't his fault. Our training for the mission included learning that there were no veterinarians in the Union army before 1863 and not many two years later.

The big man shrugged. He did not seem to place much importance on my profession.

"Corporal, have you ever heard of glanders disease?" I watched his face for some sign of recognition.

"Yes, sir, but I don't know much about it." He looked at me suspiciously as if his ignorance made me guilty of something. I hoped that an explanation would move us up in his estimation sufficiently to get us an audience with the company commander.

"It is a disease of large animals, primarily of horses, mules, and donkeys."

"What does that have to do with the major? As I said, he is swamped right now." The corporal leaned his huge frame back in his chair, and his dark eyes drilled into mine. His demeanor, from such a large personage, was almost menacing.

"There has been an outbreak of the disease in the Chattanooga area recently," I lied. "I'm making the rounds of commands looking for stricken animals. If the sick animals are quarantined away from the unafflicted, it can be kept from spreading."

The big corporal scratched his head, digested the information, and lurched to his feet. "I'll see if the major is available." He moved swiftly for such a big man and tapped the door twice before entering. Bryan and I eyed each other grimly. If we couldn't get official permission to examine the cavalry herd, there was little chance of catching sight of our horse, let alone getting any cooperation in obtaining semen to take back with us.

The corporal reappeared. "He'll give you five minutes." He moved sidewise to regain his chair. I saw Bryan's cheeks puff out a bit as he exhaled. We had reached first base.

I led the way into the office. It was a small room. There was a bed pushed against the far wall. A campaign desk sat in the middle of the room. A major and a captain were seated at an angle to one another. Neither rose when we entered. An open window behind the major above the bed and another behind the captain put the room in good light at that hour of the day.

"Good morning, gentlemen." A robust, appearing man with dark hair, a razor-thin mustache, and a hawkish nose sat straight in his chair. His face was tense as he turned his attention from the captain. "I'm Major Rogers. This officer is Captain Rumpole. I understand you are a veterinarian?" He looked from Bryan to me and back as if guessing who the vet was.

"Yes, Sir. I am Doctor Paul Smith. I am a large animal veterinarian. This gentleman is my brother, Bryan Smith."

Major Rogers studied us for a moment and pursed his mouth. "I was not aware that the Union Army contracted with civilian doctors, sir." He glanced at the captain as if seeking confirmation. The captain gave a half-shrug. "So, why are you here, Doctor?"

"Sir, there has been an outbreak of glanders disease in the Chattanooga area. It is highly contagious. I have been commissioned to make the rounds in northern Georgia to appraise the commanders of the condition of their animals." The major's eyes were already wandering before I finished the sentence. Bryan saw it too and tried to add some honey to the story.

"Sir, there is no cure for glanders. But if caught early, the afflicted animals can be quarantined to prevent the spread."

"It is known to wipe our whole herds," I added.

The major's forehead wrinkled, and he glanced at the captain again. "And what do you need from me?"

"Just your permission to inspect your stock, Sir. And the cooperation of your command should we find some afflicted animals," I spoke quickly now. The major seemed to be unusually distracted.

Major Rogers looked at us closely. "How do I know you are who you say you are?"

"Yes, sir!" I reached into my pocket and pulled out some official-looking papers. They were dummied up from actual Union War

Department communications. They indicated that the bearer had the authority to inspect army livestock. I handed Major Rogers the papers and watched his expression. His eyes dropped from the first sentence to the signature line and noted the name and rank of the signor. "Fine!" He flashed them briefly for the captain to read the signature and handed them back to me. "Get on with it!" He seemed to realize that his response had been overly brisk and stood and straightened his jacket. "I apologize for my tone, gentleman. We are in the middle of a serious situation right now. Our payroll was stolen, and a man was killed last night. We have caught the villain, but the payroll itself is not yet recovered. I'm sure that you will understand that my attention is concentrated on that. If you ask Corporal Yates to come in, I'll have him prepare the proper documents to give you the run of the corrals and any animals therein."

"I'm sorry, Sir. But, of course, we understand. I now had a reason to replace my paste-on smile with a somber look of condolence. From the corner of my eye, I could see that Bryan's face also assumed an expression of sympathy with the major's tone change. We gave the major our thanks and retreated to the corporal's desk. I passed on the major's comments, and we waited for a couple of minutes while the corporal went in, conferred with the major, and returned to his desk to write out a document for the major to sign.

We were out of the office and halfway back to the wagon before either of us spoke again. "Bryan, I'd have this same feeling if I'd just dodged a bullet," I breathed.

Bryan nodded, and we climbed up into the wagon. "Yes, there would not have been anywhere to go with this if he had just refused to cooperate."

"I guess this just proves how important it is to have the 'proper papers'?" I grinned.

"Well, now that we have the proper papers from the major to obtain the cooperation of those in his command, we just need to locate the right horse and bide our time until it is safe to return home."

"The viability of the semen without refrigeration is limited," I said. "Are you thinking that we wait until the sixth day and caper out rather than waiting until the scheduled pickup date?"

"I think it best to make our arrangements during our five-day lull and then get our mission accomplished as soon after the five days as possible. There is no reason to delay our departure unless we have an unusual situation develop. We could start today." He looked toward the corral. The three horses we could see were not our Kladruber. I looked at the sky. It looked like rain was imminent. His gaze followed mine.

"Let's head back to town and look around before the rain starts." Bryan nodded toward the clouds forming around the nearby mountain.

"I haven't seen many men the size of that corporal," I said.

"Neither have I." He climbed up in the wagon and grabbed the reins. Without further discussion, he turned the team, and we headed back toward Titustown.

13

Bryan and I were in high spirits as we drove back to town. The required five-day layover before we could leave seemed to provide a huge window in which to complete our caper's mission. Given the cordial reception from the major, the time period seemed excessive, and we fell to wondering what we could do with so much spare time. As we approached Titustown, we again met the army wagon we had seen previously, headed back through the countryside. The prisoner was no longer aboard. We passed the *Welcome* sign and entered Titustown a few minutes later. We were scarcely prepared for the scene outside the Sheriff's office. A crowd had gathered, and we could hear the raised voices a block away.

"Sheriff, Major Tom Jones ain't never stolen nothing in his life!"

"Sheriff, if we'd known you were in cahoots with that Yankee major out at Tom's farm, we would have voted for somebody else!"

The sheriff was standing on the porch in front of his office. Despite the abuse thrown at him, he seemed pretty calm. He held up his hands to quiet the shouting and then dropped them on his hips and shook his head from side to side. The young deputy we met that morning was standing on his right, and another older man wearing a badge stood on his left.

"Folks, you are getting riled up over nothing! Of course, Tom didn't steal any payroll. We all know that. Given a little time to do an investigation, the major will know it too. I don't like this any more than you do, but the Yankees have got us under martial law, and if I don't at least pretend to cooperate, there will be some Union officer sitting in my chair. Do you want that? Do you want a bunch of Yankee troops running your town for you? Well, I don't, and so I'm going to play along. I'm confident that this will work out, alright. Now, everyone, go home! Do whatever you come to town to do and stay out of trouble!" He glared at one of the men in a clump of citizens and gave him the steely eye. The man started to say something else but finally threw up his hands and turned away, taking two other men with him. With the reduced level of excitement, the other members of the crowd turned away as well.

"So, I guess the fella we saw locked up to the wagon on the way to the farm is the same fella the major says stole his payroll," Bryan said, adding two and two.

"Looks that way." I looked up at the cloudy sky, pulled out my pocket watch, and read the time. "Looks like it's about lunchtime."

We turned in the wagon at the livery and took our places at the same table we had occupied earlier.

The lunch crowd was larger than it had been for breakfast. Everyone seemed to be a local except for a few Union soldiers. We could not miss the hard looks that passed between the rival sides. I suspected that the Union boys would be as glad to go home when their hitch was up as the southerners would be to see them leave. It seemed to me that being surrounded by so much hatred could wear on you.

A large, heavily bearded man entered the Star and sat down at the table near the other window. He was about thirty years of age, and though his clothes were relatively clean, there was a raggedness to them that suggested poor circumstances. The man didn't bother to look at the menu. The old lady nodded when he ordered coffee. She greeted us a bit more warmly than she did at breakfast and dropped menus on the table. I surmised that our repeated presence and an Arkansas accent rated a more pleasant reception. She went to the kitchen and returned with a coffee pot. She poured the scruffy man's coffee and then ours before taking our orders.

A few minutes later, Mrs. Jordon carried out our plates. When she passed the big man at the window table, he said Something to her. I caught a sense of self-consciousness about him but also a sinister undercurrent that seemed at odds with his shy smile. She nodded without comment and unloaded our lunch for us. Then she fetched the coffee pot and made the rounds topping off everyone's cups. When she returned, Bryan looked up at her.

"Ma'am, that one is dangerous," Bryan said quietly, nodding toward the big man.

I was taken aback at such an assertion on such little evidence. Yet, I knew Bryan had made a study of peoples' social interactions.

"Really?" Mrs. Jordon glanced back at the man. She was putting into words my exact thoughts.

"There is a slyness there, I guess," I said.

"Yes, I see that," Bryan agreed. "And something underneath."

Mrs. Jordon did not comment before leaving us and then returned in a bit to check on us again. Bryan looked up at her. "What is going on with him?"

The girl glanced over and shrugged. "He's okay. He doesn't come in often. He tries to flirt, but I pretend I don't notice." Her eyes hardened. "He is a sight better than these Yankees!" She glanced around the room, and there was loathing in her eyes. Of course, I could understand why. In all likelihood, someone just like one of these men had injured or even killed her husband. "He's a whole lot better than that sergeant and his cronies who were here at breakfast," she added.

We nodded and dug into our food. Sarah returned to the kitchen. After a while, the big man picked up his hat and went out the door, leaving a nickel on the table. He glanced toward the kitchen; I guessed he was seeking a last eyeful of Mrs. Jordon but didn't linger. I followed his gaze, but the only person I could see from my angle was the black girl, Ellen. Again, she was preoccupied. I wondered if the man's thoughts regarding our pretty waitress were in line with Bryan's analysis of his character.

We turned our attention toward the subject of how we'd spend the coming five to ten days. Given that there was not an actual glanders threat to the best of our knowledge, we settled down to a muted discussion of how to best utilize our time in the year 1865. Perhaps a walk around the town would suggest something.

Bryon dug out a folded sheet of paper and read from the list. "Well, here's the list of 'studies' we can perform while we're here." He passed the paper to me, presumably to give me the first choice.

I glanced at the list and then had a brainstorm. "Let's get the local newspaper and see if there is anything of interest there to follow up."

Bryan accepted the paper and refolded it. "That's an excellent idea!"

"Okay." I dabbed my mouth with a napkin. "There's a pile of papers right over there."

I stood, picked up a newspaper, and dropped a penny in the little coin box. Bryan accepted one of the pages, and I opened the other.

"This isn't local, but it's interesting anyway," Bryan said. He read part of the text of the story out loud. "The Sultana steamship sank seven miles north of Memphis, Tennessee. The boilers exploded. Although the boat had a capacity of three hundred seventy-six passengers, there were two thousand, one hundred thirty-seven soldiers returning home on board when three of the four boilers exploded. Significant deaths occurred due to the explosion, drowning, and hypothermia. The rescued totaled seven hundred by other boats in the area."

We settled down to peruse any other stories. A thorough study of the newspaper revealed little of a local nature in which to sink our teeth. I wondered aloud if the local Rebel officer's arrest would be in the next day's paper. A mob hung a negro in Macon, Georgia. The Freeman's Bureau set up shop in Atlanta to acquaint the recently freed blacks with their legal rights. There was a brief story relating to the "unlikely" grants to negro families of forty acres and a mule as doing so would upset cotton production even more than was already the case. We were already aware that Titustown, in far northwest Georgia, maintained a relatively small population of negros. The farming was just above a subsistence level for most locals before the war. We could see that the blacks in the streets seemed to be moving through rather than into the town. They had all of their possessions, whether walking, pulling hand carts, or even wagons.

14

Our newspaper studies were interrupted by a commotion in the street. Several patrons moved toward the front, and we joined a few to peer out the window. A man riding a chestnut horse pulled a staggering white man down the avenue at the end of a rope. With the Macon story about a hanging fresh in our minds, I would not have been surprised to see a black man so abused, but such treatment of a white man was a curiosity.

We followed behind the rest of the Star's patrons along the short walk toward the sheriff's office. The fellow pulling the man along was a rough-looking customer. He wore the remnants of a Confederate uniform. There was a six-gun on his hip, and a carbine lay snug in a scabbard in front of his right leg. There was an odd, wild-eyed glint in his eyes, and he seemed to be talking to himself until he pulled up in front of the jail.

"Sheriff!" he bellowed. "Sheriff!" The rider was dismounting when the sheriff and his older deputy emerged from the office.

"Wilks! What are you dragging in now?" The sheriff seemed put out by the disturbance. Another small crowd of citizens was gathering. We were the second group to assemble in an hour.

Mrs. Sarah Jordon was standing at my elbow. "Oh, oh, Tubby Wilks is at it again!" I turned and noticed that the man's antics were loud enough to attract the customers' attention in other stores. Behind us, the heavy-set cook, Miss Emmy, and the girl, Ellen, were crowded up at the rear of our assemblage.

"What's this about?" I looked from the scene to Mrs. Jordon and back.

"It could be anything," she sighed. "Tubby got back from the war three weeks ago. He is addled pretty much beyond repair, according to Doctor Jenkins. He's what we call a walking wounded."

"Addled from his experiences during the war?" I asked.

"Mostly. Well, Tubby was off a smidgen before he took off with the other boys. Whatever happened while he was gone has made him worse." She turned to go back inside. "I don't want to watch him carrying on again."

I remembered that her husband was still missing. Possibly she was thinking that if he came back, there was a chance he'd be a "walking wounded" in some way, as well. She slipped away, and for a second, my eyes followed until they lit on the young black girl. For the first time, our gazes met, and I felt the first magnetic effect of those big dark eyes. She was but a child, so it wasn't that romantic notions were stirred. It was more of a sympathetic connection. I regretted the obstacles her blackness created. Perhaps she had the same concerns about my hair. She turned away, and my attention reverted to the men in the street.

"Sheriff, there is something wrong with this man!" Tubby was gathering up his rope and walking toward his trussed captive.

"Something wrong with him? Well, Tubby, dragging him in here on the end of a rope won't help him, will it?"

"I don't mean like that!" Tubby said the words angrily. "I mean, he don't rightly look human." Tubby lifted the loop from around the man's waist and stood back some. "Look at him! He's pink as a pig's snout."

"Albino," I diagnosed under my breath. I knew the condition was pretty rare. The man was tall and though still upright, appeared to be worn out from his forced walk. His tied wrists appeared scuffed and red. He was wearing a black coat, trousers, and black boots. His clothes were dusty and in disarray as if he had taken a tumble in the dirt a few times.

The sheriff took a couple of steps down from the porch and looked back at his deputy. "Boggs, see if you can talk some sense into Tubby, will you?" He approached the man and reached out to untie the bindings. "I'm sorry, stranger. Tubby gets kind of het up at the strangest things sometimes. The war, you know."

Deputy Boggs approached Tubby and looped an arm around his shoulders. "Tubby, let's go over the Star and have a beer, and you can tell me all about how you come on this gent." He made to move toward the Star, but Tubby wasn't having any of it.

"Amos, I'm telling you this fella ain't normal. When I found him, he was doing something to a big round chunk of rock out in the middle of Joseph's Creek. You know, down in the creek bottom? I was rabbit hunting, and my dog run off again, and I come around this curve in the creek, and there he was! And Amos, that rock wasn't there two weeks ago. That rock had picture writing all over it. And a scorched tree on one side of the creek bank looked like lightning hit it!"

Boggs glanced around the onlookers and nodded agreeably. "I understand, Tubby. Let's let the sheriff deal with this, fella. You and I can go over to the Star and talk about it all you want." He started toward the Star again.

"No! I can tell you don't believe me, Amos!" Tubby dug in his heels and looked around suspiciously, then brushed Deputy Boggs' hand from his shoulder. He turned around abruptly and put his foot in the stirrup and swung awkwardly aboard his horse. "I'm going home now." He reined around toward the sheriff and the freed man. "I done warned you, sheriff. Whatever happens, don't forget that."

He rode off down the street. The show was over. Some of the crowd chuckled, and the people from the Star started moving back inside. I turned to follow, but Bryan stopped me.

"Paul, I want a closer look at that fella."

"Huh? Why?" I glanced back down the street, where the sheriff escorted the strangely acting man toward his office. I looked at Bryan. His face registered concern, but I couldn't tell whether he was worried about the befuddled returned soldier or the tall, slender pale-skinned man.

Bryan pulled me aside. "We need to introduce ourselves to the sheriff, anyway. It seems that now is as good a time as any."

That made more sense than Bryan's desire to look the man over. I nodded, and we headed toward the jail.

The sheriff and older deputy seemed about to enter the jail, but the tall stranger hung back and finally slumped down into one of the chairs on the porch. He motioned toward his mouth, and Deputy Boggs nodded. Boggs went inside the office, and the sheriff dropped down into the chair next to him. We arrived before there was time for any questions.

"Howdy, Sheriff!" Bryan and I mounted the steps. The sheriff gave our redheads a quick appraisal and seemed to remember us from the Star. He rose to his feet. I looked down at the seated man and noted for the first time that he had the skin of an albino, but the hair sticking out around the edges of his hat was as black as coal. For the first time, I felt my curiosity rise. All of the Albino-afflicted people I knew about had no pigment in their skin or hair.

"My name is Bryan Smith. This gentleman is my brother, Doctor Paul Smith," Bryan said. I lifted my eyes from the seated man and looked toward the sheriff.

"Doctor?" The sheriff stuck out his hand, and we shook. "I'm Sheriff Beckett."

"We appreciate you rescuing our friend, Joe." Bryan continued. He laid a hand on the seated man's shoulder and smiled. "Joe is on our team."

"Team?" The sheriff's face registered the same confusion as I felt. I almost said the words out loud myself. I looked at Bryan with something of a double-take, I'm sure. The conversation was interrupted by Deputy Boggs coming out the door with a dipper of water. He handed it over, and the strange-looking man drank.

"Yes, sir." That gave me a second to decide that it was less awkward to play along with Bryan than not. So, I picked up where Bryan left off, although I didn't know where the heck we were going with this tale. "I am a veterinarian assigned to this area to deal with a disease called Glanders." I pulled my papers out, including the one signed by Major Rogers, and handed them over. Most people have little patience with paperwork, and the sheriff was no different. He took in the heading, then skipped to General Abrams' signature. He looked at the paper that Rogers had signed, and his jaw clenched.

"Glanders? Amos, you ever heard of glanders around here?" The lawman handed my papers back.

"Yeah, I think it afflicted Charlie James' mules' way back before the war." Amos was still watching "Joe" drink. Finally, the man finished, handed the dipper back, and straightened up.

"You are correct, Deputy," I said. "It afflicts mules, horses, and donkeys. As my papers indicate, we have contracted with the Army to make the rounds here in the north and central Georgia to look for any afflicted animals." The sheriff was looking at me strangely. I glanced over at Joe. It passed through my mind that I wished Bryan wasn't linking us up with this strange-looking fella. Any suspicion of him could splatter over onto us. With our red hair, we might seem just as strange as the albino to these men. I was sure that a lot depended on the sheriff's tolerance for odd. At that moment, he was still staring at me in such a peculiar way that it raised the hair on the back of my neck. I felt like a hammer was about to fall.

"Your accent, I'm guessing, Missouri?" Sheriff Beckett stabbed his finger at me. "Yep, Missouri!"

"Well, Arkansas." I took a quick breath and felt the hackles subside. "I was brought up in the northwest corner right up close to the Missouri line," I said. "You have a good ear." I pulled out my bandana and wiped the sweat from my forehead.

"Well, I went west for a while before coming back to Titustown. Saint Joseph mostly, but I did make it out to Springfield." He glanced toward Joe. "What's your last name, son?"

Bryan stepped in again. "Well, that's the thing, Sheriff. Joe is a deaf-mute. He communicates pretty much by reading lips and signs," he said.

"That explains why he's been so quiet all along," Boggs observed. He patted Joe's shoulder. He turned back to us. "And, don't hold Tubby's actions against him, gents. He came back from the war a bit worse off than when he left. I'll explain it all to him the next time he's in town. Once he understands, he won't give your friend any more trouble."

Sheriff Beckett stood. "Well, Deputy Boggs and I have got work to do. I'd say, stay clear of them Yankees if you can, but with your job, I guess you have to mix with them some."

"Yes, sir," I said. "I reckon we do." I refolded the papers and stuck them in my pocket. "As you know, we have already been out to visit with the major."

The sheriff frowned. "Watch out for that tinhorn soldier. One of my best friends is in the lockup because of him. No matter what his rank, he's a knot-headed Yankee for sure. He could turn on you for no reason at all."

"Well, thank you, Sheriff." Bryan put his hand on Joe's shoulder and gave it a friendly pat. The man looked up at him and seemed to be a little less spooked. Maybe the warm tone of the conversation reassured him. Bryan linked his arm with Joe's as if to assist him up, and we headed back toward the hotel with him loosely in tow.

When we were out of hearing of other people, Bryan said, "I think this fellow is a Plutonion."

"What's that?" I was confident from the man's pink skin that he was an albino, although the dark hair threw me. I wondered if the term Plutonion was some albino subset that I didn't know of. That could explain a lot.

"He's from Plutonia, a planet revolving around Proxima Centauri Two," Bryan responded straight-faced.

I stopped in my tracks and just stood there with my mouth hanging open. I knew where Pluto was. I had never heard of Plutonia. Given the dark hair, I could accept that Joe was some albino that I was unaware of. But I couldn't for the life of me fathom that this man was from a place as close as Pluto, let alone another star system.

15

Maybe it was the broad smile beneath the thick red mustache that led Joe to trust Bryan. Perhaps he just wanted to get away from the sheriff or out of the public street and felt we were the lesser of two evils. When Bryan motioned for him to come with us to our room at the hotel, he agreed. The clerk was not in view, and we made it to our room without incident.

When we were safely inside, Bryan said, "We need to shift Joe to a language we can understand." He pulled his Homey from his pocket and gave it a counter-clockwise twist, which I knew was a language setting from my training. It was a multi-pulsar-homing device like the one I carried in my pocket. He pressed one end and held it to his lips. He spoke as if to illustrate his intentions. Then he handed it to Joe and moved his mouth as if still talking. Joe nodded, and when he spoke, his first words emerged in a musical language that was like none I ever heard before. Halfway through the first sentence, his words morphed into English. He looked surprised, touched his lips, and then smiled. "This is a relief! My own translator is part of my disguise, but Tubby caught me just as I am." He held his white hand up as if to demonstrate.

"You are from Plutonia?" Bryan said. The translator changed English into the musical tones of Plutonian.

Joe stiffened, then sat down hard on the bed. His face relaxed into relief. He tilted his hat back and wiped his forehead with the palm of his hand. He looked at us closely. Aside from his lack of skin coloring, he was an attractive man with deep blue, wide-set eyes, a square jaw, and a beardless face. And there was something else.

"Bryan, he has horns." The words burst out before I could help myself. I pointed at where the hat had tilted back and revealed little nubbins of bone-like material piercing the skin at his hairline. "Holy cow, it's a good thing that Tubby or the sheriff didn't notice that!"

Bryan nodded. "Or the hat didn't come off while dealing with Tubby." In the course of the conversation that followed, we learned that Tubby was right about a new boulder buried a foot deep in the sand of a creek north of town. It was not just any rock either. For lack of a better name, it was a space-lander with an outer skin with a rock-like appearance. Joe had a small problem that Tubby had turned into a big one. The ship's propulsion system was out of whack. The burnt tree that stirred Tubby up so much resulted from the ship's swiping past it during an emergency landing. Joe had no desire to stay in the vicinity of Titustown, but now he was miles from his craft.

"So, why are you here to begin with?" Bryan looked at Joe closely. I knew he wasn't referring to Titustown specifically but earth in general.

"My partner and I are law enforcement officers." Joe moved the flap of his coat aside, revealing an object looped around his belt. On the face was a symbol that looked very much like a pound sign on a typewriter keyboard. "We are in pursuit of a criminal who escaped custody on our mothership. He escaped in a lander like the one I used."

"And he is in the vicinity of Titustown?" I asked.

"Not originally. We had our escapee located in Huntsville, Al-abama, but then he eluded us." He waved his hands. "Fortunately, we were in disguise at the time and didn't attract undue attention. My partner took off on horseback headed this way in pursuit of him. By now, he has probably reached Atlanta. I had to retrieve our lander. My partner and I were supposed to rendezvous in Atlanta unless he overtook him on the way."

"So, you are the law." I looked at Bryan.

"Yes. When I headed for Atlanta, the thrusters started acting up."

"Do you think we can help him with the lander?" I looked at Bryan.

"I don't know, but it seems worth a try," Bryan said. "Tubby seems convinced that Joe is an invader up to no good. If he tells his tale to others, they might take him more seriously than Beckett and Boggs did."

"Tubby sure didn't act like he was going to drop the subject." I turned to Joe. "Is there any chance Tubby could damage your ship? Could he gain entry?"

Joe seemed bemused at the question, and his reply was reassuring. "He does not have the weaponry necessary to damage the ship. No, he cannot gain entry, and the ship is not without defenses. If sufficiently attacked, the ship will automatically retaliate. In that case, he could be ashes in seconds."

"I was feeling pretty good up until that last part," Bryan said.

"Well, that response is unlikely," Joe said.

Thinking ahead, I asked another question. "Are there any special tools or supplies that you need to repair the ship?"

Joe nodded. "The fins used to stabilize the craft in the atmosphere retract automatically upon landing. One was bent when I hit the ground. The fin hydraulics are more efficient in drawing them in than extending them. So now the fin is trapped in the fin storage well." Joe didn't seem especially concerned. He scratched around his nubby horn in the same natural movement as I might use to scratch behind my ear.

"My thrusters were the original problem. I know how to handle that. I can free the fin with someone leveraging it outside while I work the controls inside."

"Well, we have two pairs of hands available," Bryan said. "But it sounds like we need crowbars?"

"Our best shot for those is probably the hardware store I spotted down the street," I said. "Bryan, why don't you rent our wagon again? I'll meet you, boys, at the livery stable."

Bryan nodded. He pulled Joe's hat forward and down to cover the horns. "If we can get out of town without attracting any more attention, we might get this fixed without any more dramatics."

The three of us clambered down the stairs and through the lobby. As Bryan and Joe headed toward the livery, I couldn't help noticing how odd they looked together. Our flaming red hair pretty much stretched the limits of 'normal' in the little southern town. Adding our tall pink-skinned new friend was visual overload for sure. Letting the wrong person notice those horns might get us all jailed if not hung.

I bought two long crowbars at the hardware store. The clerk gave my hair the usual quick perusal, but Yankee money spoke louder than his curiosity. In ten minutes, I was on my way with a minimum of small talk. I joined Joe outside the livery while the liveryman hitched the horses to the wagon. I threw the crowbars in the back. I climbed up to ride shotgun, and Joe folded his long legs as he sat behind us on the floor, with his back against the seat. With his hat pulled down low, throwing a shadow on his face, Joe could have been just a regular fella provided his arms were crossed and hands were out of sight.

We took off down Main Street retracing the route Tubby and Joe had used t0 come into town. I thought we might have a dilemma if Joe couldn't remember his route back to his ship. But he didn't hesitate at the junction. Instead, he pointed right, and we moved on.

We were not alone on the road. There were quite a few black men and women coming and going along our path. A group of men still wearing Confederate uniforms, mostly afoot, came into view. They looked hollow-eyed and hungry. Their shoes looked tattered, and their clothes were often in rags. We got a few curious looks, but most seemed to be concentrating on just putting one foot ahead of the other.

Two miles down the road, we came to a dry creek. I could see how that long walk being tugged along by the big chestnut could wear Joe out. Finally, we pulled off the road, and Joe pointed to the left, indicating the direction we needed to go. Bryan directed the team to a clump of trees across a neglected field out of sight of the road. I jumped down to secure the horse, then I hefted one of the prybars and passed it to Bryan as he climbed out. We followed Joe across the field and then scrambled down to the sandy creek bottom. I was thankful that his ship was out of sight of the road when we heard voices ahead.

"Damn!" Bryan murmured. The creek cut a swath about ten feet deep and twelve feet wide through the rusty-red Georgia soil. We hugged the creek's red dirt wall and moved toward a curve just ahead. As we advanced, the voices seemed to be amplified by the steep creek bank. I stuck my head out for a second to see what was happening. Three men were pacing back and forth around a large boulder measuring about eighteen by ten feet in size. It was sitting smack-dab in the middle of the creek. There was no arguing. The scene didn't just look unnatural; it seemed positively weird. The smallest of the men was whacking the ship with his sword with much clatter and no damage that I could see.

The three of us backed away a bit. I looked at Bryan. He shook his head. We were stymied. They all wore six guns. Bryan and I were unarmed. I surmised that Joe must be too, or Tubby would never have taken him. We had no option but to wait them out and hope they'd get hungry or bored. Our situation was different than Joe's. If Joe got the ship operational, he'd take off into the wild blue, never to return. On the other hand, we had a mission to keep us in the area for as long as a week. We didn't need any conflicts with these men that would lead to future harassment and interference.

16

It was already mid-afternoon when we retraced Joe's long walk and made our discovery of the three men at the creek. The presence of the men left us with no options. We conferred for a minute and headed back to the wagon. We'd try to wait them out. I was thankful that we had time in abundance at that point.

I had a million questions for Joe. I estimated from his appearance that he was probably about my age. Besides the differences, such as the white skin and black hair combo and the horns, Joe's features seemed identical to ours. My mind whizzed to my list of questions. How could life forms develop such a similarity on worlds so far from each other?

"But Centauri is years away even at light speed," I said. Joe nodded. I looked at Bryan incredulously. He smiled. "You're saying you can travel close to the speed of light?"

I was thinking of all the science fiction novels I'd read throughout my life, starting with Jules Verne. I was automatically doubtful and was about to argue the point. I looked back at Bryan. He had a funny look on his face. Then I slapped my forehead. What was I thinking? The subject was not arguable. The two of us were walking around in 1865, having traveled from 2110! I felt my eyes widen. Was anything impossible? Bryan raised his eyebrows and nodded again. It hit me like a ton of bricks. In the year 2110, earthlings had intergalactic space travel too! That was a big wow. I started to say more, but a look from Bryan made me hesitate. I let it go. Our little trick with the multi-pulsar should have been enough to alert Joe that we were not of this time. I supposed that it was possible that other cultures did not share our time-travel ability, even if they had the means to travel between the stars, but it seemed unlikely. That was something to ponder! Something in Bryan's look told me to button my lip! Our discussion was interrupted by the sound of three gunshots fired in rapid succession. The fellas down in the creek bed were shooting at something.

The only somethings I could think of were each other or Joe's lander! It was quiet for a couple of minutes after that. Then, three horses emerged from the creek and headed across the field toward the road. Tubby's two friends were upright in their saddles. Draped across the third saddle was a body that had to be Tubby! The men hightailed it to the road and then toward town. We all exchanged looks. Did they shoot each other? We ran across the barren field and down into the creek bottom. There was Joe's lander. Lying beside it was the saber one of the men was playing with earlier. When we got closer, Bryan pointed. There were three lead markings close to each other on the side of the lander. They were grazes. I could see no damage to Joe's flying machine.

"I bet one of those fellows fired at the lander, and Tubby caught a ricochet," Bryan observed.

"If they head back to town with a wounded man, it will raise a ruckus for certain." I looked around, verifying our sudden solitude.

"With other witnesses, I'd expect the sheriff to take Tubby's story more seriously," Bryan said.

With that thought in mind, we knew we needed to get down to business with our crowbars. Unfortunately, Joe had limited time to make his escape, and we had limited time to get out of the vicinity of his lander before we had company.

Joe touched a button on a device attached to his badge. A door opened on the left side of the saucer, close to where someone had directed their gunfire. He entered and came out shortly with a key-like tool to ratchet a rough-looking portion of the lander's rock facade to one side. There was the port in which he said a fin was stuck. "If you will place your bars on each side of this spot, I will be able to extend the fin. First, I need to make some corrections on the thrusters in here." He patted the vehicle's top and used the key again to slide another door to the side. That exposed other complicated-looking machinery.

"You travel the stars with this?" I was awed at the idea.

"No, this is just for local scouting. Our star-travel devices are a hundred times this size."

I looked up at the sky, half expecting to see a huge spaceship overhead. Instead, all I saw were a few puffy clouds. Even if I may have briefly visited 2110 and gone back in time to 1865, my life was centered in 1963, So, as I stood and watched Joe fiddle with his equipment, his words brought to mind President John F. Kennedy's speech about the future of space travel to the moon. I remembered his famous words in his speech at Rice Stadium in September of the previous year. I couldn't remember the details, but I remembered the essence. He said, "*We choose to go to the Moon in this decade and do the other things, not because they are easy, but because they are hard....*" Though I could only remember snippets of the rest of his speech, a thrill went through me. I didn't know the early success of that project yet, but I had just traveled through time. The two rings of connected cities I observed circling the earth suggested we eventually enjoyed some space success. Maybe our progress wasn't accomplished on the original timeline Kennedy set forth, but sometime, somehow, we had made it!

I looked at my pocket watch. About twenty minutes had elapsed since the riders took off. That meant they were in town by now. They were probably rousing the sheriff. I could see Sheriff Beckett and his two deputies mounting their horses and heading our way in my mind's eye. We needed to get a move on!

I remember the scene as if it was yesterday; Joe immersed in the bowels of his machine and Bryan pacing around us. No doubt, his mental timepiece was working overtime as well. We couldn't do our part until Joe finished with his. It was a situation where we might have to abandon him! I wiped my forehead on my sleeve and grimaced. Time was indeed running out. Bryan climbed up on the bank and reassured himself that riders were not going to arrive imminently. He descended just as Joe pulled himself out of the hatch and closed it. Joe looked at us and made a sign that I interpreted as okay. He took Bryan's crowbar and placed it just so in the aperture that held the fin. Joe held it in place until Bryan could take over. Then he turned to me and did the same with mine. I grabbed hold, and Joe looked at us with a broad smile. He patted us on our shoulders just as Bryan had patted him back in town to calm him. He jumped inside, and we heard a whir. We worked our bars in unison, and then the fins started to move outward. The motor stopped. Two independent legs protruded from the side of the boulder. Slowly the potato-shaped ship tilted up about thirty-five degrees until it was sitting securely on the two fins.

Joe appeared in the hatch one more time. He gave an up and down wave of his hand, and the hatch closed. There was a low hum that vibrated the ground. Bryan and I stepped back. There was no flame or smoke emitted. Instead, there was a pulsing that got stronger and grew to a whine. Then, the potato-shaped boulder lifted clear of the creek bank and steadied itself about twenty-five feet above the ground for a few seconds. The wind whistled past my ears as if originating with the vehicle itself. I put my hand up to shield my eyes from the disturbed sand for a moment. Then silence. When I peeped out, Joe and his ship were gone!

"We need to get out of here!" Bryan picked up my prybar from where I had dropped it and handed it to me. He clambered up the steep creek bank. I was right behind him.

We raced across the area and threw our tools into the wagon. Bryan grabbed the reins, and in only moments the wagon was rocking crazily across the field behind the galloping horses.

I held my breath and searched the horizon until we reached the road and could slow the horses. I pulled out my bandana. "That was almost as crazy and my being here," I shouted. Bryan took a deep breath and shook his head in agreement. I looked up at the sky again, half expecting to see Joe making a goodbye pass overhead. Seeing nothing, I accepted that I'd never see him again.

17

We were scarcely a mile down the road when we spotted four riders headed our way. We recognized the sheriff and Deputy Shires. The two men with them wore somber expressions. Sheriff Beckett pulled up beside us.

"Howdy, Doc." He nodded at Bryan and peered down the road behind us. "You gentlemen see anything unusual?"

We presented only puzzled expressions, and one of the men reined his horse past us a bit. "Come on, Sheriff." We told you that the big rock is down in the creek. You can't even see it from the road."

"Slim, I know what you said." The sheriff seemed annoyed by the impatience. "I'm just asking."

Slim made a face and looked back in the direction we had come. It was evident that he thought we were a waste of time.

Deputy Shires nodded. "If we're going to come all the way out here to investigate, we need to talk with all prospective witnesses." He recited the words as if they were from a book. I wondered if there was a book covering such things in 1865. It seemed possible.

The sheriff gave the young deputy a steely-eyed look that shut him up before he could say more. "You men saw the commotion in town this morning when Tubby dragged in your friend, Joe."

We nodded. "You out looking for Tubby?" I looked at the two new men and back at the sheriff. The lawman grimaced.

"Slim and Curt here, say Tubby showed them that big rock he was telling us about and got so worked up that he shot at it, and one of the bullets ricocheted and caught him right through his left eye." He frowned. The two men were nodding agreement. "So, Tubby is dead." He paused. "Where is Joe?"

"I'll swear!" I said and looked at Bryan shaking my head, then back at the sheriff.

"I'm sorry. But shooting at a rock don't make a bit of sense, does it?" I let the words drawl a bit.

Bryan picked it up at that point. "Well, Sheriff. Joe was shook-up by the treatment he got from Tubby. Best, we could make out from his signing, Joe was riding along the road when Tubby came out of the creek and put a gun on him. The next thing he knew, his horse had run off, and he had a noose around his neck. We left him in our room at the hotel. After resting up, he's supposed to head on up to Winston to do some fieldwork before we get there. That's our next stop." Bryan glanced at the two new men.

The sheriff nodded and reined his horse around. "Alright, boys, let's get this done. Show me your big rock!"

The sheriff patted his horse's neck and made a forward-ho motion, and the four men were off. I pulled out my bandana and tipped back my hat. "That is as close as I want to get to disaster!"

Bryan grinned. "As much as I'm opposed to mayhem, Tubby shooting himself was very convenient, wasn't it? I wish I could see their faces when they get down in that creek, and the rock is gone."

We rode on into town and turned in our wagon. After some exploring of the stores and shops, we found ourselves back at the Lucky Star. When our food was brought to us by another pretty gal, we mentioned that we were familiar with Mrs. Jordon and her concerns about her missing husband. The girl nodded in agreement.

We learned from her that Mrs. Jordon was off the rest of the day. She was visiting one of the farms where a friend of her husband was recuperating from his wounds. He was the young man who reported Jimmy killed in action.

My rear-end was pretty worn out by the time dinner was over. Our horseback ride into town and two trips out in the wagon interspersed with three meals sitting in the Lucky Star made me ready to lie down. The sky opened up as we were finishing up. Bryan didn't argue when I suggested a trip up to our room for some downtime.

I lay down on my bunk and thought about the day's doings. That naturally brought up some questions. I was still thinking about Joe. "So, Bryan, tell me about star travel." I put my arm behind my head and turned toward him. He had his arm over his eyes. I wanted to get my questions answered before he dozed off. I knew by then about his implanted memory appliance installed forward and over his left ear. He could pull up a galaxy of information almost as naturally as from his own brain.

"The short version?"

"That will do for starters," I agreed.

"Okay, here goes." He folded his pillow back on itself so he could prop up his head a bit. "It was actually in the 1960s when things started perking up space-wise."

"I remember," I said.

"Well, I guess you do." He smiled and continued. "Things moved along pretty well from the early Russian flyby of the moon. The old USSR put a three-person crew in orbit, followed by the first spacewalk. Then there was a flyby of Mars by the United States. Finally, in 1965 there was the first soft landing on the moon."

"Men landed on the moon? 1965?" I lifted my head from the pillow. "That is just around the corner for me back home."

"No, not yet. That landing was unmanned. Then the first plants and animals circled the moon to see what effect space had on them, I suppose." He stopped. "Maybe I shouldn't be telling you all of this. This stuff is still in your future."

"Come on," I said. "I'm interested, and you're getting my veterinarian services for free. Keep talking!"

"Well, okay. I don't think this situation has come up before. Of course, we're not supposed to share time-travel and space travel stuff with the natives, but you're one of us now." He paused. "I guess. It's not like there are rules yet so that if I tell you, I'll have to leave you here or anything," he grinned.

"Okay, good," I said impatiently. So far, this info was primarily low-grade sci-fi material. "When did we get to the moon? Let's move along!"

"Okay, the moon. That was July 1969. We landed on the moon, got samples, took photos, and made it back to earth in one piece."

"Now we're getting somewhere!"

"I'll skip the lunar rover stuff. You want to know about actual humans, right?"

"Yeah, just the human stuff." I was getting a kick out of accessing information nobody else in my time knew or possibly might never know.

"Okay, next came Mars."

"We landed on Mars! Now we are getting somewhere!" I said again.

"Not yet; I got ahead of myself. First, there were several space stations and some soft landings, and so on." He rubbed his forehead. "The first landing by humans on Mars was February 14, 2025."

"Valentines' Day!" It took me a second to make the connection. "Red Planet, red heart, get it?"

"Right. Okay, then things got serious. By 2035 we had landed on everything worth exploring that wouldn't kill us with gravity or radiation: nasty places, some of them. We thought we were done exploring by 2038. There were colonies on the moon and Mars by then. Mining operations, mostly. The pandemics that started in the 2020s came and went for a long time. Every time they thought they had one strain licked, it mutated, and they were back to square one or two. They had an impact on population growth, especially in developing countries. And by then, the sky around the earth was a minefield of space junk. The oceans, air, and freshwater sources were polluted almost beyond repair. I'll skip that part except to say that space was kind of put on a back burner for a little while, and science turned inward to give full attention to those things."

"Stars!" I reminded him and felt a thrill run through me.

"I'm getting there, okay? Here's how it went. In 2040 Doctor Phillip Domus worked on a math problem so long and complicated that it took the world's latest and greatest computer to handle it." Bryan turned and leaned on his elbow. "He was in his office on one of the huge space stations orbiting the earth. A couple of stations existed long before the ring cities were installed. Doctor Domus was running programs up, down, and sidewise." Bryan grinned. "Don't quote me on that." He poked the air to illustrate. "He hit a wrong key while entering one factor, so the equation was not what he intended. The computer stopped! As you would say in 1963, it was dead in the water!" Bryan stopped for a moment to illustrate his point. "That isn't from memory. It's from here." He tapped his noggin, referring to his appliance. "Of course, all computers were equipped with artificial intelligence by then. Very sophisticated A-I, I must point out. Doctor Domus asked the computer what was wrong, and it told him to add pi in a particular spot in the equation. So, he tried it." Bryan grinned. "You won't believe what happened next."

"So, tell me!" My excitement mounted just seeing the expression on his face.

"Bryan threw his feet around to the floor and leaned toward me. "There was a crackle like lightning. And the computer said, "add pi.""

"So?"

"So, he did!" Bryan was watching my face intently. "And there was another crackle, and the computer said, "add pi.""

"I don't get it." I threw my legs off the bed, and we were facing each other about four feet apart.

"He did that six more times."

"I still don't get it," I said.

"Well, neither did he until an assistant rushed in and interrupted him to say that the big boys at the space center on the ground were going crazy."

"Why?" I was already as confused as I'd ever been. The whole pi part and then the repeats made no sense at all to me.

"They were going crazy because the huge space station holding the most powerful computer in the world and a few hundred people disappeared for an instant. Instead of holding a continuous orbit around the earth at twelve thousand miles per hour, it disappeared! Then, after a few seconds, it reappeared in the same location from which it had disappeared." Bryan raised his eyebrows.

"So?" I looked at him dumbly. Then, I wondered, what did this have to do with the stars?

"So, its orbit was interrupted. Of course, Domus figured out later what happened. Every time he inserted pi and ran the program, an incredibly powerful force field resulted for just an instant. The space station disappeared from point B and returned to point A, where it had been a few seconds before! And it was doing that at the speed of light. Imagine what it looked like for a huge space station to disappear and reappear at point B just once! But, nine times in a row? Doctor Domus figured out later that it was moving backward in time at light speed. To the people on the ground, it looked like it was dancing in one spot!"

Suddenly I was on my feet. "I got it!" My little veterinarian brain got it! The guy had discovered time travel! Every time Domus keyed in pi, the space station, the computer, and everyone on board, jumped back in time to where they had been in orbit a couple of seconds before! The repeated "pi" was the result of the time jump!

I stalked around the center of the room for a minute while it sank in. Then, still hungry for the answer to my original question, I said. "So, star travel?"

Bryan dropped back down on the bed. "It took them a year to figure out precisely what they had and another ten years to learn to control it. But Doctor Domus wasn't finished! He realized pretty quickly that those jumps were happening at the speed of light. Some nips here and tucks there, and stars here we come!"

"Wow! So, you're saying that humans can now not only go back in time but can move through outer space at the speed of light!" I stared at Bryan. I realized I had been holding my breath.

"Doctor Domus did the equivalent of inventing the wheel, discovering fire, and coming up with e=mc2, and the public would not know about it for another twenty years."

I fell back on the bed. I was dizzy. I grabbed the pillow and pressed it to my forehead, and held it there for a long time. I just wanted to run it all through my brain some more. I must have gone to sleep because the next thing I knew, Bryan was asking me if I was interested in breakfast.

18

It was a pleasant day. The air was less sullen after the rain. As we passed through the lobby area, we could see that the natives were clattering up and down the street afoot, on horseback, and in wagons. The pretty Mrs. Jordon was back at work when we went down. She was friendly, but she looked haggard around her eyes. I wondered if she had gotten enough sleep. Bryan and I had decided that we might as well see if we could locate our prospective sperm donor. The Yankee soldier possessing such a rare horse must be known to a lot of his comrades.

Looking about, I spied Mrs. Jordon's uncle sitting against the back wall. He was a spry-looking older gent with cloudy eyes, a clean-shaven triangular face, and a sparse mustache that he would habitually run his forefinger across. Business was light, and Mrs. Jordon joined him after making the rounds to top off the customers' coffee.

She appeared almost weepy when she sat down. I could read the sympathy in old man's eyes and gestures. It was apparent that he was fond of her and her of him. After a few minutes, he made some remark that amused her, and her countenance was more cheerful when she made another round of the tables.

"We missed you last evening at supper," I said.

"Yes, I needed to go visit with one of my husband's friends. He was wounded, and not only was I concerned about him, but I thought he might have more information about Jimmy than had been passed on to me. You know how rumors are."

I said, "I hope the friend could help you out."

"Well, he was sorry enough to carry bad news, but even his information was second-hand. It's hard to keep track of things in the heat of battle." She glanced toward Pappy and smiled a little. "Pappy just keeps telling me not to give up. He says it takes a bullet to the head, the heart, or the gut to kill a Jordon, and Jimmy is made of stern stuff. But, of course, he's hinting that the stern stuff came from him." She made a wry smile. He's a Mexican War hero himself. Of course, he pooh-poohs that and won't talk about it. And just between you and me, I think Pappy thought the War of Secession was a poor cause." She stopped herself and looked at us with concern. "I beg your pardon for speaking so. I didn't mean to offend."

We assured her that we weren't offended. I remembered the battle that occurred near my hometown. There were a lot of deaths and many injured on both sides. It seemed that all wars seemed to call up more glory in the runup and the long aftermath than in the moment.

Sarah Jordon was a pretty gal, and we hung around longer than we needed to just for the scenery. Of course, she wasn't the only pretty gal around. I glimpsed the black youngster back in the kitchen from time to time. I marveled a little that a peach-cheeked white girl and an ebony-skinned black girl could be so different in appearance and yet both be beautiful in their own individual ways. Looking at them made me feel old. I was forty-five. In terms of age, either of the girls could have been my daughters. The oldest of the two was childbearing age, which in theory, could make me grandfatherly! Thinking over recent history, I thought they would be wise to keep the black girl as far away from the restaurant's male customers as possible, both Rebel or Yankee. A man who would treat a white girl inappropriately could undoubtedly be a danger to a black girl—especially one of her tender age.

While we were at the Star, we learned that Tubby's friends had returned to town with the sheriff the previous evening extremely disgruntled. All that they had found in the creek was a foot-deep depression in the sand, an abandoned saber, and assorted footprints that they assumed were their own. Although they swore that the big rock had disappeared into thin air, Beckett lost patience and headed back to town. Since Tubby had no local kin, his body was left in the local doctor's custody since he also served as an undertaker. Money was tight. Tubby was to be buried at the local cemetery with a minimum of services and expense to the county unless his friends chipped in.

Finally, after too much coffee and the Star almost empty, we gave up and went to the livery stable to pick up our horses. Again, we discussed the risk we were taking. They weren't sterling examples of horseflesh, but horses were hard to come by, and if someone were to recognize one of ours, we could be in hot water with the local constabulary. Finally, we decided that the risk was too great with us being strangers. We were headed straight for the lion's den out at the Jones' farm. Soon we were back in the wagon.

When we arrived at the Union headquarters, we could see that things had calmed down some. We stopped in at the office and spoke with the big corporal. Since we were supposedly there to inspect the herd, we could not appear to be looking for a particular horse. Instead, we inquired about the general practice of pasturing the livestock. The corporal, impatient with our questions, found a private to escort us around.

Private Evans was a middle-sized young man hailing from Riparius on the Hudson River in upstate New York. He spoke with a more clipped speech than my supposed Arkansas accent.

"Now, what are you gents planning to do?" He looked at us curiously while we explained again why we were there.

The corporal had told him nothing other than to keep track of us, I expect. We told him about our supposed mission as we walked past the barn. There was a large pasture filled with every description of horse I could imagine. We walked among them for a while, pointing out one thing or another to keep up the pretense. I loved being among so many of my equine friends all at once. My veterinary practice relied heavily on treating cows, sheep, goats, and an occasional dog and seldom provided this depth of exposure to horses. After walking about for a little over half an hour with no success, I looked at Bryan and shrugged. I wondered if it was time to panic yet. Then another thought came to me.

"Say Private, I suppose that some of the horses are out on patrol or something, aren't they?"

"Yes, Sir." I suppose Corporal Yates could fill you in on that. At any one time, I think that about thirty percent of the troopers, and of course, their horses are out on patrol. Ruffians overran the area for a while, harassing the farms, stealing livestock, and robbing anyone they could find riding alone. The rest of the time, some of them act like they're regular folks. These Rebels are never going to admit we whipped them. They are always spoiling for a fight. I can't wait to get home. My hitch is up at the end of September." He looked off toward the north and smiled. "My girl has red hair." He swung around and eyed us. "Not as bright as yours, though. You two related?"

"Brothers!" Bryan and I declared almost in unison. We left him then and walked past the two sentinels guarding the horses. We nodded at the two guards by the front door and approached Corporal Yates' desk again. He was absent, so we ambled around the room while we waited. Eventually, he came out of the major's office and stopped when he saw us.

"Yes?"

"We have examined the horses out in the pasture. We don't see any problems there," I said. "We understand that as many as a third of your men are on patrol at any one time. Is that correct?"

He shrugged. "That's a pretty good estimate. Major Rogers has his notions about how to patrol the area. There is a rotation. One troop goes out every day to sweep the area nearby. A second troop goes out for three-day intervals to look further afield. Finally, a third troop is out for a week to ten days searching the farthest locales of the major's command."

"So, if we return every few days, we will eventually have access to all of the horses in this command, is that right?" Bryan said.

"That's the size of it. If you come out on Thursdays, you can have a look at the teamsters' animals as well. They come once a week with supplies."

"Thank you for the information." Bryan and I looked at each other and turned away. It seemed impracticable to go afield in search of army animals on the move. We expected to see a lot more of the big corporal in the days to come. We climbed back in our wagon and headed down the lane. Without saying so, we realized that locating the horse we wanted would be a little more complicated than we had expected.

<h1 style="text-align:center">19</h1>

We ran into the sheriff upon our return. I figured it was best to be first in bringing up the lander business. Maybe doing so would lessen any suspicion of our involvement. Our association with Joe was bound to be lingering in the lawman's mind. "Did you find what you were looking for this morning, Sheriff?"

"No, we found a funny hole in the ground, that's all," he said. "The whole thing would be easier to explain if Slim and Curt were drunk, but they weren't." He looked off away as if pondering something. He didn't seem interested in discussing it further and changed the subject. "How are things going with Rogers?"

"Well, we didn't see him this trip," I said. "We talked with that big corporal, and he arranged for us to look at the horses in the corral."

"He's a hoss, alright," Beckett said, referring to the big man's size.

Bryan filled the sheriff in on the Union troops' daily deployment, running patrols near and far, trying to subdue the local diehards. Beckett shook his head.

"Well, as far as I'm concerned, he is welcome to them. That is probably the only useful thing he can do. He's got the manpower for that. I don't. It keeps him occupied in the countryside and leaves me and my town alone. Whoever stole that payroll did the town a favor. With no pay, fewer of the Yankees hang out in my town, bothering my civilians. If it weren't for the major jailing my friend, Tom Jones, it would have worked out fine." He paused. "Now, Rogers needs to figure out who really did it. Tom's brother, Madison, has shown up. He was a Yankee soldier. I'm hopeful he can figure out something."

"Say, Sheriff, given that we will need several trips out to the Jones farm to look at the Yankee's stock, we're going to be in town for at least a week or more. Do you suppose the townspeople and neighboring farmers would like us to take a look at their animals?"

Beckett's comments about the Army handling the renegades out in the countryside gave me the idea. I used my southern accent to its best advantage, asking my question. The idea of sitting around twiddling my thumbs held no appeal.

Sheriff Beckett pursed his lips. He took off his hat and ran his hand from his forehead to the back of his neck. "Well, I guess it wouldn't hurt. But I expect you had best keep mum about you working for the Yankees. I could write up something for you that might grease the way a bit with the local folks."

I looked at Bryan, he was nodding his head in agreement, but I caught a hint that he wasn't as excited about the prospect as I was. "That would be wonderful, Sheriff. It will give us something useful to do instead of sitting in our hotel room, killing time. And, of course, we'll be happy to do our inspections for free as the Army is footing the bill for us being here."

The free part seemed to seal the deal. We followed the sheriff in, and he wrote up a paper saying he approved our doing animal inspections in Harlon County at the owner's option. He handed it to me and rubbed his chin. "You know, I think I'll go over to the newspaper and have him print up a story in the paper for the benefit of our local townspeople. Bub McGee, over at the livery, is a good man. I bet he'd be willing to let you set up over there for inspections." He glanced up at me as if a light had come on.

"You know, that could drum up some business for him too. He fixes harnesses and does some blacksmithing. I'll go talk with him with you if you're agreeable?" I could tell that the idea of our being useful while about seemed more appealing to him the more he thought about it. So, I folded up the paper, and we all walked over together to talk with the liveryman. Everyone agreed that we'd hang around his place till noon, have lunch, and then make the necessary trips out to the military post.

As we walked away, Bryan finally had a chance to give me his opinion. "I think you should have talked with me about this inspection idea," he said.

"Why?" I looked at him. His comment confirmed my thinking concerning his skepticism. "Well, sorry if you disapprove, Bryan, but you know glanders is not the only disease of horses. There is also the possibility of strangles, tetanus, botulism, anthrax, encephalomyelitis, and colic. And some others that are less likely in this hill country. These are all real concerns of horse people, and we have plenty of them hereabouts." I cocked my head and waited for a second.

Bryan frowned and then nodded. "I guess you're right. Given that our real reason for being here is fake, I kind of overlooked that you are actually a vet," he grinned.

We saw Bub talking with a man out front. The farmer walked his horse back and asked about the free inspection.

"Yep, and this is what I do every day." I said to Bryan, "why don't you go check on the pretty Sarah Jordon and order me a bowl of soup. I'll finish up here and be over in a minute." The farmer sat on a bench and watched as I gave his horse a once over. After finishing up with its hooves, I expressed my admiration for his animal. He grinned and thanked me. That wrapped it up for me.

When I entered the Star, I immediately wished we were somewhere else. It appeared that Tubby's two friends went in right before me and sat just inside the door close to Bryan's table. It was Bryan's turn to sell our mission. He seemed to do alright.

"You boys are strangers in town," I heard Slim say. "What is your business anyway? The sheriff called the other fella a doctor?" The taller of the men rested his right hand on his hip a few inches above his holster. I didn't know if that was a posture of habit or a direct threat, but with the two of us standing there naked of weapons, it was a bit ominous given our connection with Joe.

"Slim, isn't it?" Bryan cocked an eyebrow and glanced between the two men. "Well, you see, boys, my brother, Doctor Smith, is an animal doctor. You could call him a horse doctor. He has a lot of training in treating illnesses of large animals, you know, horses, cows, and so on. We have an authorization from the sheriff permitting us to look at any animals in Harlon County that the owners are concerned about." He stopped to see if he was making any headway. Slim's hand left his hip, and he scratched his neck.

"I might have heard of that when I was in the army. I never met one, though. My old nag carried me through two years of the war with nary a scratch. It is good to have an expert around, though." He looked at Curt, who was nodding his head in agreement.

I was about to speak up and ask about the hole in the ground out in the creek, but Bryan seemed to read my mind. Before I could do more than open my mouth, he continued.

"Well, the doc is going to be over at the livery every morning this week looking at folk's stock. So, you're welcome to come by."

"Yeah, we might do that." Slim took a step toward the door, and we came face to face. "Let's go, Curt. We need to get a move on if we are going to get done in time to go to Winston tomorrow." He nodded to me. "We'll stop by and see you later, Doc."

They moved toward the door, and I spotted Miss Emmy looking our way. I waved and moved to sit at Bryan's table. She nodded.

"I'm hoping that concludes our business concerning our friend, Joe," Bryan said.

"Yes, you did save the day," I admitted. "I was going to start down a dubious road. I'm glad you stopped me." I smiled.

"Well, one thing I've learned on previous capers, two heads are better than one."

We gave the menus a look, pointed out our choices, and the pretty gal delivered our food with a smile that would soften the paint on an Arkansas stop sign.

After the girl left, Miss Emmy reappeared and stood over us in silence for a beat longer than expected. Finally, she glanced toward the kitchen, and we followed her gaze. We could see the black girl standing half in and half out of the doorway. Miss Emmy cleared her throat.

"Doctor Smith, I hate to interrupt your meal, but my girl, Ellen, has a mongrel dog that she's real fond of, and...." She looked back at the kitchen. Then, seeing Ellen lingering in the doorway, she motioned with her hand for the girl to get back to work before continuing. "As I was saying, she has a dog that seems sickly of late. She's so worried about it that she can't attend to her work properly. So, I wondered, you being a doctor, if you'd take a look at it. It's just an old dog, but the girl doesn't have anybody else." She stopped, and I could see that her color had risen. I wondered fleetingly if speaking on behalf of a person of such low social rank might strike a southerner as unbefitting her own station. I learned later that that was not the case.

"Why I'd be pleased to be of service," I said. I again looked toward the kitchen and made a point to nod and feel the pleasure of seeing the big eyes get a mite bigger.

"Thank you, Doctor. She sleeps in a storage area in the alley out back of the Star and keeps the dog there. I'd appreciate it very much. As I said, it's just a mutt, but it's her mutt, you understand, I'm sure."

I nodded again. "Glad to do it. I have treated dogs in my practice back in Arkansas, and though I can't guarantee anything, I'll be glad to look it over after we've finished eating." I glanced at Bryan. He had a faint smile on his lips. I suspected that he was not immune to the idea of pleasing a child any more than I was. I leaned forward after she left and sought to get our conversation back to more immediate interest. "So, do you think Joe's people have time travel as well as star travel?"

"I don't know. Joe didn't let on. It does seem likely. I suppose you could develop one and then the other in an opposite sequence." He paused as if considering his next thought. "The thing is, by 2110, no one has come on a Plutonian for about twenty years."

I know that I stared at him with my mouth open. "You mean they're gone like forever?"

"I don't know. History tells us that civilization's come and go. We've had to weather several pandemics. They had star travel in 1865 while we were only dreaming about it. Who's to say what stage their civilization is in by 2110? We do know that star travel means running into other star travelers very rarely. Space is a big place. Some of them can be more advanced than us. Some can be more aggressive than we are. That is the risk you take out among the stars." He paused. "Or maybe Joe's people scouted us out and decided, we, in this part of the universe, are too horse and buggy for them to fool with for another few hundred years." he grinned and shut up as Sarah Jordan refilled our coffee cups, and I stared out the window at the horses and wagons. I now knew what became of earthlings over the next couple hundred years, but there was no way to guess what became of Plutonians.

20

Bryan and I finished our lunch, and I waved toward Miss Emmy to indicate that I was available. She motioned for me to join her in the kitchen.

"Doctor Smith, this is my cook, Elsie's, helper, Ellen. She works here in the kitchen."

At the mention of her name, Elsie looked around and grinned. She was a large white woman with a fringe of gray around her temples. Miss Emmy said, "Ellen, Doctor Smith has finished eating. Why don't you take him out to see Freckles?"

"I sure hope you can help that dog," Elsie said. "Ellen sets a high store on him. She's been beside herself for two days now."

"Elsie, I want to compliment you on your cooking. The food here is the best Bryan and I have had since we left Arkansas," I said. Elsie smiled broadly.

"Thank you, sir. I'm right happy to hear you say that."

Ellen came close. Though she smiled shyly, she had a dignity about her that appealed to me. She did a little curtsey, and I followed her to the back door. The door hung up a little at the bottom, but Ellen knew to lift it a bit, and we were out in the alley in but a moment. I looked left and right. The lane ran parallel to Main Street and was accessible from the back doors of each of the stores in both directions. On the far side of the alley was a row of outhouses in various degrees of disrepair. There was a lean-to storage area built on the back of the Star's kitchen that probably stored supplies at one time. It had a Dutch door, and only the top half was closed. The shed and doors were unpainted and very weathered.

Based on its condition, I anticipated how it would look on the inside. I wondered while I waited for Ellen to open the top half if having the lower section open all the time didn't invite theft, but I then realized that the girl probably had nothing of value to steal. The shed's floor space was about eight by ten feet covered with a rag-rug. The girl's single bed, covered with an old quilt, was positioned on the left end. A dog-bed took up the far-right corner. A chest of drawers stood on the right side as well. It felt crowded with just the two of us. Bryan followed me in but backed out due to the closeness. I stood to one side to maximize the amount of light that could enter. Curled up, unmoving on its pallet, the dog was a brindle mongrel from several generations of mongrels. The general impression I got was that of a hound with perhaps a beagle mixed in. There were other possibilities as well. There were distinctive small brown spots against a lighter background. I assumed that the minor markings were the origin of Freckles' name. The whitewashed interior with lace curtains fluttering a little in the small open windows at each end suggested a much more pleasant area than I anticipated. There were no other decorations.

I knelt and allowed Freckles to sniff my fingers. Freckles was not very interested. I gauged the dog to be somewhere in midlife. I noticed that the belly was distended a little. I carefully ran my fingers from Freckles' head down across his shoulders and carefully touched the exposed underbelly. There wasn't much of a reaction. Freckles didn't whine or cry out. I pushed a little harder, but there was no increase in his response. The petting did encourage a wag at the end of his tail. It appeared that he was uncomfortable but not suffering. I was aware that this was 1865, and medications available in my time were not on a druggist shelf now. I'd have to be creative.

"What do you feed him?" I looked up at Ellen. She kneeled and placed her small hand on Freckles' head. The end of the tail thumped a few times.

"People leave lots of food on their plates," she said. "I save the meat and fat and bones. So, he gets plenty to eat."

"Well, there are two possibilities that come to mind. First, Freckles may have one kind of worm or another. If that is the case, you can help the situation by feeding him raw or cooked vegetables and cutting out the meat from his diet for a week or so. Cabbage, Carrots, onions, beets, and even garlic are good. Second, fermented vegetables like sauerkraut are good. Any of the vegetables I just mentioned can be fermented in a week or so. So, I'd suggest you set aside some of the available vegetables for eating immediately and start fermenting the rest." Ellen trained her big dark eyes on my face the whole time I was speaking.

"Finally," I said, "don't feed him bread. The yeast can create problems too." She raised her eyebrows.

"You think Freckles had too much meat?" she pursed her lips doubtfully.

"It is one of the possibilities," I said. "Now the other possibility is that Freckles has a bone splinter stuck in his gut somewhere. You should not feed him cooked bones. They can splinter and get caught in his intestinal tract. Better to give him big uncooked bones. He can gnaw the meat off of them without the danger of something breaking off and getting caught."

Ellen nodded. I suspected some of my words were lost on her, but she seemed to get my drift. I looked up at Bryan. He was bending over with his hands on his knees just outside the door. He was trying to catch my words. He straightened up as I rose to my feet.

"That's about it. I want to check on the big guy every day for a while." Ellen nodded again, and her hand trailed along the dog's back as she stood. I stepped out through the door. My eyes swept the alley again. I couldn't help but think of how vulnerable a pretty young girl was in this back alley. I felt a lurch in my gut at the possibilities. We entered the kitchen, and I made a short report to Miss Emmy. She looked relieved. Bryan and I moved back into the eating area.

I glanced around, intending to give Sarah a wave goodbye, but she had disappeared. So instead of returning to our room via the double door into the lobby, we left through the Star's front door, planning to take a little after-lunch walk. As we turned left, I spotted two figures almost a block away heading east down Main Street. I did a double-take. "Bryan, Isn't that Mrs. Jordon?" I pointed.

"Yep," Bryan agreed, his eyes squinting. "Seems surprising, doesn't it?"

"Yes," I said. Sarah Jordon was walking away, accompanied by a tall, slim young man. Seeing her with a young man was surprising in itself, given her marital status. I considered that it could be a relative. However, the biggest surprise was that he was wearing a Yankee soldier's blue cap and uniform.

"Maybe she isn't as negative about all of the Union boys as we assumed."

"Nope, appears not," Bryan said as we headed across the street. We waved at our new friend, Bub McGee, at the livery and continued down to one of the dry goods stores. I was interested in seeing as much as I could while we were visiting a time about fifty-three years before my birth. On the way, we passed the heavily bearded man we noticed trying to flirt with Sarah the previous day at the Lucky Star. He was sitting on a bench, taking the sun by all appearances. He gave no notice to us. His eyes were turned a few blocks down the street, seemingly caught up in his thoughts. We browsed about in several stores. I had visited a Civil War Museum once. Visiting here was a chance to see the same kind of merchandise while it was new and undamaged. But, of course, there were still a lot of empty shelves. I had read that merchants had many hurdles to get past in obtaining merchandise during and after the war. There was a shortage of hard currency. There were delays in moving merchandise. During the war, trade with European countries was interrupted by the Union blockade of Confederate ports. And from the coastal cities to the interior, there were more obstacles to be overcome. I asked about buying some tea out of curiosity, and the clerk said it would be arriving in a few weeks.

We walked as far as Pepper Street and were about to turn around and head back toward the hotel when we heard shouting. A block away, the young Yankee we had observed with Mrs. Jordon was facing off with a black-bearded man several years his senior. I thought for a minute that he was the man we talked with Sarah Jordon about earlier, but we had passed him sitting on a bench near the livery stable, and I couldn't see how he could have gotten so far ahead of us. Besides, this man was skinnier and wore a frock coat. They were facing each other in the center of the street. A few bystanders tucked themselves into the doorways and behind wagons and waited for things to come to a head. We were too far away to make out the conversation, but it was clear from the bearded man's body language that threats were involved. The younger man did not appear to be backing down. I had seen plenty of shootouts on television, but they were all happening out west. We were in Georgia! Watching a shootout on television in black and white wasn't realistic enough to make you feel that you were there. I had experienced actual combat earlier in my life. The situation before us was not television.

Then a peculiar thing happened. The bearded man turned his head away, and the Yankee private pulled his gun. They jawed some more, and the next minute, the man had his hands up and was shouting, trying to attract attention. A small crowd gathered and seemed to be getting pretty het up themselves until Pappy Jordon showed up. The next thing we knew, the older man and the young Yankee were herding the black-bearded gent toward our end of the street. I looked at Bryan, "Doesn't this guy look a lot like the fella from the Star sitting on that bench back there?"

Bryan nodded. "Sure does. Do you suppose they're related?"

"Maybe, but with the number of heavy beards out and about, that could be true for a lot of men." So, we followed along to see what would happen next. As we passed the bench, I noticed that the big man was gone. The three men went on into the sheriff's office. Being between meals and left to our own devices, we crossed the street and went up to our room. As usual, in my new environment, I was brimming over with more questions. But I vowed patience as I could see that Bryan needed a nap.

21

"Tell me about the stars," I said. Bryan and I were both awake after our naps, and I was getting antsy. It was too early for supper, and my childhood phantasy of traveling to the stars was nagging at me even more strongly now that I knew it was possible.

"What do you want to know?" Bryan swung his legs off the bed and put his feet in his boots.

"How many? How far? Have we ever been officially visited here on earth or just scouted like with Joe?" I could see the twinkle in Bryan's eyes. He loved it when he could access his appliance and appear to divulge information from his memory. That was easier to do if he answered one of my far-ranging questions than when responding to one of my off-the-cuff statements.

"I don't pay a lot of attention, but I know we've visited at least ten star systems. The last ship to return was gone twelve years. As far as I know, we haven't received a delegation of aliens. Our solar system is kind of out of the center of things."

"What did the people in these other places look like?"

"Well, I'd say that though humanoid, none of them have looked exactly like us. You saw Joe. He had funny skin and hair and horns. I've read that the expectation was for little green men from Mars to show up on someone's lawn in your time. There have not been any little green men from Mars or anywhere else."

"Disappointing!" To me, Joe seemed a little too close to us to be exciting in the earthling/alien equation.

"Paul, I can see that you are excited at the prospect of advanced civilizations and all of that, but I don't think people through history have given enough weight to the risk we take playing around in the universe," Bryan said. "Why?" He asked without my even saying anything. I got the feeling that he had this on his chest and needed to sound off. "Every encounter we have with other societies leaves us open to conflict. Every conflict could result in our being over-whelmed militarily by another culture." Bryan looked at me intently as if he wasn't sure I was getting the importance of his words. "The Plutonians, for instance, were doing star travel when we were liter-ally still riding around in buggies. Think about that! If they were so inclined, they could have taken us over. As bad as the civil war was, it couldn't match the likely death toll of a war between the worlds with such a disparity of forces!"

"Maybe by the time you reach that level of technology, your civ-ilization has reached an equivalent level of moral and ethical em-inence?" I had thirty years of science fiction brainwashing on my side.

"Who decides what is ethical? Someone once wrote that "the victors write history." Isn't the definition of moral or ethical deter-mined in much the same way?"

"Okay, from a more practical standpoint, our planet was nearly destroyed once. You have already said that we occupy the other planets in our system already. What happens when those resources are gone? I understand that some of those Star-gliders are carrying people to seed other earth-like planets."

"Hooked, aren't you?" He looked at me closely.

"I guess I am. But you do make some good points. Of course, there are plenty of stories that pit us against superior forces, and we still win out."

"Stories that are written by who?" He raised his eyebrows as if to say that I had just proved his point.

I thought for a bit. Bryan's tone concerning contact with other civilizations implied that time travel enjoyed benefits superior to star travel or at least fewer risks to the human race's wellbeing as it currently existed. Would that always be the case?

I mused on his words. "I guess there are two colliding impulses, aren't there? We think that the new will be interesting and will make things better. But, on the other hand, we distrust different ideas, beliefs, and appearances. Humans are just as complex in 2010 as they were in nineteen sixty-three or eighteen sixty-five. That is the one thing that hasn't changed."

Bryan nodded. "As illustrated by this war, the north and south just concluded and even Tubby's reaction to Joe."

I laid my head back and thought about the vast investment in resources and personnel it must have taken to put us out among the stars or for me to lie in a bed in Titustown, Georgia, in 1865. I could see that all of the rewards of that investment were not direct. There was a spill-over of benefits. Technological and medical advances created ways to accommodate the growing number of human beings. Otherwise, we'd eat up resources and eventually starve ourselves back to a number that the earth could sustain or kill each other off in a fight over those resources. I thought of the two rings circling the globe, supporting millions of people. My brief visit to one of the cities on the north-to-south orbital ring had left me awed and yet discomforted. I wondered if that whole system of connected cities in their giant bubbles was as fragile as it looked to me. On the other extreme, I could imagine colossal starships loaded with pioneers heading for the distant stars. Could man's craving for new, different, and better be an instinct that could lead us to the same result as the lemmings plunging over a cliff? I shook it off. Nothing Bryan said could take the excitement from landing on a virgin planet and creating a civilization from scratch. Wouldn't that always be preferable to trying to take over one already inhabited? I felt the same way about walking the streets of Titustown, Georgia, breathing the air, and getting my hands on a Kladruber in eighteen sixty-five. There was too much to see and learn about the universe for a human being to live long enough explore everything. I was forty-seven years old then. I doubted I would have enough time if I had another fifty years. I was right about that. There will never be enough time!

22

Sarah was not at work when we had supper. A different young gal brought out our food. We mentioned that there seemed to be fewer customers, and she agreed, saying that fewer soldiers had the money to pay for a meal off the post since the payroll robbery. Our inquiry concerning Mrs. Jordon brought out the information that it was the girl's evening off. A middle-aged Union corporal and a tall, lean sergeant accompanied the private we had seen with Mrs. Jordon earlier. They were sitting toward the back and eating heartily. They seemed to be hashing some things over until the private finished, pushed back his chair, and announced to his friends loudly enough for us to hear, that he would check on Miss Sarah.

Bryan and I eyed each other and caught the looks of amusement that crossed the sergeant and the corporal's faces. We weren't the only ones who considered the Northern Romeo/Southern Juliet match-up of interest. Then I saw Miss Emmy's expression and realized that interest in the relationship was pretty universally less than approving. Unlike the Union men, the aunt was not at all amused.

Bryan and I were up early the next morning and ate breakfast. I got a wave from Ellen. I took it as a good sign regarding Freckles that there was a smile to go with the wave. The corporal and private sat near the window and seemed concerned about something. They kept looking for the door as if expecting the sergeant. We left the Star and arrived at the livery by eight o: clock. We brought paper and a pencil to keep notes on any animals that might come. The brief paragraph in that day's newspaper mentioned our presence, qualifications, and there was no charge for the examination. Within thirty minutes, Bryan filled in the description, breed, age, and owner information of our first client of the day. I gave the animals a quick once over. Most were pretty fit, as it was spring, and there was grass in abundance. Even those recently in the field involved in war efforts had had sufficient time to flesh out. More horses than I expected had recovered from minor bullet and shrapnel wounds. Most just required that their hooves be dealt with by Bub, the liveryman, who cut his regular fee in half and sent them on their merry way in a smart business move. We had a lull around the noon hour, and after a quick lunch, we went back to the livery to pick up a team and wagon. Bub was so happy at all the business we had attracted for him that he offered to let us have it for free, but Bryan begged off.

"We are the ones who owe you, Bub," he said rather overdramatically, I thought. "You are providing us an office for free already. You are helping out. If word got out that we were diagnosing problems with no handy way available to solve them, people would decide it was a waste of time to come by. You're an important part of this effort. So, we'll pay for the rental; it keeps everything on the up and up."

Bub listened to that longwinded soliloquy and thought it over. The gist was that we would still pay for our rental and keep attracting customers. He nodded his understanding and grinned as he took our money.

Twenty-five minutes later, we were halfway back to the Jones' farm. As we came around a curve in the road, we spotted three Union soldiers riding toward us. We were almost on them before we realized that the second man in line had his hands bound. He was the tall sergeant we had spotted previously with the corporal and private at the Star. He was cussing and carrying on enough that one of the guards stuck his rifle in his ribs to calm him down.

"Wonder what that's about," Bryan commented.

"We'll probably know by suppertime," I said. No telephone, no television, or radio, and yet word gets around in a hurry."

Bryan nodded, and we rode on to the Jones' farm and a visit with the big Corporal at Union Headquarters. He seemed busy and suggested that in the future, as long as we didn't get into anyone's way, we were free to come and go without reporting each time. That suited us fine. We headed for the corrals.

I spotted our big Kladruber before we reached the gate. "Bryan, there he is!" I almost shouted. Bryan turned to me in surprise. A first lieutenant was coming our way. He was carrying a blanket, saddle, bridle, and a brush as he approached.

"Sir," I said. Bryan whirled around and startled both himself and the young lieutenant.

"Yes, sir." The lieutenant stopped and waited expectantly.

"Isn't that a Kladruber you were just brushing down?" I pointed.

"Yes, sir." The young man grinned. "He just arrived a month ago. I didn't want to bring him down from Pennsylvania until the shooting stopped. My family raises them."

"Well, he is a beauty," Bryan regained his tongue. "Have you been on patrol?"

"Yes. We got back last night," he said. He looked at us questioningly. I thought I detected a little concern worrying the corner of his mouth. I wanted to cut that worry short. "Well, I'm Doctor Smith. My brother, Bryan, and I have been commissioned to inspect all the Army's animals for glanders and any other infectious diseases in this part of Georgia. I pulled out my paper signed by the major. He sat the equipment down and accepted it. I could see his features relax as he read. "I was beginning to wonder what was going on when you knew he is a Kladruber. Most people don't." He stuck out his hand. "I'm Lieutenant John Scott."

"I'd like to look him over if you wouldn't mind," I said. "What's his name?"

"Of course, Doctor. But I guarantee there isn't anything wrong with him. His official name is Circumstance. I call him Stance for short."

"Of course, I'm sure there isn't! I just want an excuse to touch him," I laughed. "How did he come by the name?" We walked around the big boy and were enthusiastic with our comments. I ran my hands over him, marveling at his condition. I didn't have to lie a bit, for he was a beauty. The lieutenant was pleased with our attention toward his horse.

"Well, three years ago, I was home on leave. About midmorning my second day there, "by circumstance," I went out to the barn just as his dam was dropping him. I could see there was a problem. So I reached in and straightened things out. Growing up on a horse farm gives you lots of horse tending experience." he grinned.

"Funny," Bryan enthused. "And you got an unusual name out of it. So do you know when you'll be going out on patrol again?" Bryan asked the question as casually as he could.

"Well, next week, I expect."

"We're headed back to town in a few minutes," I said. "Any chance you will be going that way. I'd be interested to hear about your breeding operation back home."

"I'm afraid not." He patted his pocket. "We haven't been paid in over a month. I spent my last dollar for barley for the big boy over there just before we went on our last patrol."

"Well, don't worry about that," Bryan said. "We'll throw in supper if you can get away. My brother and I are excited to see him, and it's worth the cost of supper to learn more about him!"

I nodded. "Bryan is right. We're from out west, and we're always interested in the best practices back east."

"Well, he hasn't been out of the corral today." I could tell that the lieutenant was wavering.

"Well, do it for the horse then," Bryan laughed.

That comment got John past his indecision. We stood by his gear while he entered the office and checked out to go to town. He returned in a few minutes, and we walked back to the big horse and watched while he saddled him. Half an hour later, we were seated at a table ordering some home-cooked food that the lieutenant admitted was worth the ride.

"How many dams and sires do you have back home?" I asked.

"When I left home, we were keeping five dams. We have two stallions to service the dams. Kladruber horses are still pretty rare. There is another breeder in the Pennsylvania Dutch country. Our studs also service other mares to produce sturdy mixed-breed foals. Although I ride Circumstance, the main use of the breed is as a carriage horse. He is a large, powerful animal and would have been a popular target on the battlefield."

"He is a beauty," I agreed. I shuddered at the thought of Circumstance taking a bullet.

Our conversation was interrupted by Sarah's entry. She approached Miss Emmy with a distraught appearance and asked after Pappy Jordon. We overheard a mention that "Private Brumley and Sarge were in jail."

I remembered the bound soldier we met on our way out to the farm. Bryan and I looked at Lieutenant Scott, but he took no notice and thrust some more roast beef into his mouth.

The light was still good when we followed Lieutenant Scott outside and bid our new friend goodnight. He mounted Circumstance and rode rapidly out of town. Bryan rubbed his hands together with relish.

"Things are lining up very nicely. We have discovered our horse, made friends with its owner, and established a pattern for visiting the farm to continue inspections. This mission is going to be easier than I thought."

I nodded. Things did seem to be going well. We turned to enter the hotel and noticed Pappy Jordon about to go into the Star. I caught a glimpse of Sarah at the window. Apparently, she was keeping a lookout for him. We climbed the steps to the hotel as a rider came lickety-split down the way. He halted at the bench on the other side of the street. The bearded man, the Union private, had his altercation with the day before, was lounging there seemingly waiting for the rider.

Back in our room, we played cards for a few hands and were in bed early. Finally, with the stars apparently aligned to complete our mission, I slipped into a restful sleep.

A series of explosions awoke us. It was pitch black outside. Bryan was the closest to the window. He was out of his bed just after the horses thundered by. I grumbled some and rolled over.

"Gunshots!" Bryan said.

"Yeah," I said. "Tomorrow." I dived deeper into my covers. I didn't know then how important the night's events were to us.

23

The next morning, we entered the Lucky Star to find everyone in a flutter. We learned that the shots that woke us were an escape attempt by the farmer, Tom Jones, his brother Sergeant Madison Jones, and the young Private, Bronco Brumley. Of the three, only the two Union soldiers made it away successfully. The farmer, Tom Jones, was back in his jail cell unconscious with a head injury. Miss Emmy gave us the lowdown as she poured our coffee. The old west extended further east than I was aware. It was sobering to realize that people seemed just as prone to violence in Georgia as in Tombstone, Arizona.

As we were leaving, I peeked into the kitchen. Ellen turned toward me and smiled broadly, "Freckles seems to be a little better."

"I'm glad to hear that. I'll try to take a look at Freckles this evening," I said. I was acutely aware that if my home remedy didn't fix him, there would not be much more I could do. I hated to see animals suffer, just as I hated to see pretty young girls suffer.

We went down to the livery and looked over a few horses until close to noon. The area around the jail seemed unusually busy with the coming and going of another wagon and Army troops, but we had clients waiting and couldn't take the time to lollygag. Bryan wrote down the information on a pinto when a ripple of excitement up the street interrupted our work. A parade of mounted Union soldiers and two wagons passed us, heading toward the jail. Strangely, the Union sergeant and private that Miss Emmy reported as escapees accompanied them, unrestrained. Aboard one of the wagons was our new friend, First Lieutenant John Scott. He spotted us, and once the wagon stopped in front of the jail, John climbed down. He spoke with a black sergeant and crossed the street to join us. He was upset.

"Stance was stolen by an outlaw two hours ago out at a place called Carson's Junction."

"Stolen!" I felt my gut lurch. I looked at Bryan, and he looked as stricken as I felt. "How? why?" The image of the beautiful Kladruber kept passing through my mind as I imagined seeing him disappear into the darkness.

John Scott explained about an attempted payroll robbery, a shootout, and the escape of a man named John Coates. While he talked, he paced the barn until he finally threw himself down on a bench and lowered his head into his open palms.

"Surely, they'll catch him," Bryan said hopefully.

"They know who took him. That's half of getting him back, right there!" I said with optimism that I didn't feel. I looked at Bryan, and we nodded our heads in unison. We needed to believe it! They had to catch this Coates fellow. I remembered the horse I was inspecting and gave the more than patient farmer an excellent report on his horse. He grinned and rode away. We talked with John a few minutes more, trying to lift his spirits and our own. After a bit, he rose and announced he had to get back to headquarters. We wished him well.

When the payroll wagon, guards, and Lieutenant John Scott's cavalry troop rode away, we closed up our operation and headed for the Star.

While we waited for our food, we debated going out to the farm and pretending to be inspecting animals out there. There seemed to be no point now. We knew the horse we cared about was missing. On the other hand, we didn't want to blow our cover with Major Rogers or lose contact with Lieutenant Scott. Undoubtedly, our relationship with the two men remained our chief avenue to learn Circumstance's whereabouts eventually.

But it was Sheriff Beckett who provided us with an incentive to visit the farm immediately. He spotted us in the middle of lunch and dropped into a chair across from Bryan.

"Well, I guess you boys will be leaving town now, won't you?" He took off his hat and touched the back of his bandaged head gingerly.

"Huh?" I said.

"Well, the major getting orders to upend everything and move his headquarters to Clarksville tomorrow won't leave you any choice, will it?"

"Move his headquarters? Clarksville?" I twisted around to look him full in the face. My first thought was that he was kidding.

"Yeah, hasn't the major told you? He got orders to move out just yesterday. When I was out there earlier today, Rogers was madder than a hornet. And now that I've got his corporal in my jail, I bet he's in a real stir. He may have to do some work himself."

"Corporal Yates is in your jail?" My head was spinning.

"Yep." And the whole company is moving out, and I'm not one bit sorry to see them go. When they leave, I get my town back. The best thing that can happen." He looked surprised as Bryan and I stood hurriedly and turned toward the door. "Where you boys going!"

"We need a visit with Major Rogers," Bryan said.

"And Lieutenant Scott," I murmured under my breath.

The knowledge that the major's company was leaving the area gave us a reason to shake a leg. We threw the saddles on Sorghum and Billy-Ann and rode out to the Jones farm. Three days of grass and oats and a lack of exercise left the two horses feeling pretty frisky.

The major was coming off the farmhouse porch when we rode up. He glanced at our horses and looked at us sharply. "Those are army horses!"

"Yep," Bryan said. "They came with our papers."

The officer had other things on his mind and nodded acceptance. "Well, this is the first I've seen you since I got my orders to move headquarters. We're disbursing our payroll right now. We've canceled Major Jones' trial, thank goodness. Are you coming along?"

"Yes, sir. We've only had an opportunity to look at about half your horses. Reckon we'll be a thorn in your side for a little while longer," My worry had only deepened with time. I faked a grin, but he didn't seem to see the humor. I moved on, "By the way, is Lieutenant Scott about?"

"No, I dispatched him to Clarksville to assist Captain Rumpole in setting up things there."

Bryan and I exchanged a glance. We thought that we needed to keep in contact with the young lieutenant to keep up with progress in locating the stolen horse. His absence short-circuited that. We were in a bind. If John Coates was presumed to still be in Titustown, leaving town would not be a good idea. I wondered how much effort the sheriff would make to arrest him on an army offense. It didn't matter as he had his local fish to fry. Our reconnect with the major completed, we returned to town, planning to pack our gear and prepare to leave town the following day. We were not looking forward to a long ride to Clarksville. We were surprised to find several people at the livery waiting with their horses for an inspection. Bub had assured everyone that we'd be back from the farm soon, and he was right. It was almost suppertime when we said goodbye to the last owner and watched him ride away. "Free" is one of the most powerful words in the English language.

We told Bub that we were done for the day and probably would not be back the next. His face fell until I pointed out that everything I was finding required his follow-up rather than mine. There was no reason that he couldn't find those problems and deal with them himself. His eyes widened at the implications of that idea. The newspaper article afforded an excellent opportunity to bait and switch. We headed for the Star and noted Pappy Jordon in deep discussion with his great-niece. His face radiated concern. Hers was impassive as if between decisions. Bryan and I ate quickly. I stopped in the kitchen and inquired about Freckles.

"Do you mind if I look in on him?"

Ellen led the way, and we found Freckles lying in the doorway rather than on his bed. His tail wagged enthusiastically. Ellen put her hand on his head and looked back at me. "Thank you, Mister Doctor. I don't know what I'd do without my Freckles. He is my friend and my protector." There was a seriousness in her face that suggested that she foresaw a need for a "friend and protector" or might have needed one in the past. I looked about the little lean-to. I couldn't see any books or games or even crafts in the making.

"What do you do in your spare time? I don't see anything to read. Do you sew?" There was a single chair, a small table, and a little chest of drawers, but everything was bare of adornment or even personal items.

"I can't read a lick," Ellen answered quickly. I caught a little embarrassment in her face.

"Someday, I want to learn." Her words were adamant. "I keep my sewing in the kitchen. It's too dusty to keep it out here."

"I bet you could learn to read!" I felt I needed to reassure her. "Why, you are plenty smart!" The light of intelligence in her eyes had led me to make mistaken assumptions regarding her education, although I should have known better. "I'll bet you could learn in no time."

She smiled shyly. "Maybe you could teach me?" She looked up to see my response. That was an idea I had to quash.

"I'd sure like to, but I'm only going to be here for a few days. You know I read in the paper that the Freedmen's Bureau is working on setting up schools for black children and adults." Her eyes had faded slightly when I said I wouldn't be around long but brightened when I mentioned schools. I looked at the shared wall between the addon room and the backside of the Star's kitchen. This lean-to with an open door on the alley seemed very insecure to me. The equation of this pretty young girl and the lengths taken to provide a protective environment for her was way off.

I tried to estimate what area of the exterior kitchen wall was shared by the lean-to. I assured Ellen that she was welcome to my held and patted her shoulder. The big eyes looked up at me, but she said nothing. We went back inside.

"How's Freckles, Doc?" Miss Emmy asked.

"I think he's better. Ellen seems to be a good nurse," I enthused.

Miss Emmy looked at Ellen. "There have been plenty of times when she was a good nurse when our boys came back shot up. Once we had these tables covered with boys, and Ellen was right there helping out."

Miss Emmy's affectionate lauding of the young black girl encouraged me to be bold. "Could I speak with you for a moment in private, Miss Emmy?"

She raised her eyebrows and nodded. We moved out of the kitchen to a corner of the eating area. I told her about my ideas. She thought about my concerns about Ellen's safety and nodded. "I think you are right, Doctor. She showed up a few months ago looking for work. We just did the easiest thing at the time to have a place for her. A door between the lean-to and the kitchen is a good idea." She paused. "Your idea about a school for black children is a good one too. If Tom Jones weren't unconscious in jail, he'd be just the one to head up that project. I think I'll talk with Cal Jordon and a few other men. I've heard some bad things about that Freedman's Bureau. The men might see our taking on that project as a good way to discourage them from setting up in Harlen County."

With that, I rejoined Bryan, and we went up to our room. We got out our deck of cards and killed some time considering our options. While we had eaten supper, Coates had been the object of discussion at a nearby table, with the odds of catching him outweighing the cons in the estimation of his neighbors.

"Some people say Coates is already out of the County," Bryan said.

"Just as many people claim he's still around," I argued.

"You know there's just one way to handle this," Bryan said.

"Oh?" I laid my winning hand on the table.

"We're going to have to split up!" Bryan threw his cards down and leaned back in his chair. "One of us goes to Clarksville, and the other stays here."

I wouldn't say I liked that, although it made sense. "How about we stick around here for another day or so and see how things develop with the hunt for Coates."

"Okay," Bryan started unbuttoning his shirt. "One more day shouldn't hurt. We still have time before our scheduled departure. But if we don't get a break by the end of the day tomorrow, I think you need to head to Clarksville."

"I need to head to Clarksville? Why me?" I remembered how sore my behind was riding to town a few days before.

Seeing my reluctance, Bryan grinned. "Because you are the doctor whose work is our cover for hanging around the army boys and their horses."

"Oh yeah," I said. I hated it when Bryan came up with a good argument.

" One good thing about leaving Titustown is we won't have to worry about Sheriff Beckett coming up with any questions about what happened to Joe," I said. "Every time I see him, I wonder if he is mulling that story around in the back of his head after seeing that hole in the creek bed."

"Good old Joe," Bryan laughed. "I wonder where he is now."

"Maybe relaxing on a starship headed to the next galaxy for all we know," I said. I kicked off my boots and started unbuttoning my shirt. "We'll never know."

24

We were slow getting around the next day. It was almost lunchtime when we strolled into the Lucky Star. We took one of the tables looking out on the street. About halfway through our meal Bronco came in and sat down at one of the nearby tables. Close behind, the soldier they called Preacher joined him. A little while later, his friend Sarge and the Sergeant's brother Tom Jones showed up. That caused quite a stir. The major's friends among the other diners came over to offer congratulations. Even the somewhat cynical Miss Emmy joined the celebration.

I hailed her over. "Isn't that the fellow Rogers put in jail?" We knew from Major Rogers he had called off the Jones' trial. So, this party was an opportunity to connect the face with the name.

"Yes! Major Tom Jones has been released. Madison and Sheriff Beckett figured out where the payroll box was and who killed the guard!" She looked over at the laughing men. "The whole town knew all along that the major wouldn't do anything like that. I can tell you that if it had come down to a firing squad, the men of this town would have brought the wrath of God down on that Rogers." She stiffened her spine. "We may have lost the war, but before it's over, we'll be running those Yankees out of Georgia!"

Bryan and I exchanged a look. We knew that Reconstruction in Georgia was going to be a painful situation for a long time. It was another situation when knowing the future and how it would likely impact my new friends did more to lower my morale than heighten it. After my meal, I decided that I needed something to lighten my spirits, given our foreknowledge of a southerner's life with Yankees and our dilemma with the missing Circumstance. I looked around for Mrs. Jordon to order a slice of the pie, but she had disappeared. Then, I saw Miss Emmy come from the kitchen and hand a paper to Bronco. He read it, jumped up, and practically ran for the front door. I guessed that something was afoot.

I ordered and received my pie from Miss Emmy. Then, a few minutes later, the three remaining men got up, and we watched them as they mounted their horses and departed.

"Sure, busy around here today, isn't it?" I took another bite. Just as I was finishing up, we were all startled to hear a gunshot. It sounded as if the pistol was fired just out the back door of the Star. The old cook responded with a yelp. The closest customers jumped up, ran through the kitchen, fought their way through the door, and bolted out into the alley. I thought about Ellen and her dog but realized that she was safely working in the kitchen.

Bryan and I froze in our chairs. Were we destined to witness a real gunfight?

Then a young man returned through the backdoor. "Someone shot Pappy!" He passed our table and headed out the front door. "I'm going for the Doc!"

I looked questioningly at Bryan and raised my eyebrows, remembering our limitations on interfering. "Is this a situation where I'm allowed to help?"

He nodded, and we hurried out the back to join two men huddled around the old man's body. I spied some of the other men headed away, already well down the alley. I squeezed in, squatted down, and pulled up the shirt to reveal the double wound. He was unconscious. The bullet had entered through the lower ribcage and departed out the back. I knew what I needed to do. I looked around. "You, put that box under his feet," I motioned toward a small discarded fruit box and pointed to an older man who had propped himself up against Ellen's lean-to with the remains of a bottle. I could see a copious amount of blood leaking out of Pappy's right side. I tore off my handkerchief and pressed it against the wound. The bullet appeared to have missed his heart or belly, and I was relieved that I saw no signs of a sucking chest wound. Blood loss and shock were the most significant threats.

A minute later, we heard another shot that seemed to be coming from down the alley. Then there were two more. We waited. Pappy mumbled something and then was quiet. I put my finger to his neck. There was still a pulse. Then someone hurried up the alley.

"Jimmy Jordon has been shot too!" The men around me made to go down the alley. The first man held up his hand. "You're too late! Jimmy Jordon is dead! The bullet took off half his head."

I looked up at Bryan. I remembered that Jimmy Jordon was Sarah Jordon's husband. We didn't even know he had returned from the war. "Is Jimmy Jordon back and already dead?" Soon the sheriff showed up and stopped to look the scene over.

"I've got this until the doctor gets here," I said. Then, learning of the other three shots, the sheriff hurried down the alley behind his young deputy. Soon afterward, Doctor Jenkins arrived and took over. He looked at the wound and then at me. "Good thing you knew what to do."

"My first bullet wound," I said. "But a puncture is a puncture."

The doctor looked at me oddly, then nodded. I remembered then that it was a rare doctor of any kind in this part of the country who had not treated a gunshot wound at some point in his career. Doctor Yates triple-wrapped a long strip of cloth around Pappy's chest to hold my handkerchief in place while the men carried the old man back to the doctor's office.

"Whew!" Bryan blew out his breath. "I wonder if he will make it."

"I don't know," I said. "I'm sure the Doctor has plenty of experience with bullet wounds. From what I could see, it was a deep flesh wound, but I'm far from an expert on human physiology."

With the information that Mrs. Jordon's husband had returned to town to be assassinated sitting on her front porch, I remembered the girl's hopeful expression when she had talked of his possible return. The word on everyone's lips was why? "Someone moved past us, and I heard his words. "They say it was John Coates!"

"John Coates? That's who they say stole Lieutenant Scott's horse!" I looked at Bryan.

"The sheriff is putting a posse together to go after him!" Another man said.

"Now, we're talking," I said to Bryan. He and I had an additional reason to applaud an active search for Johnny Coates. An intense search for John Coates also improved the odds of locating Circumstance.

An hour and a half later, we stood on the edge of the crowd listening to the sheriff's plan for chasing down Johnny Coates. Just as he was getting into his subject, Sarge, Bronco, and Preacher showed up volunteering to assist. It seemed that the three men could be a useful addition to the posse, but the southerners were having none of it. The Union boys were not welcome. They'd track the killer down on their own, thank you very much. I looked at Bryan. "They don't need us either, do they?"

"Probably not," Bryan said.

Cal Jordon, Jimmy's father, made an impassioned speech concerning his son, and half an hour later, after buying supplies, the posse was off. We went back to the hotel and threw ourselves down to wait. Finally, suppertime came, and we settled in at the Star.

I asked after Mrs. Jordon, and the young girl told us she wasn't coming in. I glanced around. There were no blue uniforms in sight.

"I guess the major and his troops are long gone," I said.

"I bet that if the posse catches Coates, the sheriff will let us take Circumstance back to his owner since we told him we're going that way already," I said hopefully.

"The key to everything is catching John Coates!" Bryan took the menu from Miss Emmy and took a moment to look down the options before we ordered. After she left, Bryan ran his hand over his chin and fingered his mustache.

"It would be good if the sheriff's posse came up with something. I would sure like to have a handle on where that horse is before it's too late for us," Bryan said.

"Too late!" I looked at Bryan. Time had seemed to slide by quite comfortably before the theft of Circumstance. Now, of a sudden, it was an essential factor. We were leaving 1865 on May 9th, come hell or high water! That was only four days away!

Bryan and I set up shop at the stable again, but there were no takers. I thought at first that the day's events were too distracting to the citizens to encourage visitors. Then I realized that so many local horses were involved in the sheriff's posses that most of the county's horseflesh was still out scouring the county to alert the farmers of Johnny Coates' killings. We jawed with Bub a bit, but he wandered off to attend to other business after a while. We heard nothing until late in the day when the different groups composing Beckett's posse returned to town to report that they had made no contact with the outlaw or run into anyone who had seen him. The only developments were a possible sighting by a farmer of the three ex-Union Soldiers and Cal Jordon's decision to continue hunting for his son's killer on his lonesome. As we returned to the hotel, we learned that two men were found dead at Coates' uncle's farm. That brought

Johnny Coates' victim list to three and possibly four if Pappy Jordon didn't make it. I reminded Bryan that there were no antibiotics in 1865, so aside from the doctor dousing the wounds with disinfectant, everything depended on Pappy's immune system. He nodded.

"Tombstone has nothing on Titustown, Georgia," I remarked. There was a pause before he responded. I realized then that the almost undetectable delay when I touched on something Bryan did not know firsthand was because of the half-second it took him to consult his information accessory. Almost everything I knew about the post-Civil War period came from books and television programs about the old west. Bryan had instant access to stats, details, and events that I'd never know.

"You know, I wonder if all the blood-letting of the war coarsened people regarding killing," he said. I nodded, but I suspected it affected different people in different ways.

"That seems likely to me. So now the father is out chasing his boy's killer all by himself." I looked up and down the street. After the three posses returned and disbursed to their homes, the town seemed to revert to its normal sleepy posture. Supper at the Star was a somber experience. There was no sign of Mrs. Jordon. I could only imagine her sorrow for losing her husband after waiting so long for word. Miss Emmy brought us food, but her demeanor discouraged conversation. Our sitting around Titustown, Georgia, achieved nothing toward either catching Johnny Coates or retrieving Lieutenant Scott's horse.

"I think I'll go kill some more time with Bub," Bryan said.

"I'll go back to that other dry-goods store over on Pepper Street. It's the only one we missed the other day." I waved and headed that way. The town appeared quiet after all of the earlier excitement, but people in the store were buzzing over the shootings. I looked over some hats. There was a stove-top hat that I took a fancy to. I approached the clerk and waited while he rang up a couple of things for the malevolent bearded man we observed in the Star. An attractive middle-aged lady inquired about buying tea, but the clerk shook his head. "I'm sorry, Miss Taylor. I still don't have any, but I'm expecting it any day." She nodded and left me to pay for my hat.

I was pretty happy to find a souvenir that was so distinctively nineteenth century. As I approached the hotel, I decided to have another look at Freckles without interrupting Ellen's work. I ducked down the space between the hotel and the building next door to the alley. When I turned the corner and approached, I noticed that both the top and bottom portions of the Dutch door were open. That seemed a bit odd. As I got closer, I heard a noise from inside. I listened to a dresser drawer being slammed shut and another squeak a bit as if opened hurriedly. Was Ellen in her room? Given the time of day, it seemed unlikely. I stuck my head in and encountered the older man I had directed to fetch the box for Pappy's feet the previous day.

"What are you doing in here?"

The man stiffened and looked around in panic. "Searching for stolen goods." He was older and shorter than I. He rubbed the back of his hand against his tobacco-stained mouth and whiskers. His movements and breath in such a small area told me he was about two more swigs away from total inebriation.

"What stolen goods?" I was aware of his six-gun tucked into an old holster. I didn't want to provoke him into pulling it, but I was determined to confront him.

"What do you care. This place is where that black gal stays. That little thief runs up and down this here alley and sneaks into the back of the stores taking stuff."

He had a trapped look on his face, and I knew he was just saying whatever came into his head or perhaps even telling on himself. So I backed a few feet out of the doorway and motioned him to come out.

"Well, Ellen is a friend of mine, and you have no right to be messing with her things."

"What things? She ain't got nothing," he sneered.

"Which is the opposite of her stealing things out of the stores, isn't it?" I wanted to stay close enough to use my fists if he started to draw the weapon. On the other hand, I also wanted to give him room to run. "I think the sheriff would be interested in what you're doing." Although I was not very familiar with the backside of the stores, I was oriented enough to know that the sheriff's office was only about fifty feet away.

"I'm leaving. I'm leaving. I ain't taking nothing. Can't see why you're so worried about a worthless black."

"Beat it!" I couldn't help but step forward to punctuate my words. His hand moved toward his gun, but it was only reflex. He opted to step away and head down the alley the way I had approached. I looked at Freckles curled up in the corner. His tail thumped. He pawed his muzzle.

"So, you are Ellen's friend and protector," I said. The tail thumped again. "Well, I'm sure you are her friend, but I'm dubious about the protector." He gave me a mournful look. "Okay, Ellen isn't here, is she? I'll give you the benefit of the doubt. We'll pretend you are a raging lion if someone threatens her. But I don't like this lay-out at all." I petted his head a bit and stood. I stuck my head out. The strange man had hurried around the corner and disappeared between the buildings. I felt a chill run through me. It did not take much imagination to know what some low-life might do in the dead of night. I settled my nerves by telling myself that he was looking for valuables, not the girl. I told myself that Ellen was going to be okay. But I wasn't very convincing. I told Bryan about it later. He encouraged me to report the event to Miss Emmy and Sheriff Beckett. We went to bed, contemplating the likelihood that we were up a creek again in our search for Circumstance.

25

We were up early. We took our usual table at the Star and ordered. Surprisingly, Mrs. Jordon was there, but she was not herself, which was not surprising. I caught sight of Ellen. She waved shyly, and I tipped my hat before I lay it on the table. Her demeanor reassured me as to her safety during the previous night. After we finished eating, I went to the kitchen entrance and went through the routine of asking about my patient.

But it was not Freckles I was worried about now. Though relieved that Ellen was okay, I debated on whether to tell her about the old man. I decided against it. I felt like it was scary enough in the lean-to without the information about the intruder. I convinced myself that he was an old drunk and probably harmless. However, that did not remove the risk that some other younger, more lucid visitor could pose a threat to her in her living quarters. The answer to that situation lay with Miss Emmy. I had put a bee in her bonnet. I was worried that she might not act until it was too late.

I needed to know. But when I asked for Miss Emmy, I was told that she was out shopping for provisions. The improving condition of Freckles and Ellen's safe passage through another night in the shed seemed to be the only thing to celebrate starting our day. Surprisingly, Mrs. Jordon was at work but explained that Miss Emmy needed her and she needed to be busy. We did not try to converse with her except about the basics. We expressed our condolences but didn't try to prolong the conversation.

The day was heating up when we stepped out of the Star. We could feel the beginning of a Georgia summer day. We just didn't know for sure what to do next. Waiting around for other people to retrieve the stolen horse didn't seem to be paying off, but we weren't gunslingers equipped to go looking for him ourselves. And if we were, where would we look? I think we were slowly coming to fear for the first time that we might be going home with empty hands. For lack of options, we planned to spend another morning at the livery stable. There now seemed to be little benefit in joining Major Roger's unit in Clarksville. We were accomplishing nothing hanging around Titustown either.

Bryan was the first to spot the sheriff, Deputy Shires, and Cal Jordon returning to town. We were surprised, as we had learned from Mrs. Jordon at breakfast, that these men were still out trying to track down her husband's killer. Bryan waved and stepped out into the street. "Any luck with your search for Coates?"

"Oh, we found Coates, alright." Cal Jordon took off his bandana and wiped his forehead and the back of his neck. "But he got away."

I felt my heart lurch. I joined Bryan in the street. "So, he's gone?"

"Yep. The three Union boys are still chasing him. And well, I have a son to bury," Cal said grimly. He put his bandana away. "And I wouldn't be surprised if they catch him. They are smart enough, but there is a lot of luck involved, too."

I noticed a hole in Cal's pants leg. "Are you hurt?"

"Well, yes, but it wasn't Coates that shot me. It's just a scrape." He glanced toward the doctor's office. "The shooter was a black man who sneaked into our camp last night trying to steal a horse. He got one too. The odd thing is the horse he got was the one Coates stole from the Army."

"Wait a minute," Bryan interrupted. "Coates stole a horse from the Army, and then someone stole it from him?"

"Well, best we can make out, the horse somehow got away from Coates over in Alabama. Madison Jones and Bronco found the horse on the road. To make a long story short, I camped with them last night. The black man stole it during the night."

"Then what happened." Bryan's voice was rising with excitement.

Sheriff Beckett straightened up. "Well, as it turned out, Shires and I ran into the same black man on our way out to catch up with Cal. We talked with him for a couple of minutes. Of course, at the time, we didn't know that he stole the horse he rode or that he had shot Cal. The man told us he was heading for Atlanta!"

"Atlanta?" Bryan turned to me with wide eyes. "So now we know where he took the horse!"

"Maybe, unless he was lying to us," Beckett said.

Deputy Shires spoke up for the first time. "So why are you so excited about the horse? Is it sick?" He fanned a fly away and brought his horse a little closer.

"No, the horse is fine. We want to locate it because we got to know the owner, Lieutenant Scott, at the Jones farm. "It's a fine animal, and we just hated to see him stolen by that killer," I said.

"Well, Coates is gone, and unless the Union boys catch him, he is gone for good." Cal leaned forward, and for a moment, his face was hidden. But nothing could hide the pain in his gravelly voice. "We know for certain that he's somewhere in Alabama. I'm sick about having to abandon them, but like I said, I've got a boy to bury." Cal's voice caught for a second. Finally, he straightened up and reined his horse toward the doctor's office. "I'm going to check on Pappy."

The sheriff straightened his hat. "Have Doc look at that leg too." He touched the brim of his hat, and he and Shires rode on toward the jail while I squared around to look at Bryan.

"Atlanta?" He motioned toward the hotel, and we headed for our gear.

After retrieving our belongings and checking out, we returned to the Star to say our goodbyes to the three ladies we had come to know there. They were all subdued in the face of the recent killings. Miss Emmy had returned, so I called her over and told all three that we were headed for Atlanta, and I didn't know when we would be back.

Miss Emmy leaned toward her niece and put an affirming arm around Sarah. "We'll be okay. But it's hard right now!" A tear slipped out of the corner of her eye. She pretended to turn away to attend to something in the kitchen.

I was alone with Ellen for a moment until Emmy came back. Ellen was smiling faintly, but before she could comment, Miss Emmy returned. The older lady nodded toward the back of the kitchen. "I think your idea will work fine." Looking past her, I saw Bub had taken down some shelves on the outside wall. In their place, he was finishing up a large cabinet door for an entry to the lean-to. Apparently, he was a Jack of all trades and did carpentry work. I was so relieved to see that Miss Emmy was acting quickly on my suggestion that I was speechless for a moment. Pappy's shooting had undoubtedly proved that the alley was a dangerous place for a man, let alone a young woman.

Ellen saw my relief and stepped closer to me to mouth her thanks. The bright eyes were full of intelligence, and I wondered what the remainder of her life would be like? Would her young life continue to blossom, or would it fade? She had passed from slave to paid kitchen helper, but there was potential for so much more. I looked back at Bryan, who was waiting impatiently. No doubt, it was time to go. Our second detour was a quick stop to say goodbye to the sheriff. We did not say so to anyone, but we knew that our departure could be permanent. We might never see any of these people again.

<h1 style="text-align:center">26</h1>

A few minutes later, we rode out of town toward Clarksville on our route to Atlanta. It was a long ride, and we resolved to get it done as painlessly as possible. We were but a few miles out of town when we spied two familiar men coming toward us. Slim spoke first.

"Hello, Doc. You boys headed out of town?"

"Sure are. We're off to Atlanta. Expect we'll be back in a couple of days." I grinned like I did every time I employed my Arkansas accent.

Slim didn't waste any time getting down to business. He had questions that Bryan and I, riding out of Titustown, hoped we were moving beyond.

"You know, Doc, you told the sheriff and us that you sent that fella named Joe to Winston?" He cocked his head. "We're coming from there, and the folks at the headquarters say they never heard of him or you. The mention of Joe from either of these two men brought a surge of dread well before he finished the sentence.

"Well, I told him that Joe was resting up in our room before heading for Winston," I said.

"That is what he said," Curt nodded. "So, he didn't go to Winston?"

"No, he didn't," Bryan cut in. "He was so tuckered that we told him to wait until the next day. But by then, we knew that Major Rogers was relocating in Clarksville, so we sent him there." Bryan gave me a "how's that for a good story" glance. I admit I did admire it.

"There is something funny going on with you two," Slim stroked his jaw. "Yesterday, we went back out to that hole in the creek. It was washed out. Now that ain't surprising, since we have had some rain since, and it is a creek." He raised his eyebrows.

"But we got to looking around the area, and guess what? Somebody drove a wagon across that field and over in the trees not too far from that creek. And from all the stamping around the horses done, it looks like they was there a while."

"Why are you asking us about that?" I knew the answer to that question. I was hoping that he didn't.

"Well, Tubby told us that strange-looking little man, what did you call him, an Idiot Oboe?"

"I called him a deaf-mute, albino," I said. "He is not an idiot. I expect that despite his handicaps, he is a lot smarter than most of the rest of us." Even back then, I got irritated with people who abused disabled people. Given Tubby's problems, I was surprised at Slim's comment. I had a cousin who was hurt badly when he was a kid and got picked on for his shorter left leg for the rest of his life. He was called Limpy and Gimpy, and later, Chester for the deputy on Gunsmoke. I didn't think it was funny. But maybe Slim really misremembered.

"Well, okay." Slim smiled. "Tubby's story was that he found the little man with the rock down in that creek. Now, you said he was riding down the road when Tubby come on him. Them is two different stories." He looked at Curt. Curt nodded.

"So why are we talking about this now?" Bryan sensed I was running out of steam. "Joe doesn't talk, so we told you two and the

Sheriff what we understood to be his story." He stopped. "Now, from what we saw in town when Tubby dragged Joe in at the end of a rope, Tubby kind of got confused some, himself, didn't he?"

"Well, that is so." Slim pursed his lips. "He could have been confused. And when we first heard your story, we knew the stories was different, but we let it go. We was in a hurry to get to the creek. Sheriff Beckett is an impatient man, so we didn't want to get sidetracked. Later, when the big rock was gone, what with Tubby being dead, we just let it all go until today when we went back out to look around where that missing rock was. Do you know what we saw? We saw wagon tracks going out in that field. You told us you didn't know anything about it, but I bet that was your wagon tracks. And now you're saying that Joe is not where you said he was going to be. Now you have changed that story. Put all of that together, and you got the makings of a lie."

"Paul, no! Now Paul, don't get your dander up!" Bryan's voice sounded alarmed. He was making like to calm me down. He looked from the two men and back at me. I hate being lied to, and I hated that he called me a liar, even if it was true. But I don't go crazy about it either.

"Now, boys, you need to be careful who you're calling a liar. My brother Paul has been to college and medical school, and he is a certified veterinarian. He showed the sheriff his papers proving all of that. The Yankee Major saw them papers, and he permitted us to look over all of the horses in his command for glanders." He paused.

"I guess that's so." Slim nodded. "So what?"

"Well now, all that education costs a heap of money, don't you expect?" His eyes drilled the two men who nodded agreement, probably more from the fierceness in his voice and gaze than from any knowledge of the cost of school.

"Now, look at him!" Bryan leaned back in the saddle and looked at me as if in awe. "Paul is six feet, four inches tall. He weighs two hundred twenty-five pounds. Paul is as solid as a brick shit-house. He paid for his education by winning every boxing match he ever fought. He is the undefeated heavyweight boxing champion of Arkansas, Kansas, and Missouri. I'm giving you fair warning, so it is on you if you get him het up. He once bit the ear off a wild Injun. He eats rabbits and squirrels raw. Do not call him a liar!"

I could not contain my surprise. I looked at Bryan as if he was nuts. He returned my gaze blandly. "Paul, I know you don't want people to know this about you, what with being so educated and all, but It's not fair to light into these two innocent men without giving them a chance to know what they're getting into!"

Perhaps my red face and flaming red hair conveyed more fero-ciousness than I felt, but both of the men backed their horses off a couple of steps and put their hands on their revolvers.

"Now, there is an easy explanation of how them wagon tracks got there," Bryan continued. "You're right. We were out there. But it was the next day. It's on the way out to the Jones farm, where we're inspecting horses. After we talked to the Sheriff later about how the big rock was gone, it seemed even stranger than Tubby's original story, so we went out there and parked in the shade under those trees to go down in the creek to poke around. We even found this."

Bryan dug around in his breast pocket and pulled out a small item. "All we found was this bullet in the sand." I expect it is one of the bullets Tubby fired at the rock. This one ricocheted into the sand there in the creek. Remember, there were three marks on the rock. The second one could be anywhere. Of course, the third bul-let hit Tubby in the eye, the sheriff said. We looked some more, but we didn't find the other one." Bryan kicked Billy-Ann, and she moved up a bit closer to the two men. Bryan handed the piece of lead to Slim. He looked at it. "So, you see, boys, we were there, but we were there after you were." He shrugged. "And that's the end of the story."

Slim turned the bullet over in his fingers and handed it off to Curt. He looked back a little guardedly toward me. Somehow, I had pulled myself together, and with enough time, managed to puff myself up and put a snarl on my face.

Curt was the first to speak. "Well, it seems to me that that answered all the questions, don't it, Slim. These boys was just curious, just like us."

Slim nodded slowly. "Well, I guess that's so. But, Doc, I didn't mean to call you a liar. I was just trying to figure out how all the pieces fit together. I can see it now." He touched the brim of his hat. "Well, we need to get a move on to get home before dark. You boys have a safe trip, now." He reined his horse forward, and Curt did the same.

We watched them ride off. "Where in the hell did you get that bullet?" I looked at Bryan with my mind whirling.

"Right where I said I did," Bryan grinned. "We were at the Lander after they were. I did kick up that bullet just before we ran back to the wagon to head for home. We were in a hurry, and I stuck it in my vest pocket. I forgot about it until just now. I told them the truth. I just didn't tell them the rest of it!"

I rubbed my chest. My lungs hurt from holding my breath. "Heavyweight Champion in three states?" I took another deep breath. "Thank goodness one of them wasn't the state champion of Georgia!" I grinned. "But you, my friend, are the best liar I ever met!"

Bryan faked a scowl of indignation and gave Billy-Ann a kick in the ribs to get us started. Three hours later, we made but a brief stop in Clarksville to alert Lieutenant Scott of the developments regarding his horse. We told him we were headed for Atlanta on other business but would keep an eye out for his animal. He wanted to accompany us, but his duties would keep him tied up for at least another week. We did not burden him with the fact that in a week, we would be gone.

We knew that Atlanta was an important economic and cultural center when the war started. It ended the war in horrible disorder. Confederate General John Bell Hood had burned many manufacturing facilities to the ground as he tried to prevent their capture by the approaching Yankees. Union General William Tecumseh Sherman's occupation oversaw more destruction in the countryside and city proper. With Atlanta taken, most of the residents had to leave town for a while as Sherman used its facilities to advance his efforts toward taking Savanna further to the southeast.

By 1865 Atlanta was far from full recovery, but many of the residents had returned. A lot of other people were joining them. When we entered the city, Peachtree Street churned with people. Former Confederate soldiers and black men, and women, now referred to as freedmen, lounged along the streets. Dodging among the natives was a more prosperous appearing group that we judged to be northern carpetbaggers looking for bargains in the ashes. Aside from a few stragglers, it was apparent that most of the returning Rebels on their way further south had already made their way through the area.

Bryan and I left our horses at a livery stable and walked a short distance until we found lodging. After obtaining a room in a small boardinghouse, we explored. Atlanta was a lot larger city than I expected. The population was officially around twenty thousand, but I suspected that another ten thousand people were transients who occupied the shanty towns, alleys, and private homes serving as boarding houses. Our immediate question was how likely were we to find Circumstance in the time remaining? I acutely felt the weight of that dilemma. We eventually went back to our room and tried to develop a plan, but our stomachs had other ideas.

"Let's go talk about this over supper," Bryan said

<h1 style="text-align:center">27</h1>

Unlike the now abandoned Titustown, Atlanta swarmed with Union troops. Unlike the southerners, they had pay in their pockets and were thick on the walks and in the cafés. And they seemed to have a lot of time on their hands. Finally, we slipped into a restaurant and ordered our dinner.

Bryan interrupted our eating. "I hope I'm just paranoid cause we already have a lot on our plate right now. But that Rebel over there is staring at us." He had spotted a tall man in a Confederate uniform to my rear who seemed more than casually interested in us. The man arose and was now standing close behind me. I jerked my head up and kinked my neck around for a better view.

"What do you do to your hair to make it that red?" The man leaned forward and inspected my hair closely. Then I felt his fingers spreading my curls as he examined my scalp. I stood up quickly to get clear of his curious fingers. We were about the same height. He was well tanned and wore his black locks almost shoulder length. I felt my hackles go up. I knotted my fists. If he wanted trouble, I'd oblige, though my heart wasn't in it.

"I might ask you the same question." I faked a smile and pretended to be inspecting his hair.

He smoothed the back down protectively. "I just let it grow!"

"So, do we."

Still focused on my hair, he said, "Interesting."

"What can we do for you?" I asked. He seemed more curious than belligerent. I opened my clenched fists and felt the moisture on my sweaty palms evaporate.

"Don't know yet," he said. He and I also shared eye color. He glanced over at Bryan. "You two together?"

"Pretty much since we are brothers," Bryan said. He was still seated. Maybe he was less intimated than I was.

"Nah!" He looked back and forth between us to appraise the difference in our heights and facial features.

"Paul got height from our old man. I got his brains and good looks." Bryan grinned.

"What are you gents doing in Atlanta?" The man dropped the subject of our hair and pulled out one of the spare chairs to sit down.

"I'm a veterinarian. The Army dispatched us to inspect local army horses for various diseases," I said. I hoped that the mention of our governmental connection would encourage him to go away. But, since he didn't seem so inclined, I sat down too. Strangely there was something about his eyes that was familiar.

"We're primarily looking for horses with glanders," Bryan added.

"Never heard of that. I'm George." He stuck out his hand, and we shook all around. I assumed that we had passed whatever yardstick he required. I reached for my fork to finish my meal. George grabbed it up and poised it, tines down. Then he put his arm down close to mine. I watched dumbly, not knowing what the man was going to do next. I had the feeling that he might stab me with it. Instead, he leaned forward and pulled his sleeve back an inch or so. With a tine of the fork, George pricked the back of his wrist. Then he lifted the skin about half an inch. It seemed to stretch an unusual amount before it parted. But instead of bleeding, it revealed a half-inch of white, almost translucent, under-skin. I stared for a moment, unsure of what I saw, and then looked into his eyes.

"I go by George, but you can call me Joe." He grinned.

For a moment, I was too stunned to take it in. Then I leaped from my chair like a scalded cat. Standing over George, I remembered the horns. The tousled blond hair and fake scalp hid everything. I dropped down in my chair and motioned to Bryan, who looked as surprised as I. "It's Joe!"

There was a moment of silence between us while Bryan caught on. His eyebrows went up, and the shoe-brush mustache lifted in a grin. He slammed his fists on the table hard enough to make the plates and saucers rattle. The talk around us stopped for a moment. We looked around. Suddenly, the restaurant crowd seemed too close for comfort. Bryan nodded toward the door. The three of us rose from the table and headed outside. Joe couldn't stop laughing. "I'll have the image of your face embedded in here forever!" Joe grinned and tapped his head.

We staked out a bench around the corner in a less crowded place, and Joe filled us in on the state of his search.

"Before being stranded in Titustown, my associate, Harry, and I located our man. We had a gunfight with him, but Bad Dog got away and headed for Atlanta just as we closed in.

"Bad Dog?"

Joe grinned, "Yeah, that's the way our translation gear renders his name in English. Anyway, Harry headed east, trying to keep track of him on horseback. You know what happened to me. We got back together this morning. We haven't had time to talk much. We split up to search the saloons looking for him." Joe gently scratched the place on his fake scalp right over one of his horns. I watched, fascinated, waiting for the phony scalp to part and the horn to protrude through the skin. "At least in disguise, we have fewer problems with the locals. What are you two doing here?" Joe's eyes glanced out on the crowd and then back to us.

"Well, we are searching for a black man who stole a horse from some fellas who were after another bad guy," Bryan said.

Joe tilted his head. "You are looking for a horse thief?"

"No, we're looking for the horse," Bryan said. "He is a special breed. But unfortunately, we wouldn't recognize the man who took him if he sat down with us like you just did." Acknowledging Joe's apparent confusion, Bryan tried to clear things up. "You see, a killer by the name of John Coates stole a horse from a Union soldier stationed in Titustown. We're after that horse. After more killings, a posse was after Coates. The man got away, but the posse recovered his horse. Then, the night before last, a black man sneaked into their camp and stole the killer's horse. He said Atlanta was his destination. So now we're here looking for him trying to regain possession."

Joe smiled. "You are never going to believe it, but my associate, Harry, is disguised as a black man. And he's the man who borrowed your horse."

Bryan and I stared at each other.

Joe straightened. "There is Harry now." He pointed at a heavy-set black man who was searching the crowd as smaller people dodged around his considerable bulk. He spotted Joe and joined us. He looked at Bryan and me suspiciously and then searched Joe's face.

"Harry, these fellas are Bryan and Paul. They are the men who rescued me over in Titustown."

Harry's face relaxed. "Whew!" He looked us over and smiled. "I was afraid George got himself into more trouble." We shook hands.

"These boys are looking for that horse you stole over toward Birmingham," Joe said.

"Yes, he belongs to a friend of ours, and he's anxious to get him back. You're having him sure simplifies our search!" Bryan grinned. I felt my constricted chest relax, as well. Our dumb luck was more than I could believe.

"Oh?" Harry frowned. "Well, boys, I hate to break bad news, but that horse was stolen by Bad Dog twenty minutes ago."

"What?" My excitement at finding Circumstance sputtered like a car running out of gas."

"Yep, I spotted Bad Dog over by that livery stable?" He pointed further down the street. "I was circling to get a better angle on him, and he must have spotted me because the next thing I knew, I lost sight of him until he rode off with my horse!" He is as slippery as a Taziion eel."

"Good grief!"

"Not only did he get the horse, but the saddle I bought yesterday."

28

After we shared the details of the John Coates saga with the two Plutonians, the four of us concluded that our Kladruber had to be the most often stolen horse in history. Knowing that he was in Atlanta did not diminish our dilemma very much. Was the scoundrel planning to stay in the local area, or would he head out for some distant destination?

"Can you think of any reason why he'd want to hang around here," Bryan said.

"No, we can't." Joe scratched through the fake skin over his horn. "Him knowing that we are here looking for him makes it even more likely that he will head out of town. The big problem is we don't know which way to expect him to go."

"Well, the Fleedle located the horse once. Can't it do it again?" I looked at Bryan expectantly.

"That is still a possibility," he agreed.

Harry's face wore a frown that deepened as he looked back and forth between Bryan and me and Joe for a moment before he came to the logical conclusion. "They aren't from around here, are they?"

Joe turned toward Harry and nodded in agreement. We grinned. "I didn't have time to mention that, did I?" Joe knew we didn't fit in because he had already seen our language translation technology back at the hotel in Titustown.

I started to explain, but Bryan cut me off. "No, we're not. Like you, we are wearing disguises."

"So, where are you really from?" Harry leaned forward. He pointed to our redheads. "You are certainly not trying very hard to be inconspicuous."

Bryan grinned. "Sorry, our protocol does not permit us to disclose that information," he said. "However, you're welcome to stick with us while we search for our horse. We should anticipate that Bad Dog will probably move on out of this area from what you say. Maybe he has ditched or wreaked his lander as Joe did. In any case, it's too late in the day to try and trail him. How about we send out the Fleedle tonight to locate him and then get an early start in the morning?"

I nodded. I didn't care to spend the night on an unnecessary campout. "With the Fleedle, we do have an advantage," I said.

Bryan reached into his pocket and pulled out the matchbox replica. In addition to a few matches, there was also something else. The beetle-sized Fleedle expanded its wings and flew straight up out of the box. It seemed to orient itself, then moved to a position facing Bryan. "Find the horse you viewed earlier," Bryan commanded. The Fleedle did a corkscrew bee-like circle and disappeared, flying north.

"Our horses are in the livery stable across the street. How about we meet you, fellas, in the restaurant at six A.M tomorrow?"

Joe and Harry nodded. As we turned away, I heard Joe say, "Too bad we don't know which horse at the livery Bad Dog rode in on."

"I think I'll know it when I see it, Harry said. I got a glimpse when Bad Dog rode away from Huntsville. Let's look for a gray horse at the livery in the morning and see how that works out."

Bryan and I were chowing down the next morning when Joe and Harry showed up. They ate little. I wondered if Harry's robust-looking disguise included padding as well as fake skin. He didn't seem to be eating enough to maintain his heft. After breakfast, we retrieved Sorghum and Billy-Ann and found Joe and Harry waiting in front of our boarding house. "You found the gray horse," I observed.

Harry smiled. "I found a gray. I hope it is the right one!"

"How will your "Fleedle" find your horse?" Joe asked.

"I suspect that it has already found it. Starting here, it flew in an ever-widening circular pattern. It flew its pattern until it picked up the homing device it had attached to the stallion when it found it originally. Once it finds the animal, it will return to us and can lead us to its location."

I mounted Sorghum. "And I was beginning to worry!"

"Well, finding the horse does not guarantee that we can gain access to it. We'll just have to wait and see." Bryan looked at the six guns on Joe and Harrys' hips. "You are better equipped to deal with this Bad Dog fella than we are. So we'll try to stay out of your way and concentrate on the horse."

I looked at the men's six guns. Although Bryan and I were familiar with the weapons and could handle one in a pinch, neither was eager to do so.

The four of us were riding north toward the edge of town when the Fleedle intercepted us. It circled Bryan twice to get his attention. We were anxious to get started. He nodded, and off we went. We were pulled up at a stream watering the horses when we spied a rider at a junction ahead. He rode through the crossroads, going right to left across our field of vision. The man was aboard a black horse that was galloping at a good clip. We mounted, and our Fleedle continued straight forward and then veered left at the junction. We could not make out the details of the horse and rider from the rear.

"It's too far to know for sure, but I think that was our Kladruber!" I stood in the stirrups and followed the receding horse as best I could. "Well, the Fleedle is leading us in that direction!"

"Let's ride!" Bryan motioned to Joe and Harry. We started in pursuit behind the rider, who was now half a mile ahead headed northwest.

"Well, this is going to take a while. Our best bet is to follow along until he stops," Bryan said.

We rode for another mile and encountered a rider coming back toward us. He looked us over carefully, especially Harry. I wondered if Harry's disguised as a black man would serve to get him more attention than he might want. When the rider passed without a quibble, I concluded that the Plutonians' appraisal of the situation might have been on target. Maybe black men were so ubiquitous in the region that he might indeed move with a high anonymity level among the populace. Perhaps the fact that Joe dressed as a Rebel soldier tended to equalize the equation. We skipped lunch and were about twenty-five miles out of town when we stopped and built a fire for supper.

"Well, today and tomorrow will tell the tale for us, I suppose." I kept my voice low as we were trying to keep our schedule limitations to ourselves.

"Yes." Bryan looked concerned.

"At least if we find him, we'll have total control, won't we? Neither Lieutenant Scott nor anyone else will be around to interfere. We thought we'd have to do a song and dance for permission for the sperm donation."

Bryan looked at me and hesitated before he said, "yes, we won't have to do a song and dance." From that moment of hesitation, I knew that the term "song and dance" must not be part of his background knowledge, and he'd accessed the meaning of the term from his appliance. I grinned. "It's been a long time since I tried to do a "little soft-shoe." There was another pause. Bryan was concentrating again before he smiled.

"You're toying with me, aren't you?"

"Just a little!" I laughed. Joe and Harry looked over questioningly. Finally, we shut up and lay back with our heads on our saddles. I've never slept well out-of-doors, but after a long day in the saddle, I think I was asleep before Bryan was. Even after several days in the nineteenth century, my brain still didn't fully accept it.

29

The next morning, I dragged in a good-sized fallen branch to break up for firewood, and Bryan made coffee. We had only purchased a sack of biscuits at the store in Atlanta, thinking we'd keep things simple, and they would do for us given the short time we had left. We walked the horses down the slope to the water and conversed in private.

"How strict is our eleven-day time limit? I was wondering about that as I dozed off last night. Is there any give and take at all?"

"The length of a caper is established upfront," Bryan said. "When our time is up, we are automatically recalled."

"Oh. I didn't remember any mention of that. Maybe I dozed in class? What about when you and I were at the roadside park?"

"That was an emergency recovery that occurred after my recovery period and within my trip limit. We can initiate recovery whenever we want after five days, but a trip's time limit, once set, is inviolate. When it is time to go, we go!"

"There's no way to short-circuit the clock?"

"Oh, sure. We can lose our homing devices. If that happens, our pickup will be unsuccessful, and they will send Fleedles to find us. But we will be in boiling water. These little trips cost a bundle, and we get only one shot at our mission. We will be picked up on time, successful or not."

"You mean that this is our only shot at finding our Kladruber?"

"That's the size of it."

I chewed on that while we climbed the slope to rejoin Joe and Harry. They were looking at a map of the area.

"The map shows at least three possible turnoffs ahead between Titustown and us for Bad Dog to take. If we didn't have your Fleedle, we'd be in trouble," Joe said.

It occurred to me that kind of trouble might be closer than they knew. If we ran out of time, the Fleedle and we would disappear, and they'd be on their own. I wondered what it was like to see someone suddenly vanish before your eyes.

Bryan picked up his saddle blanket and spread it out on Billy-Ann's back. "Time's wasting." Billy-Ann's shivered just then like she knew something.

I kicked at the embers and poured water on the fire. "Yep. We need to get a move on!" I could practically hear the clock ticking.

The Fleedle moved ahead at a good clip, and we followed—the horses plodded along for several hours before we spotted smoke off to our right. The Fleedle stopped in front of Bryan as if anticipating further orders. Bryan pointed and reined his horse under some trees.

"The Fleedle indicates that the horse is up in that camp." He looked at Joe and Harry. We all dismounted, and the two men checked their guns. That got my attention. Despite all the showdowns that I'd viewed on TV, the real thing gave me the creeps.

"Wait a minute! If you go charging in there throwing lead, you might hit a horse!" Shouldn't we at least see how things stand first?" I looked around at the others, almost in a panic.

"Of course. We weren't planning on charging in," Joe laughed.

"Well, checking your guns made us wonder," I said.

Bryan nodded his agreement. "Let's see how close we can get."

"Let Harry go first," Joe said. "Stealth is his strong point."

"Okay, then," I said. Bryan nodded again.

We tied up the horses and sat down on a fallen tree to wait. I turned around to wish Harry good luck, but he had already slipped off into the trees.

Fifteen minutes later, I was drinking from my canteen when he returned. His news caught us by surprise.

"He has five men with him." His eyes swept us. "And they are all carrying these." He reached down and patted his weapon.

"He must have just run into these men, you think?" I felt our recovery of the Kladruber move a couple of steps further out of reach. Joe and Harry were outgunned.

"Five men is a challenge," Joe scratched where his concealed horn should be.

"Did you spot the horses?" Bryan asked.

"They are tied up about ten yards from their camp."

"Any chance we might steal one or all? Bad Dog and his friends would be at a disadvantage without horses," Bryan said. "We'd like to get our Kladruber out of the area as quickly as possible." The danger that gunfire posed for the other horses weighed on me. Because of our protocol, the threat to the men with the Plutonian outlaw weighed on Bryan.

"Maybe." It was Harry's turn to scratch his horn area.

"Horses or not, if they scatter out in these woods, there is no way to keep track of them," Joe said.

"We are no help. We don't even know what Bad Dog looks like," I said. "Wait a minute. Fleedles rounded up these two horses for us. How about we send our Fleedle into their camp tonight to run the horses off?"

"That's a great idea," Joe said. "But if the horses are hobbled or tied securely, the Fleedle may not be able to get them moving."

"What else can a Fleedle do?" I looked at Bryan.

"They are a reconnaissance tool. Aside from buzzing around and annoying horses into moving in a particular direction or depositing tiny objects like a homing device, they don't have any way to influence anything."

"We're up a creek," I said.

"Maybe not!" Bryan held up a finger.

"Harry, since you are so stealthy, how about you sneak into camp. You release whatever bindings there are on the Kladruber." He turned to the other Plutonian. "Joe, you set up on the other side of the camp. Once the horse is free, you and Harry can fire your guns to scatter the horses. The men will be running around like ants in an anthill. Our Fleedle will corral our horse on the run and guide it to us, and we'll be on our way."

"I doubt that Bad Dog will give up without a fight," Joe said.

"That probably is true of the others also," Harry said. We don't know what connection if any, they have with Bad Dog, but once the shooting starts, they are going to start shooting back."

"That's a problem for me," Bryan said. "I don't like it. Even if the other men are outlaws, we aren't supposed to interfere with them. If they aren't, even wounding them is far from our protocol."

"You have your mission, and we have ours," Harry shrugged.

We looked at Joe. He cocked his head and reluctantly nodded in agreement.

"What do you think of Bryan's idea?" I was tired of the standoff. We were running out of time, and jawing wasn't getting us anywhere. It seemed to me that the protocol dealt with what we had control over. We had no control over the two Plutonians.

"It's worth a try," Joe said. "But let's make gunfire a last resort. Harry, you release all of their horses. I'll see how things stand in camp.

Harry rechecked his gun, and the two men slipped away into the trees. Bryan and I had nothing to do but wait. I didn't expect that to last long. I imagined the scenario of Harry approaching the horses and releasing them from their restraints. But then, I heard a horse whinny. I grimaced. Was that going to alert Bad Dog or one of the other men of our shenanigans? For lack of anything else, I climbed aboard Sorghum. I wanted to be ready to scram when things broke loose. Bryan mounted as well, and we sat for another long five minutes.

Afar off, we heard scattered horses' hooves and movement through the trees and brush. Bryan motioned for us to head for the road. Just then, Joe and Harry appeared out of the trees with a tall man dressed in black.

"Ah, you stuck around," Joe said.

"Nowhere to go," I replied. I peered at the third man. I knew he would be wearing a disguise, but I was still curious. "What happened to the others?"

"I was lucky. Bad Dog was camped a few yards away from them. I got him out of camp and never had to fire my weapon. I don't think I roused anyone but let's go on down the road a spell. The movement of the horses could have roused them even if we didn't. I don't want us to be found." We moved down the road as quietly as possible. As far as we could tell, none of the other men had awakened. Once we stopped, Bad Dog looked from Joe to Bryan and me. His disguise was what on Saturday morning TV would be "The old prospector's" outfit. He had a bushy mustache and a battered hat. He searched our faces in the semi-darkness and addressed Harry.

"What's your connection with these two?"

"You stole my horse, which I stole from some friends of theirs," Harry said.

"Well, you won't find him standing around here," Bad Dog grinned.

"We don't have to worry," Bryan said. He's got a homing device on him."

Bad Dog seemed to study on that for a minute, then smirked as he reached in his shirt pocket and produced an object. He held it out in the moonlight. "Homing device? Like this?"

Bryan gasped and strode forward to take the small item from Bad Dog's hand. He turned on his heel and came back to me. He held it up in the faint moonlight. It looked much like a cocklebur. "How did you find it."

"I like horses. Your horse needed brushing. I knew right away that it wasn't a natural burr."

"That puts us up a creek," I said. "As long as Circumstance was carrying the homing device, everything worked fine. Now that they are separated, everything changes."

"It sure does. There's no telling where Circumstance is now." Bryan dropped the homing device in his pocket. "The Fleedle can search the countryside once it's light, but the lack of a homing device changes things. He could be anywhere."

I felt my anxiety mount. Had I just wasted a week of my life for nothing?" But something nagged at me. "Can you direct the Fleedle to search a particular area?"

"Yes," Bryan peered at me through the darkness.

"Okay! "Horses have a natural homing instinct of their own. So circumstance may head back toward Titustown now that he's free," I said.

"That's a long way to travel. You think that's possible?" Bryan looked dubious.

"I think he will at least head that direction. And I doubt he'll travel very far tonight. Tomorrow, when it gets light, let's send the Fleedle out to scout the way back and see what happens."

We rode another mile down the road to create a safety area between ourselves and the other riders. Then, not daring to build a fire with Bad Dog's earlier companions in the vicinity, we hunkered down. Harry tied Bad Dog securely to a tree, and we dozed off. Everything was on hold till morning.

30

I was the first to awaken. I shook myself and looked around. We were all sprawled about like we'd been dumped out of a wagon. I nudged Bryan, and he roused. We went off in different directions to take a piss and returned to find the three Plutonians up as well.

"Fellas, we need to get a move on," Bryan said. We saddled our horses and turned to shake hands with our two Plutonian friends. We nodded at Bad Dog and mounted.

"So, you will take him back to your mother ship in your lander?" I asked Joe. I was still enthralled at the idea of star travel.

"Well, we have to collect the lander he escaped in first."

"Good luck getting back home," I said. I remembered Bryan's comment about Plutonians disappearing from the galaxy. That could be a year in their future or a century. Nothing I could say would affect the outcome, whatever that was.

"Same to you," Harry answered. He smiled. "Wherever that is."

"Finding our horse could be harder than getting home," Bryan said and reined about to begin our journey. Our brief consultation with the map and the sun on the horizon told us we'd be going northwest. We had to assume that Circumstance would take a similar route. The odds seemed to be stacked against us now. If the horse had a weak homing instinct, he could be anywhere.

Bryan instructed the Fleedle to fly a zig-zag course back and forth, keeping within a quarter of a mile on either side of the road. He released the Fleedle, and it disappeared. Bryan and I had about two days to find the horse and obtain our sperm sample, or we'd be going home empty-handed. That fact weighed on us. But, as important as time was, there was no reason for us to hurry forward. If the horse strayed off the road, we'd never spot him. If he roamed too far, the Fleedle would never find him either.

Slowly we trotted along the road, eating our breakfast of cold biscuits as we went. A couple of hours passed. We saw no sign of the horse nor the Fleedle.

Around lunchtime, we stopped to wipe the sweat from our brows, water the horses and ourselves. "This is a longshot, isn't it?" I said.

"Yep, and it gets longer as the day passes." Bryan lifted his canteen and took a long swig. Just then, we heard the sound of hooves coming around the curve in the road. Three rough-looking men rode up and halted before us.

The oldest of the men spat a wad of chewing tobacco and pushed up the brim of his hat. "Howdy, strangers."

"How are you boys," I said with my exaggerated Arkansas drawl. I noted two things right off. First, all three of the men were sporting six guns, and trailing behind them was Circumstance! He whinnied. I let myself think that he remembered Bryan and me fondly, but that was unlikely given our limited exposure to him.

"Where you boys headed." A smaller man stood up in his stirrups and stretched his legs.

"Titustown," I said.

"That's a fer piece away." The third man wore his blondish hair shoulder length. He eyed us and seemed compelled to join the conversation. "We're headed that way ourselves in a few days." The hair sticking out from under his hat reminded me of Joe. I kind of wished Joe and Harry with their guns were with us just then. Something was coloring my opinion of the three men toting the horse I wanted so desperately.

The big man spat again. "You from there?"

"No," I said. "We're from Arkansas. I'm a veterinarian."

"What's that?" The third rider pushed his hat up as if to make room for some new information. His cheeks bristled with a new growth beard, while the other two men looked like they had sworn off shaving a long time before.

"Well, I'm a horse doctor, cow doctor, such as that." Their speech gave me an idea of how educated I wanted to seem to them without making them anxious.

"That so?" The big man spat again and tugged at his long beard. "You know, we have got us a sick milk cow hanging around our barn. I reckon a look-see by a doctor would be a good thing." He looked over at his companions, who nodded.

"What about you?" He looked at Bryan.

"Well, I help out the doctor here." He nodded toward me.

"Well, you talk different than him, don't you?" The little man had a puzzled expression on his face. Bryan had overdone the drawl some. It was more cracker than Savanna southern.

"Well, actually, we're brothers," I said. I lifted my hat to expose more of my red hair. It was a perfect match for Bryan's mustache.

"We talk a little different because Paul has had a heap more education than I have." Bryan grinned and winked as if the education part was some kind of a joke.

"Well, as I said, we got us a sick cow. You seem to be the man to take a look at her."

I trained my eyes on Circumstance and nodded affably. "Well, I'd be glad to have a look. Are we far from your place?" Staying in the vicinity of the big horse seemed like a great idea at the time.

"No, you just passed our road back there." Then, for no apparent reason, he touched the butt of his revolver. The other two men saw that and did the same.

I looked at Bryan and swallowed. I read a half-suppressed threat in the motion, and it gave his previous questions a disquieting undertone.

"Well, let's get going," I said. "We're unlikely to get to Titustown today anyway."

The three men nodded to each other. The middle man even allowed himself a grin through tobacco-stained teeth.

"That's a fine-looking horse you're leading there. I don't know that I've ever seen one just like that before," I looked back over my shoulder as I reined Sorghum around.

"Yeah, we were just talking about that when we run into you boys." The smallest man grinned again. "We just come on to him a minute ago. He was just standing beside the road, eating grass." He looked at the big man and realized he was the only one of the three celebrating.

The big man gave him a milk-curdling stare and spat again. It was a shut-up look, and it worked. The little man pressed his lips together and ran his hand across his sweating brow. He pulled the hat forward and nudged his horse with his stirrup.

"We go to the left once we get around the bend up here," the big man said.

"I didn't catch your name," I said, hoping to help us through our little sticky place. "As has been said, I'm Paul Smith. Bryan is my brother. We have kinfolk in Atlanta."

"That so?" The three men seemed to be straining to think of a Smith they might know in Atlanta.

"Yes." I didn't venture anymore.

"Well, I'm Luther Tatum. My brothers are Tater and Thaddeus," the big man said.

"Glad to make your acquaintance," Bryan hastened to assure him.

He just grunted and nodded.

We turned up a lane and found ourselves facing the most dilapidated house of our travels.

"The cow's out in the back of the barn," Tater said. He pointed, and we reined our horses that way. The gate was hanging on one hinge, and the other end depended on a wire wrap. Tater climbed down from his horse and tied up to the post.

"We can get off here," Luther said.

I exchanged a look with Bryan. This visit was not going to be a simple house call. Nothing untoward had happened, but we both had an eerie feeling that we were in the soup. We weren't sure what the rest of the ingredients were, but we could feel the temperature rising. Belatedly, I realized that we had in our possession a year's wages for all three of these men, and our horses, as poor as they were, would be prized specimens hereabouts. If there was ever an oops on a caper, we were right in the middle of one.

31

Luther dismounted and threw the reins of the Kladruber to his youngest brother and pulled open the gate. Bryan and I followed him through. We all headed to the back, where we found the milk cow running loose in a small corral. She was an older animal for a milker. I could see that she was suffering from bloat just as Freckles had been. Her left side was distended some, but I have seen much worse. I cast my eyes around, looking for a source of the problem. Bloat in cows, like with other animals, is usually caused by the food that they ingest. Some feedstocks are very high in nitrogen, leading to excess gas release as the cow digests its food.

"What does your animal eat?" I walked to the gate that opened on a pasture.

"Just grass," Luther said.

"Nothing else?" I looked at the three men. They were all shaking their heads negatively.

"You sure? This cow has bloat, and often it is caused by the animal eating something new or different than it's accustomed to."

I went over and pressed the swollen left side. "You're sure?" I looked over the cow's back and gauged with my fingers how bad it was. From my new vantage point, I spied corn tassels a few feet above a side fence. I walked in that direction and propped up my foot as I looked at a very weedy garden area. In addition to the corn, there were tomatoes, onions, and lettuce. It was easy to see that the plantings were pretty much on their own once they got started. Then, in a far corner, I spotted several rows of vegetation that I did not recognize. I pointed and looked around at the four men who followed me over.

"I don't recognize that."

"That's peanuts!" Thaddeus grinned. "I done bought some raw peanuts at the store, and I thought, why am I buying something I can grow." He took his hat off and wiped his brow. "Looks like they're doing real good, don't it?"

"Goobers!" Luther interrupted. "I ate more goobers during the war than I could stand. They're wasting space if you ask me." Tater was nodding his head in agreement.

"They're green enough," I said. "Any chance that cow grazed over there?"

"She sure did!" Thaddeus nodded his head in agreement. "She rubbed on that board right over there," he pointed off to the corner of the barnyard to our right, "and it came off. Then, she took herself into the garden and ate whatever she wanted for at least a half-hour."

"Well, there's your problem," I said. "Peanuts have a high concentration of nitrogen. By eating the peanut bushes and leaves and maybe even some green peanuts, your old girl over there was eating more nitrogen than she is used to getting. The problem is that she can't fart fast enough to keep up with the gas production. But since it was a one-time thing, I think she will be okay in a couple of days. If you want, you could feed her some onions. That slows down the nitrogen release, but the milk will taste like onions for a while." I grinned at the three men. "So, there you are!" I noted that counting Freckles, Ellen's dog, and this cow, I was devoting a lot of doctoring time to animal bowels. But that wasn't surprising.

I glanced at Bryan. He was smiling broadly and edging toward the gate. "Well, I guess that solves your mystery," he said. "I guess we better get back on the road. You know, Paul, we might make it to Titustown tonight after all." We all walked to the gate, and Luther opened it again so everyone could pass through. I was beginning to breathe a sigh of relief when the big man did the unexpected. Luther looked at his brothers. They were looking back at him as if awaiting his next move. "I'm right glad we run into you boys," he said. He reached down in no apparent hurry and pulled his colt from the holster. "Now, you boys empty your pockets of anything valuable."

"What is this?" Bryan feigned indignation more from duty than surprise. I didn't bother. I just turned my pockets almost inside out, leaving my little Homer in a fold, and hoped we'd see the sunset.

Thaddeus looked over the loot and grinned. "Good God, almighty! Look at all the money!" He grabbed up the wads of folded greenbacks and spread them out to see how much they were collecting. He held up the fanned bills. "Look, Luther, Tater!"

"That's real good. Put them bills back in the saddlebags." Luther looked at me. "I figured what with you being a doctor, you'd have some money but that a sight more than I expected." Luther pointed toward the road. "Now if'n you take a long walk and don't cause no trouble, you're going to be okay. If you start smart mouthing or whining or cussing, then I might have to shoot you. Just be glad that you're white men. If'n you was black, I'd have to shoot you where you stand." He looked at Tater. "Go search them. Make sure they don't have one of the little guns like the gamblers use."

Tater did as directed and approached Bryan. He was distracted by Thaddeus, who kept smoothing out the wrinkled and creased bills into separate piles. Whether or not he could read, he appeared to have a basic grasp of numbers. Tater went over us hurriedly, patting us down, and turned to his brother.

Watching Luther conduct his business, I was worried that there would eventually be shooting, regardless of our cooperation. How could he hope to get away with a robbery at his front door if he let us go? He had an answer.

"All right, now before I let you gents go, there are some things you should know. My pa is the sheriff of Dixie County. You is in Dixie County. It won't do you no good to go crying to him. He knows how to treat Yankees just like we do."

"Yankee! We aren't Yankees!" Bryan was so taken aback that he forgot his accent. He didn't sound like a Yankee, exactly, but he didn't sound like an Arkansan either.

"Well, you ain't from around here, are you? You are also riding Union Army horses. These ain't the best, but horses claim a high price in Georgia right now, and unless we know better, anyone riding a Yankee horse is a Yankee." He motioned with the barrel of his gun for us to move lively on down the lane.

Thankful to be leaving under our own power, we did move as quickly as possible and were soon standing in the midafternoon sun at the junction of their lane and the county road.

I was so thrilled to walk away with my hide that I made a little joke. I quoted Oliver Hardy from the old *Laurel and Hardy* movie shorts. "Well, here's another mess you've gotten me into." Bryan did a double-take, and I waited out the pause for him to access his device. He looked at me and said, "I didn't mean to." He tried to be a sport, but you had to see the movie. I could tell he was missing the humor. I was just glad to be alive.

"Well, that pretty much kills our chances," Bryan said soberly.

"Maybe not," I said. "It's going to be a long night. We'll just wait for a while and go back for our horses and our stuff after dark."

"Go back!" Bryan frowned.

"We have one more day to work with on this. We'll hide out here close by, and maybe we'll get lucky, and they will leave again. If they do, we grab our three horses and head for Clarksville. That's only about ten miles away. That's where Lieutenant Scott is. He'll be so glad to get his horse back; he'll let us have what we need without a problem."

"I have a better idea." Bryan pointed down the road. "We head out now and fetch the good lieutenant to rescue his horse."

Sometimes Bryan had the perfect plan. Sometimes his ideas were a stepping stone to a good plan. This plan seemed to be one of the former We lit out. But we were short a couple of things. No water, no food, and neither our legs nor feet were ready for a ten-mile walk. We were limping before we hit the three-mile mark. I looked at Bryan, who was about fifteen feet ahead of me and the words from the movie continued running through my head, so I repeated them, "Well, here's another mess you've gotten me into."

Bryan stopped, turned around, and looked at me askance. I could tell he wasn't in the mood to respond. I gave him a little finger wave and grinned. We were still alive, and that counted for a lot to me!

32

After another mile of trudging down the country road, I felt too sorry for myself to make any more jokes. Hoofing it for help seemed like such a good idea when we started out. Not easy, but doable. Letting the good lieutenant rescue his horse seemed pretty sensible to me, compared to risking our hides. If everything went according to plan, we would still have time to accomplish our mission.

On the other hand, when had everything ever gone according to plan for us? I felt that, in a way, even the army was letting us down. Major Rogers' idea of multiple patrols of soldiers covering the countryside seemed like a good idea on paper but fell short in practice. We had been riding and now walking the Titustown-Atlanta road going in both directions, and the only soldiers we had run across were hanging out in bars, restaurants, and street corners in Atlanta. I remembered the old lament, "There's never a cop around when you need one," almost a century before I first heard it.

Bryan was limping pretty severely when he angled off the road to a lane leading downhill. The sound of a rushing stream promised some fresh water and shade. Bryan slumped down and took a drink before refilling his canteen. I estimated that we had walked about a third of the required miles to get us to Clarksville. I sat down nearby and leaned back to survey the sky through the canopy. My body wanted to close my eyes and let the time run out. So, what if we didn't accomplish our mission? Surely, some other groups would be successful. Maybe all of them would be. Nineteen out of twenty wasn't bad!

But my conscience would not let me alone. Who knew where the beautiful Kladruber would end up? My sense of justice was severely mutilated by the fact that three worthless idiots could get away scot-free with all of our possessions plus a valuable horse belonging to an honorable officer of the United States Cavalry! And what if there was never another mission to try and save the breed!

Then my memory took me back to the old and crippled remnants of the last herd of horses on the planet. By the time I hashed that over I was ready to fight a horse-inspired civil war right then. I looked at Bryan. "We've got to do this!"

He nodded and pulled off his boot to inspect his blisters. Pausing, he held up his hand to hush me. He seemed to be listening to something. He touched his lips with his index finger. Amid the chirping of nearby birds, we could hear the clop-clop of horses' hooves out in the road. Given my recent ruminations concerning the cavalry, I was hopeful of rescue. Being less optimistic, Bryan headed for a stand of timber to the right of the lane to conceal ourselves. I followed. We crouched down. I was eager to hail the riders. Bryan was probably ready to head back into the trees. As usual, Bryan's instincts were better than mine. The three riders were leading three horses. It was the three brothers, and they were leading our two horses and the Kladruber! We looked at each other excitedly.

"Our horses!" Bryan exclaimed.

"They're taking them to Clarksville?" I couldn't believe our luck.

"Sure looks that way. That's pretty stupid given that we told them that's where we're going."

"We said Titustown," I reminded him.

"Well, it's the same road." He hobbled toward the road to keep them in sight. I could tell that the sight of our horses energized him.

I was too, but I didn't think we could keep up at the pace they were holding. We hurried out into the center of the road and caught sight of the men rounding a curve a quarter of a mile ahead. We hurried toward that curve and arrived in time to see them round the next one. They had traveled about half again farther than we had. We were panting from our exertions. I didn't see how we were going to keep that up. Then they surprised us again. They turned up a lane and disappeared. By the time we reached it, they were already dismounted in front of a house as dilapidated as their own. I wondered if it was a relative. We hit the brush and sat, catching our breath for a moment. I knew they had brought the horses for something. Were they planning to sell them? Were they distrustful of leaving them back at their place? We sat in the bushes, tired and hungry. I looked up at the sun, now well down toward the western horizon. Now what?

As dusk approached, Bryan and I circled the clearing, hoping to discover what we were up against and develop a plan. Altogether, there were four men and an older woman. The men sprawled on the front porch while passing a jug of milk, cider, or moonshine back and forth between them. My bet was on the whisky. The more they drank, the louder they talked, and we were privy to every slurred word. Finally, just before dusk, they got a call for dinner and filed inside. I felt my stomach growl. Bryan and I had not eaten since we munched on a couple of biscuits right after leaving the Plutonians that morning. The six horses were left to stand at the watering trough. Edging around the clearing, we found two more horses in the pasture behind the house.

It didn't seem possible that the three men were going to leave the horses there all night. Were they planning on riding back with them or putting some or all in the pasture here? If that was the plan, we were in terrible shape. There was no way that we could steal three bareback horses. Nor could we steal them parked out in front of the house. Or could we?

Given the choice of trying to get the horses back saddled or unsaddled, we did not doubt which was preferable. I doubted that either of us could stay on a barebacked horse for five minutes. Bryan was thinking the same thing. He brought his head close to mine. We were back to plan A that we had tried before.

"If we can let all of the horses loose, we can take out with the Kladruber and delay them following." He looked at me questioningly. I nodded. I had just been running all of the reasons it was essential to save this mission through my mind. It was easier to continue down that path than do a reversal and think about the risks. So I let the negative thoughts simmer on a back-burner, and the positive ones take the lead.

The men were talking loud enough for us to be sure that they weren't wandering off. We edged out of the trees. Step by step, we moved closer to the six horses hitched to the post at the front of the house. Once we cleared the first one hundred yards or so, we could keep the horses between ourselves and any observers at the house. When we reached them, I felt confident that we were almost home free.

Bryan grabbed three of the reins and passed them to me. He took up the other three, and we started to lead the animals away. The farther we got from the house, the more confident I was that this would work!

Walking six horses is not a silent activity. They make six times as much noise, just walking, as does one. Then there is the thumping into each other, the squeak of saddle leather, and the grunts and whinnies. Every squeak brought up my hackles. By the time we got to the edge of the yard, all these things were going on at the same time. Finally, someone in the house noticed.

I heard the shout and froze for an instant. Then the fear spurred both Bryan and me into action. We clumsily mounted and reined toward the road. Then the shooting started. I ducked down, laying my head on Sorghum's neck like I had seen Jock Mahoney do on his television series, *The Range Rider.* Unfortunately, Bryan didn't have late nineteen fifties television programs to fall back on. He was sitting straight up fighting just to stay in the saddle when the bullet found him. I heard him cry out in pain. I was riding with my eyes shut to keep them from being whiplashed by Sorghum's mane. I opened my eyes and twisted my head toward him. He was clutching his right shoulder while he looked at me wild-eyed. He couldn't do that for long. I watched, horrified as he tumbled from the saddle onto Billy-Ann's rump. I lost him from sight for a moment and then looking back, I saw him sitting on the ground.

Billy-Ann took his quick dismount as a signal to stop, as did the two horses he was leading. I pulled up. I was a hundred feet ahead of him, and the men on the porch were running toward us. I couldn't leave him wounded. I had a decision to make, and I made it. I turned my horse about and headed back. In the westerns I watched on television, the guy on horseback raced to his fallen comrade, then they linked their arms together, and the fallen man was swung up and behind the rider. We should have practiced that before we needed it. Bryan did manage to get to his feet. I stuck out my arm, and he must have had a general idea of my intentions, if not the details of how the maneuver worked. He reached up with his good arm. For an instant, I thought we would manage to pull it off, but that was before his full weight came to bear. Instead of him swinging aboard, he pulled me off Sorghum. We were lying in a jumble when the three brothers reached us.

"Well, look at this," the youngest brother hollered shrilly. I glanced up. I was still stunned by my fall. He looked rapidly between

Bryan and me and back to his brothers. "These boys done followed us!"

I let that pass. I was more concerned with Bryan's injury than anything else. The combination of being shot, falling off his horse, and then my falling on him had to take a toll. I propped his head up. He was still breathing. My hand touched his shoulder and came away slick with blood.

"We've got to treat this shoulder," I said. By the position of Bryan's bullet wound, I could only surmise that he had half-turned to look behind us as he was shot.

"Maybe." Luther, the oldest brother, made a face.

"What do you mean, maybe?" I was dismayed that not helping Bryan was even up for discussion. "Let's get him to the house." I was full into my order giving doctor mode, and for a couple of minutes, it worked. The men halfheartedly carried Bryan into the house and dumped him on the sofa.

The old woman peered at him and went for a towel. "Don't you go bleeding on my couch, young man!" she screeched. I didn't discern any sympathy in her tone.

I ripped some of the buttons off Bryan's shirt in my hurry to get a look at the wound. I felt around on his back, and I could tell that the bullet did not go all the way through. From the look of the injury, it seemed like the bullet had passed under his clavicle, through the ribcage, and then lodged against the scapula. The bullet was still in there. The wound was bleeding profusely. The distance from barrel to target had slowed the bullet enough that it didn't go all the way through. The scapula could also be cracked or broken. I had no way to tell.

I put my head down close to Bryan's ear. "You need to go home." He nodded. "Not in here!"

I remembered that outdoors was the best place for a caper pickup. Somehow, I needed to get Bryan back outside.

33

I looked around the circle. The old woman was nervously rubbing her hands together. She had tucked a towel under Bryan's wounded side in the interest of preserving her sofa. Her elderly husband slumped down in a chair and watched the proceedings as if it were a spectator sport. I did not have time to deduce the relationships between the older couple and the men. Perhaps these were grandparents. Neither of them seemed too concerned as to Bryan's chances of recovery.

I pressed the towel against the bleeding, but I was just providing window dressing, pretending that I was accomplishing anything. I was glad Bryan was at least awake, but he was starting to show signs of shock. That is often a prelude to going unconscious. He must have realized that as well. He was shivering uncontrollably.

"Take me outside!" he cried out the words with great urgency. "Take me outside."

I looked at the startled expressions on the three men's faces.

"I'm dying! Take me outside!"

I didn't think he was dying, but maybe there was damage not apparent to me. Perhaps he was just trying to motivate the men to carry him outside where an emergency caper could occur. I knew we needed to get a move on.

"Let's take him outside," I said. "The bullet hit an artery. He is dying."

Bryan raised on his elbow again and spoke with wide-eyed clarity, "*Thessalonians 4:16 says: For the Lord himself will descend from heaven with a cry of command, with the voice of an archangel, and with the sound of the trumpet of God. And the dead in Christ will rise first.*"

I knew Bryan had accessed his appliance. I admired his quick thinking. I looked around at their startled faces. "That's from the Bible!"

The old lady clasped the towel to her bosom. "He's right." She looked with wonder as Bryan's face lit just then by his animation and lamplight, reflected from his light-colored skin. "Take him outside!"

"A man should die under the stars!" I proclaimed in my best imitation of a prophet's voice. "A man should die under the stars!" I made to sit Bryan up. Thaddeus and Tater, filled with a kind of awe at the off-the-cuff Bible talk, helped me get Bryan to his feet. We drag-walked him out the front door and into the yard. I pointed with my free hand to a spot well away from everything. Bryan gave me a pained wink and crossed his arms over his chest as we lay him out. He crooked his finger for me to bend near and whispered. "Let's get out of here."

I looked around at the gathered clan. Just past the family, my eyes could still make out the Kladruber. All of my concerns about him and the last dying herd on earth crowded into my mind. This caper was the last resort. Bryan, through no fault of his own, needed this caper. I did not. For my peace of mind, I still needed at least one last attempt to get this animal back to his rightful owner and a sample of his semen transported into the future.

I looked at my friend's features, fearful that he was seriously hurt. I remembered in a flash all that we had gone through in such a short friendship. "You go ahead. I'll follow if I need to," I said into Bryan's ear. I stepped back.

"Now, everyone, turn your backs!" I commanded. "Give the man some privacy in his last moments!" I felt the shakiness in my voice as I grabbed Tater since he was the smallest and forcibly twisted him around to face the house. Then I grabbed Thaddeus. He half-turned, and I grabbed his arm to complete the movement. By then, the others had caught on. Luther turned sluggishly. I realized that either fewer swigs or a few more swigs from the jug could have made dealing with all of them impossible. The old man and woman, who had followed us out, turned obediently. I glanced back. Bryan pulled his honing device out of his pocket and twisted it.

Curious, I only half turned my head. I wanted to see what a capering looked like from the outside. I felt the barometric pressure drop around us with a swoosh of air. A translucent box-like object about the size of my AMC Rambler appeared to materialize around Bryan. He raised up and lunged to the center to lie flat. It solidified for just a moment and then disappeared in a blink. Bryan was gone. The wind was so strong against our faces that the harsh air movement tended to make us close our eyes and hunch forward. In the five seconds that followed Bryan's caper, everyone straightened up, and one by one, glanced around to reorient themselves. Then they looked back to where we had last seen Bryan, no doubt expecting to see his stiffened body.

"He's gone!" Grandma cried out. The menfolk looked at the spot, then scanned the area beyond out to the tree line. One by one, they remembered Bryan's words about the stars and turned their eyes heavenward. The sky was black and broad and starred. I was searching my brain for a logical explanation. The old woman was faster.

"Demon!" The old woman pointed toward me. "Demon!"

"Good grief," I said out loud. For a moment, the old lady's words seemed funny—most people back in my time in the twentieth century reserved witches and demons for Halloween. But then, my smile faded as I realized that the old woman was entirely serious. The younger brothers looked at Luther for guidance. He seemed stymied for a moment.

"You should hang his ass," the old man said gruffly. He was speaking his first words in my presence. "You should hang his ass from that yonder tree!" He pointed at the dark silhouette of an oak tree, now casting a huge circle of shade in the moonlight.

"Yeah, let's string him up." Tater eagerly agreed. Thaddeus was starting to nod his head. Finally, Luther seemed to reach a decision. "Go get that fancy horse we found!"

I put my hand in my pocket and felt my homing device. In the excitement over the money in the saddlebags, no one had searched us. I wished I had already used it. I felt a moment of dismay that I had not gone with Bryan and left these hayseeds with a mystery to ponder for the rest of their lives.

"Wait!" The old woman pointed skyward toward the moon. "We have to wait!" She tottered to Luther's side. She grabbed his arm and looked up with a toothless glare, and pointed. "The moon must be full to protect us from the ghosts and spirits."

Luther shook his head in dismissal. "We hung them three blacks last week by that same moon. There weren't nothing ghostly about that. Tater, go get a rope."

"But blacks ain't got no soul," the old man said. I could see him puff up some at his wisdom concerning such things. "Everybody knows they ain't blessed with a soul."

"That is so!" The old woman seemed to weigh his words against the present dilemma. "You must hang this demon-possessed white man under a full moon!"

I was thinking about what a pair she and the old man were. Expertise in the hanging of human beings! I still had a caper option, but I just couldn't abandon Circumstance to this crowd. Aside from capering, I could think of only one other possibility. I pulled out my homing device and triggered it. A pale blue light beamed outward. I held the device below my chin, like we did with flashlights as kids, to give ourselves an eerie appearance. Then shining the beam upward, I bared my fangs. The whole thing was straight from my Halloween days. I'm sure that I took on a ghostly appearance, and indeed they all shrank back.

"Get thee into thy house," I said in my best seventeenth century, *King James* version of a ghost voice. I pointed the light toward them. "I command ye on penalty of death! Get thee into thy house!" I stalked toward them. I was ready to twist my homing device should anyone balk. But they didn't! The old lady took off at the closest thing to a run that she had probably done in twenty years. The old man staggered close behind her. The three brothers backed away for a bit and then turned to mount the porch. I gave them one last chance. "Get thee into thy house!"

I followed them as far as the grazing horses that had wandered back toward the porch after Bryan's unseating. I grabbed the Gladruber's reins and mounted Sorghum. In a last bit of nostalgia, I snatched up Billy-Ann's reins, circled the blue light overhead in a wide circle as if it was a torch, then pointed it toward the house. "Cursed be yea if you leave this house this night!" I rode with the light shining toward the heavens like a living Statue of Liberty as I scattered the other three horses as best I could. I did not dare look behind me as we descended the slight slope down to the road and turned right toward Clarksville. I bent low over Sorghum and closed my eyes again. At any second, a twin to Bryan's bullet could have found me.

Galloping down the road in the light of the moon, I didn't know if I was running from the real bad guys or imagined ones. I hurt in every joint. The saddle battered my butt, and I dreaded every stride that Sorghum took. But I rode on for another couple of miles. Finally, I slowed to a walk and then stopped, listening intently for the sound of pursuers. I couldn't believe that the three men would allow me to ride off with three valuable horses without more effort to retrieve them. I was right. I heard an urgent shout afar off. Then the thunder of galloping horses. "Shit!" I started forward again. I was going to be caught for sure! I saw a break in the trees on the inside of the next curve and headed straight into them. There were several cedars together, just past the edge of the road. I kicked Sorghum's ribs, and he breasted the brush, and I jumped from the saddle. I positioned the horses to take full advantage of the cover. I pulled their heads close and tried to quiet them. It was a reflex move as the men couldn't have heard them over the noise they were making, but I was panicked and taking no chances.

The three men thundered past and down the road. The quiet settled well before the dust did. I stood panting and stroking the horses for a long time.

What to do? If I continued and they stopped and turned about, I'd ride right into them. There were plenty of oak trees surrounding us, and I did not doubt that the men had brought a rope with them. The success of our mission required that I stay with it. Either capering home or being discovered again by the Tatum boys would be the end of my contribution to the future of horses.

I patted my pocket where I had thrust the homing device earlier. Strangely I didn't find it. I felt around the pocket again. Then my back pocket. I moved the reins to my right hand and touched my left front pocket. The back. My jacket pockets. My homing device was gone! I had lost it back in the lane, on the road, or during my frantic plunge into this wood! My foolproof backup option was suddenly gone!

I had to search for it. I walked about the immediate area, but I could scarcely see my own feet. I wondered what was next. I pulled out my pocket watch and held it close in frustration. It was only ten o'clock. That was good as it gave me time to complete the mission if all went well. I walked the horses back to the road. I was hesitant to go forward, leaving my homing device even further behind, and for fear of coming on the Tatum boys coming back. I felt something crawling on the back of my neck. I felt around until I was able to hold it between my fingers. I couldn't see it, but it felt like a tick! "Dammit!" I walked the horses to the other side of the road and looked back. I glanced down to my right. There was a blue glow among the leaves. It had clicked on by itself from the fall. I picked up the device, thanking my lucky stars until I felt an indentation in the center. I held it up in the sparse moonlight. It had a deep crease on one side. It looked as if one of the horses had stepped on it. That didn't look good. Maybe the blue light meant it was still fully functioning? Perhaps that meant nothing. I didn't know.

Stay or go? Both felt like a disaster waiting to happen. I petted the three horses and tried to come up with the best case. The best case would be for me to mount up and continue toward Clarksville unimpeded, find the Lieutenant, and obtain his assistance in getting my semen sample. I resolved to try that regardless of risk. I mounted Sorghum, and we headed back north. If I rode slowly, keeping the noise down, maybe I'd hear the Tatums coming, if they returned, and have enough time to hide before they were on me. I froze at even the remote chance of them finding me. With the homer possibly damaged, my backup escape route might be gone. As a practical matter, I could be totally on my own. I rode on.

34

As I rode north toward Clarksville, I came out of the forest canopy after a few miles, and the moon lit my path. That made for better riding, but it also gave me fewer places to hide if I came on the Tatum boys. I couldn't expect them to ride on forever! How desperate were they to retrieve the horses and put a loop around my neck?

I looked over at Billy-Ann and the big Kladruber, Circumstance. They seemed discontented with something. Even Sorghum seemed off somehow. I took it to be exhaustion. After only a short time in the Titustown area, I wondered if any of the three horses truly knew the way home. The foothills looked lovely in the moonlight. I looked up and vowed that if I ever again found myself in the twenty-second century, I'd arrange to visit the moon. And Mars! Hell, why not the stars? Of course! I'd see some far-off planet circling some star I had yet to know. But, unless they needed a veterinarian, I would just be extra baggage on such a voyage. I had but an inkling of the immense expense that such a trip would cost some government or organization. Then, I thought I heard the sound of horses again. Damn!

I searched the roadside. There was nothing but brush shoulder high to the horses. Far across the field, I could see the darker shadows of the forest. I didn't have time to get that far. I'd just have to rely on the semi-darkness. I moved the three horses as far into the brush as I could. I positioned Billy-Ann behind the two darker-coated horses, but it still felt like we were in plain sight. I watched helplessly as the three familiar men approached; Luther, tall, Thaddeus, a bit shorter, and Tater, the smallest of all. They didn't stop! I couldn't believe it! They rode on at full gallop. I wondered, crazily, if shining my blue light on myself somehow produced some permanent condition rendering me invisible.

Then another group of riders thundered past. A troop of ten men wearing Union Blue went by only moments behind the Tatum brothers. Then the sound of insect life started up again. Finally, I was able to breathe. I gave a mental tip of my hat to Major Rogers. His troopers were riding the roads. They were searching for the bad guys, after all. Things weren't as bad as I'd imagined. Though I was almost falling out of the saddle from fatigue and still had several long miles to go, I resolved to make it to Clarksville.

As we approached Clarksville, I was asleep in the saddle. I had no trouble locating Major Roger's new command post at a farm on the edge of town. Since Bryan and I had met briefly with Lieutenant Scott at the headquarters, I had no idea where in the camp he was located. Would I be allowed to roam around as freely as Bryan and I could at the Jones' farm? There was sunlight on the porch as I rode up with my two extra horses. I told a guard stationed at the gate that I needed to speak with the lieutenant. He looked me over and directed me to go to the headquarters building. It was a low one-story building with two columns on each side of the door. There were two guards stationed there. Through the window, I could see an Officer of the Day lounging inside. I repeated my reason for being there to the guard with the corporal stripes on his sleeve. He yawned and said I was to wait inside, so I introduced myself to a second lieutenant and to wait until the commanding officer arrived.

I sat down against the wall and ate another blasted biscuit. I was exhausted. I was beginning my last day in this era, and whether I was successful in my mission or not, it seemed like the most important thing in the world to me. Well important, along with a meal and a good night's sleep.

Nudged awake, I opened my eyes. Major Rogers stood over me. "Doctor Smith?"

"Major!" I struggled to my feet. The man pointed toward a doorway through which I could see the chair in front of the desk.

"Sit over here. We have a couple of things to clear up," Major Rogers said.

"We do?" I was immediately bewildered.

"Yes." He pushed the door open and motioned me inside. Of course, I was happy to oblige, though his expression was anything but friendly.

"Have a seat," He said again, but his tone had an unfamiliar edge. He pulled his chair out and sat down. He steepled his fingers and looked at me over his fingertips. All of my previous interactions with him had been cordial if distant. Back then, with his attention focused on his stolen payroll and then his orders to move his headquarters, Rogers passed me off as unimportant. Now, with those issues out of the way, he seemed fully attentive to our discussion. Something was cooking, but I had no idea what it was. He pulled out a drawer, shuffled around inside, and brought out a telegram.

"According to this, you are unknown to the staff at regimental command and certainly have no orders or authorization to treat military livestock." He pushed the paper toward me. I grabbed up the telegram. A quick scan verified his words, and I knew I was in the shit. I played the only hand I had.

"There has to be a mistake." I tried to keep the stress out of my voice. I leaned back leisurely. With Bryan long gone and time running out, there was no defense except distraction for me to go with.

"If you look at the three horses I brought in, you'll see that one of them belongs to Lieutenant Scott. His Kladruber was stolen almost a week ago by John Coates at the scene of the second payroll robbery attempt." I waited.

"I'm aware of that, but what does that have to do with the fake orders!"

I shrank back at his choice of words. "I told you there is a mistake about that."

"I think the mistake is on your part, trying to pull this stunt! You might not even be a veterinarian."

This man denying my veterinarian credentials burned my ass. I took a deep breath. "Major, I assure you I have done nothing illegal or even questionable. I'm exactly who I said I am, doing exactly what it said I was doing. So what could I possibly gain from a charade?"

"I don't know. So, I'm withholding judgment until the kinks are ironed out of your story!"

I knew then that the way the major had it figured I was guilty of impersonating a government contractor. Bryan and I were riding U.S. Army horses without authorization, and I was in possession of a stolen horse. All of his suspicions were accurate.

I pushed hard on the only clear truth available to me. "If you will just consult with Lieutenant Scott, I'm sure he will be happy to confirm that his stolen horse is outside and that he was relying on me to bring it back to him if it was recovered. You know yourself that I brought it in. If I was up to anything illegal, why would I return that valuable horse.?" It was my turn to lean forward aggressively and raise my voice.

"Lieutenant Scott is back in Harlon County with a troop searching the area for another crop of outlaws plaguing the locals." He scratched his head and leaned forward, putting his face only inches from mine. "Speaking of your irregularities, where is your brother?

You come trotting in here with an empty saddle and no explanation for his whereabouts."

"Bryan got called back to Arkansas for a family matter," I said. "I put him on a train in Atlanta." I sat back smugly, pretty satisfied with myself to come up with that so quickly. But, I didn't like the way the conversation was going. The major seemed determined to lay on the perceived misdeeds without limit. It reminded me of Mrs. Jordon and the Sheriff's description of Rogers' handling of Major Jones' supposed crimes back in Titustown.

The major leaned back in his chair. "I could jail you right now, but I do recognize Lieutenant Scott's horse out front. So, I'll tell you what I'm going to do. I'll give you the benefit of the doubt. You can walk away, but you leave the army stock here."

I felt a flood of relief. Free to go! I was tired. I thought of the horses outside. They were tired too. I could walk out the door, find an empty pasture, and do an emergency caper back to the future, or I could wait out the day and let the scheduled caper happen. But neither option was close to completing my mission. Neither option assured the continuation of the Kladruber in the twenty-second century. I'd disappear from 1865, forever a failure. I remembered my visit to the herd of mutated horses in Wyoming. How pathetic they were! I wondered if there was any wiggle room at all. I forced my voice into a more amicable tone.

"I know you think you are generous, Major. And by your light, you are. But I'm disgusted that headquarters got things so messed up. I am a veterinarian. I have not stolen any army horses." I paused.

"My patience has run out!" He suddenly stood, indicating the end of our conversation. I rose from my chair and warily opened the door to the outer office. My mind was spinning, trying to come up with another angle. I knew I had to keep the conversation cordial.

"Well, you don't give me any choice," I said. "Best of luck to you and your command. These are dangerous times for everyone in the south." He followed me to the front door; I stepped out on the porch. I turned and extended my hand. The major shook it. Within the hearing of the two guards, we said our goodbyes. Then lady luck intervened. Just as Major Rogers turned to go back to his desk, a rider arrived in a cloud of dust. He pulled off a saddlebag and headed toward the door. I figured the young man was a messenger. I stepped out of his way, and he hurried inside just behind the officer. It appeared that a new set of "proper papers" had just arrived! I looked around. Circumstance, Sorghum, and Billy-Ann stood patiently at the hitching post five yards away. I stepped down and walked to the horses. I had an idea. As far as the guards knew, the Major and I were still on good terms. Without a pause, I mounted Sorghum. Giving the reins of the other two horses a tug, I rode down the lane toward the road. Major Rogers struck me as a man with a one-track mind. I didn't know if or when the man would give me another thought, but I intended to make myself easy to forget by getting out of his sight as quickly as possible. I still had the wild-ass idea of completing my mission.

<h1 style="text-align:center">35</h1>

As I rode toward Titustown, I realized that Circumstance was more antsy than usual. Despite the miles we had covered, he danced and nudged Billy-Ann regularly. On her part, she nipped at Circumstance twice and Sorghum once as we traveled away from the farm. Sorghum seemed to grow more possessive and tried to pull away from the path I intended to place himself between the other horses. I suddenly realized that Billy-Ann was entering estrus. I had been so preoccupied with my problems retrieving Circumstance, avoiding the Tatums, putting miles between myself and the chance of being captured that I just hadn't been alert. Of course! It was mid-May! This month was within the most likely time frame for a mare to ovulate. Both Circumstance and Sorghum were reacting to that occurrence accordingly. Nature was at play. I wondered if Billy-Ann enjoyed having multiple suitors. We needed a haven where I could use Billy Ann's condition to help me acquire the semen I needed. Was it possible that everything was finally going to come together?

A safe-haven! Where could I have the accommodations and another set of steady hands needed to facilitate the semen collection? I expected Lieutenant Scott and Bryan to help out, but both were out of the picture. Scott was the most likely, but he was on patrol. Who knew where? The chances of finding him were slim. There was only one place that sprang to mind, Bub's livery stable in Titustown! I reined Sorghum hard to the left and tugged the other horses' reins. Time was running out, but somehow, I was the closest I had ever been to accomplishing my mission. I shrugged off the likelihood of a cherry on top, the off chance I'd run into Lieutenant Scott and return his horse to him personally before I capered. I pulled a biscuit out of my saddlebag and took a bite. Old biscuits are a nasty thing to put in your mouth, but I didn't care. I just wanted something in my stomach. I chewed on it for a long time and swallowed. I glanced behind me. I admit I was nervous. Major Rogers could already have walked out on his porch and realized that the three horses were missing. Would he bother to send a troop after me? I looked back again.

There was a cloud of dust. "Shit!" I reined the horses into some trees. I was sick of riding. I was sick of hiding. I was still hungry. I was dead tired. I thought of the Lucky Star and the food that awaited me there if I could get to Titustown. I wished I knew the countryside better. I wished I knew of a shortcut. The troop passed. I gave the riders a fifteen-minute head start while I wondered how Bryan was doing. Surely with the medical advances by 2110, he was doing fine. But what if being injured like he was, degraded his ability to withstand the stresses that a caper would put on his body? I thought about the foreign object lodged in his upper trunk. That couldn't be good! "Shit!"

I kicked Sorghum up a gear. Nothing motivates me like the thought of food. We came around a broad curve. There was no sign of the troops. I realized that we had reached the junction. One road led to Titustown. The other was a road to Winslow. I knew that there was an army post there. Maybe the troop was headed there. Perhaps they weren't even after me! I went left and kicked the tired horses into a gallop. I rode them hard. I could feel the time-draining away. I rode up to Bub's livery late in the day and secured the three horses. Bub saw me and came out.

"Doc, I was wondering when I'd see you again!" He shook my hand. "Where's Bryan?"

"Well, Bub, I'm not sure about that myself. When we got to Atlanta, there was a telegram waiting. So I put him on a train headed north. He had to deal with a family matter." I motioned toward the three horses. Would you take the mare around back to the pasture? She's in heat, and both of these big boys are as antsy as hell."

"Can do. I'll put the boys in the corral. How long are you going to be here this time?" He looked hopeful. I surmised that business might have eased off after Bryan and I left.

"Well, not long, I'm afraid. I need to duck into the Star and get something to eat. I'll be back in a bit." I ignored his disappointment. I couldn't do anything to change that situation.

I hurried into the Star and picked out a table by the window. I was sitting down when Miss Emmy rushed to my elbow.

"Doctor. Did you just ride in from Atlanta?" Her face contorted with concern. I could see that she was anxious about something.

"Yes, Ma-am. Is there a problem?"

"Yes. There is a big problem. Sarah has disappeared! She covered her mouth anxiously.

"Disappeared?" I scanned the room. There were a half dozen customers. Then, through the kitchen doorway, I caught sight of Ellen. She still seemed unaware of my presence as yet.

"Yes, disappeared. We held Jimmy Jordon's funeral today. Of course, we were all upset, especially Sarah, as you'd expect. After it was over, I put her to bed. I needed to come in to help the girls. Quite a few people were in to eat earlier, right after the funeral. So, it was at least an hour before I went to check on her, and she was gone!"

My head was spinning. Titustown was a small community. How many places could there be for a girl to disappear? Hiding out was my first thought. Upset people do strange things sometimes. And I hated to think about it, but sometimes people harmed themselves. So I ticked off some of the possibilities that came to mind.

"I guess you've touched base with her friends." I watched her nod. "Checked all the stores?" Another nod. "What about that Yankee fellow, Bronco?"

"She said goodbye to him the day Jimmy came home." He and Madison and Preacher are still over in Alabama trying to track down John Coates."

"You don't suppose she'd ride out that way, I guess," I said, still thinking out loud. "People do strange things when they are upset."

"I know they do, but she wouldn't do that. Besides, the only place she could get a horse or wagon is over at Bub's. He hasn't seen hide or hair of her either. I'm just beside myself. At first, I thought maybe she got up and went home with Cal's family after I put her to bed, but he hasn't seen her either." She was wringing her hands.

"Have you talked with the Sheriff?" I asked.

"I'm going to. I'm waiting on Cal. He's searching through the stores one more time. If he doesn't find her, we're going to go see Ben." She looked further down the street. "There's Cal now."

"Well, if it's any help. I just got in from Clarksville a few minutes ago, and I didn't see any sign of her along the way." She touched my arm in appreciation for the information and stepped away. I watched Miss Emmy hurry to join Cal Jordon in front of the Star, and they turned toward the Sheriff's office. I sat down, and a pretty gal came to take my order.

I was as puzzled as Miss Emmy. Mrs. Jordon was a lovely girl, and I was baffled by her disappearance. The idea that she had met with misfortune on top of losing her husband was troubling. The other problematic aspect was that this was a mystery that I would probably never see solved. If she didn't show up in the next few hours, I might never know how her story ended.

I found my eyes drifting toward all the places where I had seen her so often; the doorway to the kitchen, the back of the eating area sitting with Pappy. I had an eerie feeling that she was hiding in plain sight though that made no sense. I leaned closer to the window to search the street. In a little bit, I'd be gone forever. I could appreciate, as never before, how long forever can be. I ate quickly. I didn't enjoy the food as much as I expected, probably because I was concerned for Mrs. Jordon. I ducked my head into the kitchen to greet the cook and Ellen. The cook smiled at me and turned back to her work. Ellen's pretty young face beamed. She pointed toward the back of the kitchen. I could see the larger than usual cabinet door that Bub had installed.

"Mr. Bub finished my door two days ago!" She grabbed my arm and led me over. She opened the door. It was two steps down into the small room lit with light from an open window on each end and the open bottom half of the Dutch door. Freckles was lying in the open doorway. He caught sight of me and jumped up to come and greet me. His tail was going sixty to nothing.

"He's okay?" I petted him and could feel nor see any sign of bloat.

"Yes, I did what you said. Freckles didn't get any bread or meat scraps, and I made some kraut." She said proudly. "Today is the first day that I gave him just a little meat." Her luminous eyes searched my face.

"Well, he looks fine. I guess you are a good nurse," I said.

She grinned and nodded. "One more thing!" She picked up a menu.

"Chocolate!" She put her finger below the word and moved her hand over to the next word, "Lemon!" Then she pointed to the top. "Menu! Miss Emmy has decided to teach me to read," she said excitedly. "I am learning three new words each day." Her eyes searched my face.

"That is wonderful! I bet you'll be reading and writing and doing arithmetic like crazy!" I couldn't help but grin.

"Yes! And she said that if I read well, I can help teach at the new school for negro children."

"School?" I remembered my brief conversation with Miss Emmy about educating black children. Miss Emmy didn't let any grass grow under her feet.

"Yes, they are already planning to build it out at the edge of town." She glanced away, apparently a bit embarrassed to exhibit so much excitement.

"Well, I am happy," I said. I remembered my mission then. I lay my hand on Ellen's shoulder. I have something important I have to do. I'll have a present for you a little later."

"Present?" She looked puzzled.

"Yes, but I have some things to do first." I patted her shoulder and moved toward the door. I hurried across the street to the livery. Bub was inside the barn, working on some harness.

"Hey, Bub. I'd like to breed that mare. Suppose you can give me a hand?"

"I expect so." He stood, and we walked toward the back where the mare was in view. "Which of your studs are you going to use?"

"Well, I think I'll go with the Kladruber first. Then I'll give Sorghum a try," I said.

"Well, I've got a stall over here we can use," Bub pointed off to the side.

I looked the area over. I needed to keep Bub a bit in the dark regarding the whole procedure for my plan to work. If he saw me siphon off Circumstance's ejaculation, it would just raise a lot of questions. "Okay, let's think this through," I said. We'll bring the mare in, and you can stand on the other side of that gate to the outside. You can hold her head while I bring on the stallion. That stall is pretty narrow, so there won't be much room for her to maneuver.

Let's unsaddle the two males. I'm sure you have plenty of blankets available to drape her?"

"Oh, sure." Bub pointed to a pile over against the wall.

"That's great!" I walked out into the pasture and grabbed Billy-Ann's reins. "Big girl, I know you'd like a foal that is half Kladruber. But don't forget Sorghum is a pretty stout boy too. He's a fine horse. And, maybe after I'm gone, Bub will give the big boy another chance before turning him over to Lieutenant Scott. Whichever of these guys sires your foal, you can be proud of the colt or filly you drop. Just cooperate, and everything will turn out great!" I grabbed the halter and led her toward the stall.

Both Circumstance and Sorghum were pawing the ground by now. Billy-Ann was starting to formulate. She whinnied. She pawed the ground. She wanted to play hard to get, but I didn't have time for that. I left the saddle on her and piled on several blankets. To prevent injury, there needed to be some padding.

The equipment was little-changed from what I had in my time. The collector we brought was about three feet long and six inches in diameter. I went over to Sorghum and removed the collector and specimen vial hidden deep in the otherwise empty rifle scabbard. The vial was half the size of a hotdog. It was self-cooling using a battery half the size used in hearing aids in nineteen sixty-three. It would cool its contents to about thirty-seven degrees Fahrenheit. Time was running out. I inserted the liner and brought Circumstance to stand about six feet behind Billy-Ann. She looked around and made a kicking motion.

Circumstance lifted on his hindlegs a bit and tried to paw the air. The big boy's penis started to extend. I pulled the reins and encouraged him to approach Billy-Ann. He lifted on his high legs and balanced one leg on the blankets and the other on the side of the stall. This process was not going to be easy. Usually, you have someone at the head and a second person to pull the mare's tail to the side and help keep the stallion in line. The third person grabs the stallion's extended penis and thrusts it into the collector.

All in all, it takes about ten seconds for the stallion to ejaculate. There are two to five billion cells in a mature horses' ejaculate. About fifty percent are active.

"Okay, Bub, hold her head," I called.

"Got it," Bub yelled back.

"I released the reins and trusted Circumstance to position himself. The big Kladruber knew what to do. As someone once said, "This wasn't his first rodeo." Up went the front legs. I grabbed and pulled on the collector. Circumstance lunged. Twice, three times. It was over.

I Quickly backed him off and walked him out the door into the pasture. I led in Sorghum. He was just as excited as Circumstance was. The difference was that I let him deposit his sperm where he intended. Billy-Ann snorted. Sorghum snorted. We were done.

"We're done, Bub." I led Sorghum away and set him free in the pasture. I gave him a good petting and said goodbye. He looked at me with satisfaction in his eyes. I moved to the Pinto and unsaddled her. I put her back in the corral. She also received some loving on Bryan's behalf. Finally, I grabbed Circumstance's reins and brought him back inside. I stroked his massive head and rejoiced silently as he nuzzled against my chest. I unsaddled him and breathed a sigh of relief. I kneeled and opened Sorghum's saddlebag and found the rest of the money that Thaddeus had stuffed inside. I didn't bother to count it. I took out enough for Bub and crammed the rest in my pocket. I stood as Bub approached. I picked up the fake scabbard, and he and I walked to the front of the livery. I gave him some money. "Bub, I'm leaving town. I'm not sure when I'll be back. This money is to cover a couple of weeks of care for the horses. If I don't make it back, you are welcome to Sorghum and Billy-Ann if you can keep the Army off your back. The Kladruber belongs to a Union cavalry Lieutenant by the name of Scott. I'd count it a personal favor if you'd see that he gets his horse back?"

Bub nodded and searched my face. "I've got a feeling that the odds are you aren't coming back?"

"Well, that's how the odds seem right now," I said. We walked to the front of the barn, and I looked down the street. I knew my time was short. But, at that moment, time seemed to get a lot shorter. Catty-cornered down the street, still mounted, in front of the sheriff's office, was Major Rogers. I wouldn't have been surprised by soldiers, but I did not expect the major in person. I tried to duck out of sight, but I was too late.

36

Major Rogers caught sight of me and pointed me out to a sergeant. The man spoke to two of the troopers, and they reined about and started in my direction at a gallop. Their hands were reaching to pull open the flap on their holsters. From my perspective, that was totally unnecessary!

There was no time to spare. I had one more errand to run before I finished my mission, and it looked like my time was running out. I ran out the back of the barn and dodged left. I slipped through the side gate, which I knew would slow the horsemen a bit. I had to stay free for another two hours or use the homing device for an emergency pickup. Either way, I had one more errand to run. I mentally kicked myself. I should have taken care of it before I left the Star. I doubled back around the side of the barn and headed toward the street. I glimpsed the last soldier entering the front of the barn as I paused. There was no way for the major to miss seeing me as I darted across the street behind the dismounted troop. Rogers spotted me and pointed again.

"There he is, get him!"

"Give me a break," I murmured. I ran into the Star and turned into the kitchen. The cook and Ellen looked at me, startled at my sudden appearance. I grabbed Ellen's arm and pulled her toward the new door. I felt resistance, but I was insistent.

"I don't have time to explain. Just come with me. Please, trust me!"

The big eyes widened. Ellen seemed to sense my urgency then. She nodded, and I opened the door. There were two steps down to the floor of the lean-to. I skipped a step and steadied Ellen as she followed. I saw that the lower half of the Dutch door was open, so I swung it closed and locked it. I remembered that it was almost invisible from the outside when closed. I'd have to count on that. I turned back to Ellen. I lay the small vial of semen on the top of the chest.

"Okay, listen carefully. The soldiers are after me. I can't explain, but I am going to go away. I won't be back." Fear fled across her face. She looked back toward the doorway. The cabinet door was ajar. She pulled it all the way shut. I reached into my pocket and extracted the green-backs I had retrieved from Sorghum's saddlebags. I grabbed Ellen's hand. "Open your hand!" The fingers flew open. I laid the thick wad in her palm. "This is for you. Hide it where no one can ever find it." I looked around the bare room. "Not in here!" I looked into the pretty young eyes now filled with surprise. "This is for you. I want you to learn to read and write and do arithmetic. I want you to travel and see the world. I want you to go to college. There is enough here to get you started. Don't let anything stand in your way!" I looked at her closely. "Do you understand?"

Ellen nodded, but when she looked up at me, she said. "I don't know how."

"You are young. No one can do everything at once. So just conserve your money and go one step at a time. You don't know how right now, but you will figure it out. Trust me! Do you trust me?"

"Yes, Mister Doctor," she said with finality. "I do." I heard her words, but I also saw the confusion. I repeated.

"Remember, hide the money where no one can find it. Use it to get an education. Use it to build your future. You don't have to do everything at once. Do it one step at a time!" Ellen nodded.

We could hear the soldiers in the kitchen behind us. We heard them fussing with the back door and then running down the alley. I held my breath. If they forced their way into the lean-to, I was a goner. In their hurry, they did not. I squeezed Ellen's thin shoulder and bent over to crack the bottom of the Dutch door, and looked out. I hesitated as I could hear more soldiers in the kitchen. Again, I held my breath. If they opened that cabinet door, my goose was cooked. I whispered. "Remember, keep this door locked at night! Goodbye."

The big eyes grew larger. The girl nodded. "Goodbye!" Ellen whispered. I grabbed the vial of semen, and cracked open the bottom of the Dutch door, and ducked down to peer out again. I could not see anyone, so I went through the doorway and closed it swiftly behind me. There was a field past the row of outhouses. I just needed to make the field. Between the large walnut trees, there were great open spaces and the way for me to caper away forever.

I ran. I picked a spot maybe a hundred feet away, past the Star's outhouse, halfway to the big walnut tree. I pulled the homing device from my pocket. I felt the crease on the side where one of the horses had stepped on it. I stroked it with my thumb as I ran. If the emergency homing device didn't work now, what hope was there that it would work when my assigned pickup time arrived? I could feel the dread come over me. Finally, I reached the spot I was targeting and dived to the ground. The grass was only two feet high there. I hoped I'd only be there for a moment. I didn't even take time to glance around. I held my breath and brought my hands together so I could twist on the two ends of the tube. It wouldn't turn! It was so small; there was so little to grasp. I realized that the crease had thrown the threads out of alignment. I pulled and pushed, trying to turn it enough to separate the two ends and break the connection. I couldn't move it! In exhaustion and despair, I lay my forehead down on my crossed arms and held my breath.

I knew that the grass wasn't tall enough to provide sufficient cover. In but a moment, I heard footsteps running down the alley behind me and a yell. There were rapid thumps of heavy footfalls coming closer before Union Cavalry boots stopped beside me. Two pairs of gloved hands grasped me by my upper arms. I palmed the ballpoint pen-sized homing device in my right hand. The equally small vessel of Kladruber semen was in my left. The two men lifted me to my feet, and I opened my eyes. Two young troopers held me snuggly between them. Around the corner of the Lucky Star came Major Roger's husky figure, still mounted. His mouth twisted in anger.

"Bring him here!" His horse pranced a few steps, and he looked away. I used the moment to pretend to stumble. In doing so, I dropped the contents of my hands into my right and left boots.

The men brought me to stand at the head of the major's horse. I reached up to give it a friendly pat. But it tossed its head as if to convey the major's anger and say hands-off. I looked up, but the man's head was in the sun, which glowed like a halo leaving his face in shadows.

"I go against my better instincts and see where it got me?"

"Oh, come on, Major. I borrowed the horse to get to Titustown. I told you as much when we talked earlier. Just let me go, and I'll be out of your hair. I'm headed back to Arkansas."

"No. I'm going to see to it that you spend some time in jail," he said.

"Give me a break! I haven't been in your way, and I haven't interrupted your work. I haven't actually stolen anything. Just let me go! I promise you'll never see me again."

Just then, the jail's back door opened, and Sheriff Beckett came out with his two deputies. "Howdy, Major. I heard you were in town. I wasn't expecting you back so soon."

"Sheriff." Rogers turned in the saddle as the three men approached. He looked back at the two soldiers holding me. "At ease, men."

"Hey, Doc! So, you're back again too?" Deputy Shires stepped around the major's horse and shook my hand.

"Well, I'm only here temporarily," I said. By now, Beckett and the two deputies had come to stand with Shires. Beckett motioned toward me.

"Major, I appreciate your sending Doc out to do those inspections," Becket took off his hat and ran his hand over the top of his thinning hair. "He's made a lot of friends for you here in Harlan County."

Major Rogers' eyebrows we up, and he looked over at me. "He has?"

"You bet. When Doc wasn't out inspecting your stock for that glanders disease, he's been doing inspections here in town. He never told you about that?" The sheriff looked past the major for a moment and raised his eyebrows at me.

"Well, the major's been busy what with the payroll robbery and moving his headquarters," I said. "I expect that's quite a load."

The sheriff nodded. "I expect." He eyed the two soldiers bracing me. "So, Major, what brings you to town so soon? Everything's been pretty quiet here except for the murder of old man Coates, his oldest son, the shooting of two of our citizens, one of them dead, and a missing girl today."

"I did get word of the shootings." The major dismounted and stood facing the group of us. "Do you think John Coates is responsible for the missing girl as well?"

"Well, I don't see how he could be. Deputy Shires and I just got a report the other day that he is over in Alabama.

He turned to me. "Doc, Bub stopped by to tell me you left that fancy horse at his place with instructions that he was to turn it over to the army at the first chance?"

"That's right, Sheriff. I'm afraid I'm finished with my work here in Georgia. I put my brother, Bryan, on a train in Atlanta. I'm taking the next stage northwest. We've got some family business to take care of in Arkansas." I glanced over at the major.

His mouth was working like he was grinding his teeth. I hoped that the sheriff's laudatory remarks were taking their toll on his intentions toward me.

"So, have you found any glanders?" Major Rogers eyed me.

"Fortunately, no." I saw a look of satisfaction across his features. "But I think a lot of people hereabouts have had their mind's relieved about the condition of their animals. What do you think, Sheriff?"

"Well, I think that is true. Bringing in the Doc, here could be the most positive thing you've done for the folks hereabouts." Beckett glanced at his deputies. They were nodding agreement.

"Well." Rogers motioned toward the two soldiers to move away. "That's real fine." I wasn't aware that the inspection project has been so successful." He adjusted his cap. "Well, we need to move on. I thought it would be good for me to get out of the office for a bit. Remember, Sheriff, if things get out of hand, get word to me. My patrols in the area are constant. We can't stay in any particular area as long as we'd like, but you can count on us to come when called. "He mounted his horse and sat back to survey our little group.

Sheriff Beckett grinned. I suspected that he was happier to see the major leave than he would ever be to see him arrive. "Well, Major, don't be a stranger!" He lifted his hat, and the officer reined his horse about to ride between the jail and building next door toward Main Street.

37

Sheriff Beckett and his two deputies stood with me as we watched the major ride away. "Well, Doc, I guess this will be the last time you see the good major," Beckett said. "I wish we could say the same. What did you do to get cross-ways with him?"

"How did you know?" I was startled by the question.

"One of his troopers said they were here to arrest you and throw you in my jail. I've had all the dealings I want to have with Rogers. I want to be the one to decide who gets arrested in Harlan County."

"Well, I appreciate your help," I said. "He and I did have a misunderstanding." I looked at the sun. It was a little less than two hours till my scheduled pickup. Because of the damaged homey, I didn't know if it was going to happen or not. I was dead tired, and I couldn't get my concern for Bryan out of my head. I remembered what Preston had said about "here" time and "there" time. It didn't seem important until your "here" time forced you to wait in a worried and exhausted state before you could join "there" time.

On the one hand, I thought he'd be fine, but on the other, I needed to know for sure. I was ready to go. "I think I'll go see Bub for a minute." I waved so long to the men and headed between the buildings. When I came out on Main Street, the major's troopers were disappearing down the street. The last one had the reins of three horses in hand. "Goodbye, Stance, Sorghum, and Billy-Ann,"

I murmured. I did feel a sadness sweep over me. More so than I experience saying goodbye to most people. Bub was standing outside the livery.

"Well, I see the major collected his horses," I said as we joined each other.

"Yep." Bub turned to walk back into the barn. "Them army horses could be a problem for me somewhere down the road. I'm glad to be finished with the whole thing. I guess you want back that money you left with me earlier?"

"Nah, keep it. I appreciate your help." Bub nodded and turned away. I still had almost two hours of waiting ahead of me before my scheduled pickup. I watched him retreat toward the back pasture and suddenly felt a huge wave of fatigue wash over me. I was tired. I wanted a nice soft place to lie down. I knew where that was if I could get to it. I called after him.

"Say, do you have any pliers?"

"Sure, over in that box." He pointed. "Help yourself. I need to take the wagon down to the feed store." I noticed then that he had the team hitched up. He climbed aboard, called to the horses, and moved forward out of the barn. I watched for a minute, then walked over to the box. There was an assortment of tools, as you'd expect for a man of so many talents. I found a pair of pliers in one corner and another buried under a pair of leather gloves. I looked around. Seeing that I was alone, I walked out into the corral and over to one side to be out of sight from Main Street. I pulled out the damaged homing device. Using the dented spot for traction, I got a good grip with the pliers in my right hand. I clamped the pliers in my left hand down for a solid grip on the notched end of the tube. I looked around again, and feeling the power that the additional leverage gave me, I twisted the notched end violently. The two sections parted. A blue light spread out from one section. A yellow light beamed out from the other. I didn't take but a moment. I tossed the pliers away from me. They landed with a clink near the corner of the toolbox just before the air started swirling as if I was the center of an enormous suction device. I sat down in the dirt, brought up my knees, lay my forehead against them and put my palms over my ears and let my hands soften the rush of sound.

I let my eyes flicker open for just long enough to verify the lightning-lit hieroglyphic flashes around me. I forced myself to take a long ten-second breath. Then came the sudden silence. When I opened my eyes, total darkness enveloped me. I remembered Bryan's command. "Light!"

I stood, extended my arms to the side, and braced myself as decontamination began. So much had happened since I stood in this same spot and felt my hair stand on end and my clothes tugged away from my body.

Then everything stood still. I opened my eyes. The same dark gray walls greeted me. I felt in my pockets. The two sections of the homey were in my right pocket. The vial of Kladruber semen was in the other.

The door opened. Preston Andrews and Louise Dubois entered. I handed the vial to Preston and the homey to Louise. "Mission accomplished! How is Bryan?"

Preston put the vial in his pocket. They seemed to be relieved about something. Preston reached out to shake hands. His left hand was on my shoulder. Louise put her hand on my arm.

"What's wrong?" I looked at each of them closely and repeated my question. "How is Bryan?"

"How are you?" Louise searched my eyes.

"I'm fine! How is Bryan?" I asked again.

"Bryan is going to be okay," Preston said. "I assume you know about the bullet wound?" He glanced at Louise.

"Well, yeah! That's why he made the emergency caper. We were together."

Louise put her other hand on my arm. "Good, we didn't know but that you were separated. Bryan arrived an hour ago. The wound was the first thing we saw. It suggested the possibility that you were hurt or killed. We didn't know what to make of your not coming with him. We have been debating on whether one of us should caper in to check on you or send a flight of Fleedles."

"An hour ago?" It took me a minute to realize that my return caper could have brought me back to innumerable possible arrival times. "Why didn't you just ask Bryan?" This was ridiculously confusing.

"Bryan has a serious concussion. He was unconscious when he arrived. Did he fall?"

"Yes, he fell off of his horse when he was shot. But he was able to stand." I straightened. Of course! He could easily have suffered a concussion when he fell. I had not even considered that.

"Bryan is in a rehabilitative coma," Louise said. "We haven't had an opportunity to talk with him." Preston moved toward the door. "If you're okay, let's go sit, and you can tell us what happened."

I nodded, and we moved to the door. We proceeded down the hall and ducked into a conference room. "In the confusion of the shooting and chaotic aftermath, I was more worried about him bleeding out than anything else." I searched their faces. "Bryan is going to be okay?"

They nodded.

"Good, I want to go see him." I stood, and they rose as well. We walked the length of the hall past the classroom, where I received my initiation into capering. I caught sight of Dr. Ortley through the transparent partition. He was pointing at the sign on the wall.

Comprehensive, Anonymous,

Pre-pandemic Era Research

My memory of my first day in the class flooded over me. All of that seemed so long ago as if I experienced that two hundred forty-five-year interval in real-time. We turned and passed through a set of double doors. A short walk later, we opened another set of double doors. There was Bryan. A transparent helmet covered his head. His eyes were closed. There was a hose protruding from his mouth. He looked to be sleeping. There was a dressing on his shoulder that covered his collarbone.

"You're sure he is going to be okay?"

"Yes, the coma is induced to prevent swelling. It's precautionary," Louise said.

"He was coherent when he capered out," I said, thinking out loud. I pressed my hand on my forehead. "He stood up after he fell off the horse. I never gave a concussion a thought. We walked him all around before I could get him to a clear area for his caper. That's the worst thing I could have done! Shit!"

"It's okay!" Louise put her hand on my arm, trying to reassure me. "The doctors say he'll be in this coma for another six hours or so. "They'll bring him out of it, and he'll be fine!"

I looked at Preston. He was nodding agreement. Suddenly I felt the exhaustion roll over me again. "I need to lie down."

"Okay. First, you did not sustain any injuries?" I shook my head. "You're not dizzy, nauseous?"

"I told you, I'm tired," I said crossly. "I need sleep. I haven't slept in at least twenty-four hours."

"Okay, Louise, can you take Bryan to his room?"

Louise nodded, and we moved toward the door. In a few minutes, I was in my own room or one that looked just like it. I slumped to the bed and was out like a light in half a minute. My last memory was a gentle female hand pulling a blanket up to my shoulder. Or maybe I imagined it?

38

When I awoke, my head felt like I was coming out of a bank of thick fog. I rubbed my forehead and closed my eyes again. I wasn't ready. I wondered if I would ever be ready. Then I must have dozed. When I opened my eyes again, the buzzer on my door was going off. I shook off my muddled condition and opened it.

"I think the term is rise and shine," Louise said.

"You think?" She gave me a good reason to keep my eyes open. The blouse was blue; the tights stretched over her long legs were a match. The short skirt was yellow.

"Well, my appliance has some limitations. I request morning greetings in English. Just requesting morning greetings, and I get an unending supply in every language. They don't necessarily make sense to me." She grinned.

"Well, I think 'rise and shine' referred to the sun and bright shiny faces." I smiled back. "How long did I sleep?"

"Ten hours."

"You're kidding!" I shook my head to orient myself. "Then Bryan is awake?"

"Yes! And he has been asking about you. He says he left you in a precarious situation."

"Yes, and I guess that his remembering that is a good sign," I said. I looked down at my wrinkled 1865 outfit. I was reminded of sit-

238

ting in the dirt in Bub's corral at the beginning of my caper. And I imagined the scent of horses. So, I was able to bring something of Circumstance, Sorghum, and Billy-Ann into the twenty-second century! I took a deep breath in satisfaction and grabbed my hat from the chair out of habit. "I want to check on Bryan first before I do anything else!" We hurried to his room and entered. He was sitting up, rubbing the area over his appliance.

"You're up!"

I walked over to his bed, and he grabbed my hand. "Glad you made it!"

"Me too." He was interested in how things went with the Tatum boys. He doubled over laughing when I told him about the witchcraft ploy I used after he disappeared from the field. But he thought the funniest story was Major Rogers' wilted resolve to throw me in jail when Sheriff Beckett bragged about my contribution to the community and how well it reflected on him.

"That Beckett is no fool." Bryan wiped his eyes.

"He's not," I said. "Or he wasn't."

Bryan closed his eyes. I took that as a sign that he needed rest. I told him I needed to get cleaned up. As hesitant as I was to wash away the residual hints of my visit to the century of the horse, I went back to my room and did just that.

After a couple of days of observation, Bryan was up and about as his usual self. We sat down with Preston and Louise and went through the chain of events that led to the achievement of our mission. Louise was interested in the sociological aspects of our caper. We discussed the day-to-day interactions of the southerners and the Yankees that we observed. My interactions with Ellen sent Louise to search the historical record. Finally, she found the girl there. Ellen Pauline Smith did go to college. She graduated at twenty-five years of age. The blurb concerning her life described her as "an Educator who viewed teaching as a form of Christian service."

Louise looked up. "You made a big impression there, Doctor."

"Funny, I didn't realize that her last name was Smith. Everyone just called her Ellen," I said. Bryan and Louise stared at me for a long moment before it dawned.

"You don't think?"

"You have a better idea as to why her middle name was Pauline, and her last name was Smith?" Louise smiled.

"Well, she was smart and pretty, and I encouraged her." I looked at Preston.

"Nothing wrong with that," he smiled. I hugged myself as inconspicuously as I could. There was no reason to mention the wad of greenbacks I gave to her. I felt such enormous pride in Ellen, almost as if she was my own child. It took her a while, but she graduated from a negro college right along with the boys! I hoped she had a good life. She probably had descendants in my time and possibly even the present time. That moment was one of the times that the consequences of my capering hit me like a bus.

The week would have dragged for me except for my lively repartee with Bryan and Louise. We hung out together often. Every day, I asked about other caperings that had concluded successfully with additional breeds. The American Saddlebred and the Andalusian from Spain came in shortly after I did. The Pinto, Quarter Horse, and others arrived on succeeding days. The promise of each breed made my heart sing! But there was another question ledged in the back of my mind. Did I want to sit around and wait for another mission? And the stars! I learned that the next star mission awaited the starship still under construction. It would be years! I kicked myself for the decision, but my response was no. I had a home and a practice. I had lifelong friends. I was ready to rejoin them for my "here" time.

"You ready to go home?" He looked at me closely.

"Well, I think it's time. Every adventure comes to an end, I guess. I need to get back to reality while it still feels real," I said. Although I had not been gone long enough for anyone to miss me, I had been gone long enough for me to miss my life in Oklahoma.

"I can understand that." I'll schedule you in for tomorrow morning?" Preston said.

I wanted to go home, but I was conflicted. Bryan and Louise, and I had built an affection for each other over my time here. I reflected on Louise. I'd have welcomed a spark, but our circumstances doused any effort I made to ignite one.

"Okay." I was relieved to have the decision made, to be committed to a plan of action.

The following day, I ate a subdued breakfast with my three friends. Then, I stopped by to say goodbye to Professor Ortley and continued to the capering platform.

"We will deposit you in a clearing across the road from the campground four hours after you left," Preston explained. "There is no reason for you to take unnecessary chances. You can approach cautiously to make sure your two black-shirted friends have left the area."

Bryan handed me an envelope. "Here's your going away gift," he grinned.

"Oh, what is it?"

"The title to the Ford. It's signed and notarized. So all you have to do is sign your name or anyone else's name you want in the Buyer's spot." He pointed.

"Well, thanks!" That was a pleasant surprise.

"There aren't a lot of perks in this job other than the experience itself."

I looked over at Louise. Suddenly she was in my arms. The soft, the rush of breath, the smell of her a hundred times better than a horse. "Be safe!" She kissed me then, on the lips. Not urgently, but with friendship. She stepped away as the door to the caper platform opened. We did a kind of group hug then, before I was suddenly alone, huddled with my head on my knees and my hands over my ears.

The rushing noise started. I counted—five seconds of black with lightning, then ten and silence. I was almost afraid to look. In a bit, I heard a bird chirping. I opened my eyes. I was sitting on the ground, listening to cars pass fifty feet away. Then a semi-tractor rig roared past. I stood and approached the road. Across the way, I could see the little AMC Rambler and the Ford Country Sedan station wagon parked where Bryan and I had left them. For a moment, I just stared at them, trying to let everything in my head concerning my previous many weeks settle down.

Were all of those memories real? Was this even real? Was anything real? There was a third car there too. It was a 1957 Chevy. It was black with a white top. A man and woman and two young children were sitting at the picnic table. I scanned the rest of the area. It all looked normal, or at least the way I remembered normal. I crossed the road and absently broke off a stem of Queen Ann's lace. I intended to go directly to my car, but the man caught sight of me and waved. I walked closer. I wanted to absorb as much of reality as possible, and I had another motive as well. "Say, which way are you folks heading?"

"Claremore," the man said.

"My friend was picked up earlier. He had to leave his car. I'd give you twenty bucks to follow me into town."

"Twenty bucks? Sure."

I handed the young man the keys.

He bent and picked up the basket Bryan and I had left behind only a few hours before. "I wondered why this was here." He was looking at the stem in my hand. "You, picking weeds?"

"Well, I am," I said. "This plant is called Queen Ann's lace."

"I've been looking at it. It's quite pretty. What do you do with it?" The wife swung around to face me.

"Well, my friend sells them to florist shops to use as a filler in flower arrangements."

"I've seen that!" She looked from me to her husband and back.

"It's quite common," I agreed. "I guess it's time for me to get on my way. Are you folks ready?"

The man nodded, and they called to the kids chasing each other among the trees. I dropped the sprig of Queen Anne's Lace into Bryan's basket. I opened the back door, and set the basket in the seat.

"I'll take it easy, so I don't lose you," I said.

They looked at the little AMC Rambler and had the good grace not to laugh. While they followed me in, I thought back over my adventures in 2110 and 1865. It seemed unlikely that I would ever have such an experience again. I went into my office and puttered around for a bit watering the plants and such. I was to be gone a week.

Six months later, I was about to head out for an appointment when I heard a knock at the door. I looked out the window. I could see the backsides of two red-haired people looking back toward the Rambler parked out front. I felt a lurch in the pit of my stomach and headed toward the front door. I held my breath as I opened it.

THE END

About the Author

Charles Reed is the author of four other works. *Tracks to Harlon County – Twenty-One Tale of Life and Adventure.*, *Trouble in Harlon County* (First novel of the Pursuers Serie*s)*, *Mission in Harlon County* (The second novel of The Pursuers Series), *Justice in Harlon County* (The third novel in the Pursuers Series),

Charles was born in Saint Louis, Missouri. Because of his father's occupation, he moved frequently throughout his early years. During that period, he attended twelve schools in four states. When not writing, Charles is an avid reader of biography, history, mystery, and science fiction.

Charles has run three marathons, three half marathons, numerous *Tulsa Runs*, and ridden his bicycle in the *Free-Wheel across Oklahoma* six times. In addition, Charles has traveled in Europe, the Orient, and North and South America. His first air travel was to Southeast Asia, where he served as an infantryman with the 101st Airborne Division.

Finally, Charles is also a "throw the seed down and see what happens" gardener.